D1600472

JOURNEY
— *for* —
JUSTICE

BRAD ARBUCKLE

Journey for Justice Brad Arbuckle

ISBN: 978-1-7782622-1-0 eBook
ISBN: 978-1-7782622-0-3 Paperback
ISBN: 978-1-7782622-2-7 Hardcover

For more information email: arby51@hotmail.com

Sometimes in your life you find someone that completes you.
I am one of those lucky people.
I found my wife Lynn.
It is to her I dedicate my life and this book.
Without her I am not.

1

Hard Rock Cafe

LAURA HUDSON FELT and looked absolutely beautiful. The tropical breeze caressed her freshly bronzed body. She danced with her hands above her head, in some world that was known only to herself.

She was enjoying a holiday of a lifetime with her husband, Brent. She had been ecstatic to exchange the harsh winters of Canada for the warm, white sands of Australia. Brent had surprised her further by then making yet another of her fantasies a reality. The love of her life had whisked her up in his arms and transported her from Australia to the land of three hundred islands. So now she was in Fiji, on the dance floor of the Hard Rock Cafe.

Laura's body sensually swayed with the music. When she twirled, her sundress would balloon in the breeze of the open-air patio, showing more body than she would ever dare to back home in Canada. It was of no matter here; she was with her husband, and she knew he relished other male eyes feasting on her body. It was their special foreplay.

At lunchtime, Brent had returned from snorkeling in the waters surrounding their island paradise. He had explained in detail to Laura about all the colorful fish and even an octopus biding its time shadowing unaware prey.

This was their date of the day: drinks and dancing. An unwritten custom in their marriage had always been that no matter what, they would share a "Date of the Day." Even if it meant just a walk and holding hands.

The Treasure Island afternoon sun was hot. No doubt about it, cocktails with crushed ice would be the drink of choice until it was time to hail a water taxi to go into town. Not being much of a drinker, by the time the sunset appeared, Laura was very lightheaded and had donned a permanent grin. She was in heaven and feeling giddy about how the naughty girl within her was coming to the surface.

Brent sat on a stool in the open-air patio and sipped on a local, limited, Hard Rock lager beer. He noticed that the attendance at the bar was increasing. Not so much with tourists from all over the world but with locals, and mostly men. He thought it was odd, and his warning flags were raising their ugly heads about this situation. Not to worry, though, as he just saw four single girls arrive and take their place on the dance floor.

They integrated Laura within their group.

Still in her own world, Laura either failed to notice these girls or just didn't care.

Brent paid attention, and what he saw before him stirred

his manhood and the lusting beast within himself. In front of Brent swayed five erotic creatures oozing with sexual prowess. Their bodies were expelling a conscious aroma of women in orgasmic heat. He believed Laura was the finest goddess in the orgy playing itself out within his mind. Brent, being the voyeur that he was, decided that another round of beer was warranted.

He ordered one for himself and an ice-filled mudslide for his wife.

She would need it, as her body was glowing from dancing to the seductive Fijian music.

Suddenly all eyes were diverted toward the parking lot. It seemed that a caravan of shiny black Cadillac Escalades, polished to look like mirrors in the moonlight, had arrived. Each vehicle had the Fijian government symbol on the rear doors.

Brent mused to Laura, "This looks awfully official."

Laura replied with half a sarcastic grin. "You think so?"

Each driver in the parade of black beauties hustled out of their vehicle and, in unison, opened the door for their distinguished passenger. Four gentlemen of obvious pedigree exited the shielded world of wealth and were about to join the rest of the partiers at the Hard Rock Cafe.

The gateman to the patio stood rather stoically and was aware of who these four men were. They walked in and were shown to an area next to Brent and Laura. The Hard Rock Cafe staff scurried around like field mice, gathering tables and chairs and putting them together. From inside the Hard Rock, two burly gentlemen were hauling around finely upholstered, plush sectional seats to form a semicircle. The last touch was bottles of fine wines and liquors. Laura could tell that these bottles didn't come from the same cupboards that served most patrons.

As these gentlemen walked closer to Brent and Laura, local customers were addressing them by rank. Most assuredly they were military. Laura didn't know how high up their official ranks were, but she knew they were classified as officers and not to be messed with by the Fijian public. Laura noticed that they smelled of alcohol and were checking her out. These military men taking a good look at her assets was neither alarming nor made her feel awkward. It was normal. What didn't seem normal was that they had been drinking like drunken college kids. There was also the fact that although they were military officers and addressed with respect and rank, none of them were wearing uniforms.

Beside Brent and Laura was now boisterous with the bravado of the four men entertaining the four dancing nymphs from the dance floor in the posh setup. Laura couldn't determine if the ladies were enamored with these Fijian big boys or just petrified to death by the thought of displeasing any of them. It was not her concern; she was here tonight with her husband and was herself warming to the sexual spirits of the alcohol she had been consuming.

Brent couldn't help but secretly check out the chicks and the pecking order that was developing among the out-of-uniform military men. The guys were way over their alcohol limit, and he sensed that, at some point during the night, trouble lay on the horizon. Brent thought he and Laura should only have one last drink before discreetly making their exit.

Before they could finish their next drink, four well-built, young men who were obviously tourists entered the bar. There was instant recognition and karma between them and the four local women entertaining the military men.

Brent sensed the tension in the air between the young tourists and servicemen. His instincts were screaming, "Pull the plug!"

Laura looked into Brent's eyes and said, "I want to dance."

Brent whispered, "No, it's time to go home."

Laura acted like she didn't hear Brent and started a seductive chair dance at their table. She again asked Brent to follow her onto the dance floor.

Brent just shook his head indicating no.

Laura went to the dance floor and started her highly sexual, come-fuck-me dance. She unwittingly attracted more of an audience than she'd expected. The four guests of honor and the quartet of young stallions were also watching her dance of seduction. Everyone noticed that, during her mating dance, her parasol-paneled sundress spiraled deliciously upward.

She crooked her finger beckoning Brent to the dance floor, but a big, bold, and bawdy man of the Fijian military came forward instead.

He grabbed Laura and quickly nestled into her. He proceeded to cocoon Laura within his arms.

Laura was alarmed, but the amount of alcohol she had consumed that day lowered her resistance to confrontation. She also had confidence that if anything went wrong, her Prince Charming would rescue her.

Brent's alarm bells were hitting decibels unknown to him since the bar fighting days of his youth. In the instant it takes to blink, he had already surveyed the incident happening right before his eyes.

The man was big and likely, very skilled at fighting.

He had three other friends.

Numbers were not on Brent's side.

Things looked bleak.

On the upside, the cup could be half full.

They were military men and therefore should have some sense of decorum and a modicum of respect.

The guy just might be a friendly sort who simply liked to dance.

"We are at the Hard Rock Cafe on the patio with several people dancing and drinking," Brent thought, "so what could happen?"

Brent decided to remain seated and stay quiet. That did not mean that he wasn't full of adrenaline. He was ready to pounce like a panther stalking its victim if he saw any indication that Laura was in danger.

Laura knew she was in trouble. Her seductive finger movement had not enticed her intended Romeo. Instead, she was being hugged by a man she didn't know, and he smelled like rum.

The man steered her further onto the dance floor before he introduced himself as Etak.

Laura didn't give a damn about who he was, but she fully understood the position that she and, for that matter, Brent were in.

Brent was witness to this but knew Laura could handle herself with overaggressive men.

To Laura, the slow music seemed to get even more unhurried. Etak was now fully interwoven with her body and pressing his stiffened manhood into her home base. She tried to create distance between herself and the perpetrator. This wasn't going to happen, as Etak was dedicating himself to staying in proximity to his goal. Laura knew the words of the song they were dancing to—and when it ended. She could hang on that long. Laura was no schoolgirl and very wise in the ways of lechers.

Etak's hand slid from Laura's lower back to directly on top of her ass.

Laura knew she had to draw a line, but she also knew that if Brent saw what this guy was doing, shit was going to hit the fan. She was afraid that Brent could get seriously hurt by these Fijian military men. She decided to give up her ass in favor of escape, which lay ahead at the end of the song. For her, it seemed that this dance would never end.

Etak took Laura's hiding his actions from her husband as permission to advance the troops. He started invading her body with his hand under her sundress and felt her nakedness outside of the thong she was wearing. His other hand played tag with the sides of her breast.

Etak had crossed Laura's red line. Laura pulled away from Etak and shouted at the top of her lungs, "Fuck off, and leave me alone!"

2

THE GOODBYE

TWO MONTHS EARLIER

MORNING WAS FAR from being awake. A fall chill filled the air.

"Goodbye sweetheart," Laura said as she embraced the love of her life. "Have fun living in the bush this week. I hope you see what you're going for, but I hope you don't shoot one," she whispered.

Brent quietly chuckled and gave the mother of his children a full-body hug. It was time for him to leave.

They created just enough space between them so they could enjoy a lover's farewell kiss.

Brent turned from Laura's caresses and left to go on his annual moose hunt.

With tears in her eyes, she watched until his truck and trailer passed out of sight. Laura closed the front door of their home that had housed so much love over the years. She felt cold and headed to the kitchen to pour herself a cup of coffee. She hoped the time it took to drink her java would act as a transitional bridge to get the day from darkness to dawn. Laura knew she would be busy for the entire week and a half ahead of her before she and Brent flew off on their vacation of a lifetime.

In no particular order, she thought about a good cleaning of the house, getting ready, all the documents and money they would need, and packing the suitcases while being very careful not to pack too much as the overweight penalties were pricey. Just as important was to take Brent's dress uniform to the dry cleaners and get it returned before his retirement party. There were too many chores to deal with logistics right now. Laura decided to start the house cleaning first because she wanted to make sure that if her daughter-in-law and grandkids came to visit, the house would look perfect.

Her two boys, James and Michael, had said they would be in for a visit after their father returned from the hunt but before Laura and Brent left on vacation. That time period seemed so far away, but James had business. James always seemed to have business, and Michael was away on an assignment with the military. James had promised to take a few days off just before Brent and Laura departed for paradise.

Laura took a moment to reflect on her life. The verdict came back faster than Cupid's arrow. This put a smile on her face and caused an extra beat in her heart. Laura was hopelessly in love with the man she had decided to spend her life with. The two offspring that their lovemaking had produced, sent forward into this world, were two of the finest sons that anyone could ask for.

Both their babies, James and Michael who everyone calls Mike had turned into outstanding adults who were respected in their workplaces and communities. Even more important was that they were both loving husbands and fathers. Still, she had to admit her boys were very different from one another.

James was naturally endowed with a superior mind. His elementary school teachers had always slid advanced learning lessons into his backpack before he returned home from school every day. Neither of his parents had had to sit beside James and direct him through processes or equations. He had figured his way through problems and, best of all, solutions by himself. In high school, James had taken all advanced courses. His grade abstracts in his junior and senior years had always been at the top of the class.

During his university years, James had had to take part-time work to monetarily assist his education. Laura thought she and Brent had done the best they could, but the cost of quality education outweighed the quantity of money they'd been able to afford. This had led to their oldest son applying for and succeeding in being a part-time hire for Meredith Reinsurance as a file clerk.

True to James's work ethic, he had decided that if he was going to have to fetch files all day, he would make the file system work for him. James had gone on to redesign the entire system so efficiently that it had caught the eye of the Canadian chief executive officer. James had worked part time for Meredith all four of his university years and completed his bachelor of science degree with distinction. He had stood first in his graduating class.

Laura and Brent had never had to worry about James joining the real world. Meredith Reinsurance had been waiting at the exit door of the University of Guelph to offer him a career in reinsurance. The job offer had come with good money and had been a big promotion from the position of file clerk. He had started as a junior underwriter.

James had gained, from working his university years at Meredith, a basic understanding of the reinsurance business. It was simply layering on top of the risk that a conventional insurance company couldn't assume if anything catastrophic occurred with their client's business. For that, reinsurance firms made plenty of money. The pressure would always center around the underwriter's tolerance for risk and his ability to read and decipher data. Cold, hard facts without emotion were 90 percent of the critical thinking behind any deal entered into.

James never let his corporate life interfere with his personal life. He was fulfilled outside of his career through the love and grounding of his husband, Daniel, whom he had married straight out of university. They were both devoted parents who would stand in the way of a bullet for their young son, Brady.

Meredith had always been on his ass to make some real money and exert his expertise in the American market. They had often wanted James to transplant his family from Canada to the United States. James had thanked Meredith for their gracious offers but always turned them down. Daniel and Brady always came first. He had not even thought of uprooting and transplanting them to a foreign land. It had been a done deal; James's family would remain homegrown.

Within a few years, Meredith Reinsurance had canceled its Canadian operations.

But word of James's prowess and abilities had made it all

the way up the chain to the big boss of the entire enterprise structure. The CEO, Rudolph Lidster, had flown James to Bermuda for a meeting with the shareholders. Rudolph, surrounded by a cloud of smoke hanging in the air from a Cuban cigar, had laid the big bomb on James.

Meredith would supply all the seed money for James to start his own fledgling cyber reinsurance company in Canada. This start-up business would cover identity theft, data breach, and cyberattack. Furthermore, Meredith would act as a safety net for any losses the new company couldn't absorb for the first three-year period. For this, Meredith Reinsurance would take 35 percent ownership of James's fledgling company for three years.

James had said yes to Meredith and graciously thanked Rudolph for his grand gesture.

Rudolph had asked James what he would name his new enterprise.

James, with a big grin, had retorted, "Hudson Reinsurance, naturally."

Laura couldn't help thinking that James had made all the correct decisions. Hudson Reinsurance was a glowing success. His three years with Meredith were complete, and the business was now entirely his own. Brent and Laura's son was now flying a corporate private jet to meetings all over the world. He had over fifty employees in his corporate office in Toronto. James was about to take Hudson Reinsurance from private to public. All that remained were the hoops he would have to jump through with the Regulatory Commission. Then his initial public offering would hit the stock market.

Where James was calculating and thought strategically, his younger brother, Mike, was always laid back and surveyed every situation. You would never find Mike in a circle of people and holding court. He would lurk in the outer limits of the group until he had some comprehension of what was going on. Once he had a grasp of the subject matter being discussed, he would feel comfortable enough to weigh in.

Mike was so laid back and easygoing that some of his teachers had thought he'd exuded boredom and disdain for the education he had been learning. In fact, the opposite had been the case. Mike had savored every bit of knowledge imparted to him. Mike's problem had been the useless bullshit that had come along with the mere tidbits of useful content he could use in real life.

Mike had believed his thirst for knowledge was quenched more from outside, rather than within, the education system. Mike had walked the forest and picked out plants and berries. He had then sought the appropriate book to read to become educated in these previously mysterious floras. This, to Mike, was education. He'd already had the skills to read and write with the best of them. He hadn't needed any teacher to school him in history, geography, or science. That knowledge could be found in books. If he'd wanted to know something, he would look it up himself.

Mike had been interested in someone pointing him in a direction that would enthuse his curiosity. Everything real-world had interested Mike to no end. Sitting in a classroom, listening to the teacher regurgitate a slew of facts they already had memorized because this was their tenth year teaching the same old shit, hadn't interested Mike.

The bottom line was that school hadn't really been Mike's thing. Learning about real life had been. Still, Mike had received great marks all the way through school. He'd also gotten the same comment year after year: "Mike could show a little more enthusiasm during class."

Like his brother, Mike had been accepted into the University of Guelph. His mindset had been totally different from James's. Mike had taken bachelor of arts courses. This had been a recommendation from his brother, James. James had inferred that one didn't need as in-depth a degree like the one he had; all one really needed was a "Degree that says you can be taught." In other words, any degree would suffice.

That was exactly what Mike had done. He had really taken a minor in arts and majored in the sciences of human tendencies outside of the classroom.

He'd become quite the card player, with poker being his specialty. Mike had learned to count cards, calculate odds, and discover tells in his opponents. It had been like he was stalking prey using their own inclinations.

He'd used most of his excess time to get a good workout in at the weight room. Four years of pushing weight had turned Mike into an incredible specimen of a human being; he'd become chiseled.

Many years of stalking the bush with his dad and studying the flora had made Mike quite bush savvy. He could survive in any forest because he knew what he could and couldn't eat. Brent was a wealth of knowledge when tracking game, increasing the possibility of staying alive in a hostile atmosphere. Mike had it all: brains, brawn, and the looks of a Hudson.

Bachelor of arts in hand, Mike had had to decide what was next in his life. He'd needed a job. The corporate world or being a municipal civil servant hadn't interested him. Mike hadn't been sure he'd had the stick-to-it-ness to ever make a success of a start-up business.

Laura, too, had had a deep curiosity in what Michael would do after graduation. What better way to find out than to track him down and discuss his future endeavors? Perhaps she could provide some guidance, if needed.

Laura's youngest son had followed her home from Guelph a week later after his graduation. This had been her chance. She had met him at the front door of their family home and given him a big hug. She had been very aware of how strong and handsome her baby had become. She had felt the power in his arms but also the gentleness in his embrace.

Laura had sat Mike down in the family living room, and she'd asked her son what his plans were now that he was a university graduate. She had not expected the reply she'd received.

Her son had gone on about not wanting to be a corporate guy or an entrepreneur. She'd listened to him say he wanted to be a public servant. That had sounded good to her, but then the bombshell dropped. Laura had heard the words come out of Michael's mouth. Her motherly instincts had tried hard to block her fears from rupturing her soul. She'd heard the words "Canada's military."

Laura had put on a poker face that even her son couldn't see through. "That's nice. Can you tell me more about your plans, dear?"

As Mike had given her his reasons, Laura's mind had been elsewhere. Her baby wanted to put himself in harm's way. At this point, the expense of four years of university and higher learning had meant nothing to her. Her baby, in her mind, was going off to war!

Laura had calmly excused herself. She'd smiled at her son and said, "I need a bathroom break." She'd needed time; she'd needed space; she'd needed to cry. Laura had also known that nothing she could say would dissuade her son from joining the military. She'd opted to look for the positive.

In the bathroom, Laura had shaken her head. "What's positive about this situation?" She knew her son. Laura had sensed that Mike was still trying to find himself, and the military would give him a chance to further develop. Discipline was the number one thing he'd learn. A sense of duty and belonging to a team wouldn't hurt Mike either.

In the end, she'd returned from her bathroom break and, before sitting down, she'd kissed her baby on the forehead. She'd told her son that she knew Canada was respected for peacekeeping throughout the world, so his risk of injury or death wouldn't be too substantial. After all, her husband was a firefighter, which had inherent risks of its own.

She'd risen once again from her chair and approached her son. She'd held her arms wide, asking for an unspoken hug. Her son had also risen and put his arms around his mom. Through glassy eyes, Laura had told her baby that "Whatever you choose to do, I will be behind you 100 percent."

With the unconditional support of his parents, Mike's decision had been confirmed. He'd gone to the recruitment office and enlisted in the Canadian Armed Forces. He'd gone to boot camp for ten weeks. He'd excelled because of his superior physical fitness and mental acuity. In no time at all, Mike had been elevated to team leader.

Mike, in his superiors' opinion, was a rare breed. He was a strategic thinker, a physical specimen with practically zero fat content, and he had the ability to multitask in stressful situations. On his posting application, in all areas where it had asked his preference as to where he wanted to be posted,

Mike had replied, "Wherever my superiors think I would be of best service."

In the end, it had been his ability to track and shoot in stealth mode that had sealed his fate. Mike had been assigned to Dwyer Hill, which was located outside of Ottawa—the capital of Canada—in the province of Ontario. Mike would hold the rank of private and be assigned to general duties.

Mike and James had laughed, and James had told him that "You are their bitch."

The traditional boot camp graduation party had been a festive occasion where goodbyes had been said, and recruit assignments had been revealed to others. The libations had been kept to the proverbial spiking of the punch bowl. It hadn't been a night to get carried away, as all recruits had been under increased scrutiny. Plenty of Mike's classmates had been headed for Trenton, Ontario, where he'd expected that he would also be assigned. A few had been assigned out West, and one or two would go to the East Coast bases. When Mike had informed some others where he was headed, their eyebrows had gone up immediately. Mike had seen the surprised expressions and felt the celebratory pats on the back. What he'd come to realize was that Dwyer Hill was the home of the Canadian Special Operations Forces Command and the home base for Joint Task Force Two.

JTF2 was on par with, and held the same respect as, American SEAL teams and Special Forces. There were a few distinct differences between JTF2 and SEAL teams. The first and most distinct was the degree of secrecy around their missions. When SEAL Team Six had taken out Osama bin Laden, the head of the al-Qaeda organization, everyone had learned that Neptune Spear was the code name for the operation.

A book had been written and the team members had been interviewed on mass media. In the JTF2 world, this would never happen. In Canada, only two persons outside of Special Operations Forces Command ever knew about operations conducted by JTF2: the prime minister of Canada and the minister of defense. That was it!

Family and friends could communicate with their loved ones, but never during missions.

When it had been time for Mike to leave his parents' house and begin the four-hour drive to Dwyer Hill, Mike had gotten a hug and a pat on his back from his dad, and then he'd shifted his attention to his mom and cuddled her in his arms. The hug had been longer than usual, and Laura had cried gently against his chest. Laura had trembled in fear that something would happen to her baby boy.

After two years at Dwyer Hill, Mike had made the rank of sergeant in Canada's elite commando force, JTF2. Laura hadn't dared ask, but she knew that Brent had often asked himself the question, "We know what Mike does, but what does he do?"

Brent had tried to have conversations with Mike about what his job entailed. Brent had known every time before he'd asked what the answer would be.

Mike, with a smile on his face, had always responded, "If I tell you, I'm going to have to kill you."

Now, in the days before her vacation, Laura danced around for the rest of the day, going from chore to chore. She always saved her two favorite tasks for last: seeing to the floors and vacuuming the carpets. Laura always did the dusting first. She didn't like this activity too much because it was so finicky.

Her cell phone rang. The call display showed it was her daughter-in-law, Nicole. "Hello, Niki. How are you?"

Niki replied, "Great. Do you have a minute to talk?"

"For you, I have all the time in the world," Laura joyously replied.

"That's good, Laura. I have some time on my hands the next few days. I thought I would take advantage of Mike being on assignment to come up your way and visit with friends and, of course, bring the grandkids to have a visit with Nana. If I leave in the next hour, I should be at your house in the early afternoon."

Laura, with glee in her voice, told Niki, "Get your ass in gear, and get here as soon as possible."

Niki replied, "That's what I'm going to do. Is there anything I can bring?"

"Nothing," said Laura. "Drive carefully, and tell Hank and Catherine, I love them and can't wait to see them. I also have some of my homemade strawberry jam that Hank loves so much."

"OK," responded Niki. "I will see you shortly. Love Ya. Bye."

"Love you too," answered Laura. "Hurry up," she said before she hung up the phone.

3

HUNT CAMP

BRENT'S CAMP WAS an orphaned railway passenger car that was sitting on a redundant spur line. The car's guts had been hollowed out. Primitive wooden cupboards had been built. The hunt gangs over the years had wired a kitchen area, and a stove and fridge had been added. Over time, the rows of passenger seats had been removed, and a series of single beds, complete with finely aged mattresses, had been added. This poor man's vacation residence was not airtight. Everything electric was powered by a generator that was parked outside, a little distance from the train car so no one in the car would breathe in the exhaust fumes waffling through the air. Most of one's money went toward buying fuel to keep the generator fed.

The entire inside of the railway car lived a charmed life. It was used by hunters and First Nations people alike. The out-house was as one would picture it, except it had to be moved from time to time over the years as the holes filled. In bad years, the shithouse had been located on a bit of a hill. Snow would fall. If someone had to take a dump at three o'clock in the morning, it should have been classified as an Olympic sport. One would slip, slide, fall, and be frozen before one even started their business. Then, to add insult to injury, the person before might have used the last of the toilet paper. The one good thing about a successful outcome was that one was able to hone their downhill skiing skills. Making it back to bed had felt like winning a gold medal.

The hunters who frequented this rail car included First Nations people of the Ojibwa tribe.

When Brent had first started to hunt this area some thirty-plus years ago, he'd looked at these original inhabitants with a jaded eye. He hadn't known them and, therefore, his initial instinct had been not to trust them. How wrong he'd turned out to be. Over the decades, they had taught him about bush wisdom and life lessons that he would go on to use for the rest of his existence.

Brent's number one mentor was Clinton Strathroy. He was an elder in the tribe. Brent and Clinton had been friends for over two decades. Brent thought of him often and wished he had just a little of Strathroy's temperament.

Brent had also gotten to know Albert Medford. Albert was a young man and strong as a bull. What wasn't to like about him? He was always the one who carted in a load of wood to stoke the not-so-airtight stove. Albert was also the generator starter and one of many who made sure Brent safely got out of the bush before nightfall.

The lessons he'd learned from all his Ojibwa friends were greatly appreciated: little hints that sharpened his sniper skills, how to track and hunt down both animals and humans alike, and how a prey animal's instincts could be used against it.

These Ojibwa people had become his friends. These hunters without fail knew when Brent would make his trek to camp. They would show up and greet him. Brent knew the hot coffee would always be his treat, and that he would probably also throw in a week of lunch munchies. After the day's hunt was complete, they would return to their own homes to be with their families. One would always stay at the camp until he was sure Brent had gotten out of the bush and returned to the rail car; he would wait until Brent was able to start his generator and get enough power to turn on his stove. Brent would then have heat and cook for the night.

The Ojibwa men would always have a beer before their exit. This was a fair trade-off for Brent. In return, he had security and a feeling of peace. All and all, the hunt camp was never trashed or vandalized. It was as if a bastardized version of the Marquess of Queensbury rules were in effect: enjoy your hunt but leave no footprint.

The camp was located about forty kilometers outside of Geraldton, in northwestern Ontario, a sixteen-hour drive from Brent's home. Every year, he drove up in the last week of October and hunted during the first week of November. It seemed odd to Brent that, in all his time hunting, he'd never once felt the urge to go visit nearby rural towns.

Brent had retired just a little more than a week ago. He'd achieved the rank of district chief with the Mississauga Fire and Emergency Services. He had to admit that he felt good about how he'd handled himself. His professionalism and strategic thinking during the emergencies he'd dealt with had put him in fine stead with his ranking officers. The shining star, to him, was the respect he'd earned from the personnel under his command.

His gala retirement party was scheduled a few days after the hunting trip. Over two hundred of his brothers and sisters had bought tickets for the event. He was almost as nervous about being the center of attention as he'd been on the day he'd gotten married. Brent didn't know what kind of night it would be. Would it take the form of a roast, or would others prepare speeches to give everybody a glimpse into his career? Brent did know there would be a speech given on the Medal of Bravery that he and his fellow firefighter Steve St. Louis had been awarded for one specific emergency response. It would likely be given by the fire chief. With women and family members in attendance he would laugh at the flowery speech that might come out of the fire chief's mouth.

It was not yet light in the woods, and all Brent Hudson had was a flashlight to illuminate the bush trail he was negotiating. It was the same path that Brent had meandered on for most of his adult life. He loved to hunt and felt very comfortable in the woods of Northern Ontario.

The air was nippy, but that was to be expected. Sir Weighs-A-Lot, his Remington .308 rifle, seemed heavier and that wasn't expected. He was getting old. Brent, all through his life, had truly enjoyed the outdoors. He loved how, at dawn, the forest became alive. Even if no game was in sight, he could watch chipmunks scurrying from tree to tree or making a racket on the forest floor. Often, they would holler back their indignant replies to bitching blue jays.

Black squirrels would be the next to awaken. They were much quieter in the trees but, on a floor of leaves, they would make any hunter alert. Hunters wouldn't be able to discount their travels, as the squirrels would somehow sound like bigger game as they surveyed the area ahead of them. Sometimes, little flocks of finches would fly from tree to tree in a tight formation, and Brent would always wonder how they never collided. None of those flitting finches seemed to be in charge.

If one sat back and used one's senses, the forest would sound like an orchestra, complete with a woodwind section.

Brent was just arriving at his hunting stand. The stand consisted of a ladder with twenty-three steel steps. Five and a half square meters of floor space had one meter walls on all four sides that acted as a windbreak. The walls also acted as a gun perch to steady his rifle on when the time to kill approached. Brent was not what anyone would call a tree hugger, and he fully understood that the concept of culling the herd was needed for a balance in nature.

He called his hunting stand the Trojan Horse after the contraption Greek soldiers had left as a gift for the goddess Athena at the gates of the city of Troy. That had been no true gift to the people of Troy but, in this case, it was a gift of comfort to himself. Brent reflected on how difficult his Trojan Horse had been to build. He had not been able to justify the expense of new lumber while raising his family, so it had all been built with scrap lumber.

For years, he had taken two weeks of vacation to hunt. The first week had always been used to transport scavenged materials for the Trojan Horse. When the Trojan Horse had finally been completed, he'd used the first week of subsequent seasons to scout his hunting area and make mental notes of the changes that had occurred over the last year. The second week had always been the opening of the hunting season for moose: the reward for all the work he always put into the first week. This year, he would only hunt for a week.

Brent scaled the stairs of the Trojan Horse and unlocked the trap door that doubled as part of the floor. It was like looking into the attic of his house, except his roof was now a daily mural of different skies. Brent hauled himself into, and stood up in, the game stand. It was still dark, and dawn remained a short time away. He took this time just to stand still. The silence was broken by a blue jay squawking about something invading its space.

Brent sat down on his throne: a rustic, old spin chair on wheels. It had long since lost its value scooting around office floors, but it was the best chair in the forest. He remembered it well. It fit his butt, and when he leaned back, the chair gave just enough so that he was able to warm his face in the sunshine. The arms of the chair were positioned just so Sir Weighs-A-Lot wouldn't feel like a tonne of weight resting on his legs.

He traveled ever so slightly in his chair, which made the wheels squeak. Not much, but enough to scare his prey if he wasn't careful. Brent was always on the alert for any unnatural movement or sound that was not created by the wind. He settled in and scanned the forest from left to right, very slowly. He favored whatever direction was upwind from the Trojan Horse.

Brent heard a dog barking far off in the woods. He knew that bark. Like humans, dogs had a distinctive voice, and this voice could only belong to Blackie. This dog belonged to his Ojibwa family. That meant that they, too, were out hunting moose.

Brent marveled at how Blackie was a razor-sharp tracker. This dog could capture the scent of moose. He would then alert everyone in his hunting party with his barking. Blackie had an unusual, canny ability to turn an animal and head it back toward his strategically stationed humans. When the dog finally caught sight of game, and if it was heading in the proper direction, Blackie would turn into a herding dog. He would stop barking and just alarm the target enough to keep it moving toward his masters. When Blackie stopped barking, the voice of a high-powered rifle would be heard shortly thereafter. His success rate was legendary among the First Nations in the area.

Brent gave Blackie his due, but he also knew of a dog that would have rivaled his intelligence: Duchess.

In his youth, he had been a paperboy for the Globe and Mail newspaper. No matter the weather, whether rain or shine or a cold that froze a person right to the bone, the paper had to be delivered. According to Brent's dad, if the paper wasn't at the customer's door by six o'clock in the morning, it was of no use to them. Brent had been the chief operating officer of a fledgling delivery business. He'd even had an employee that he'd paid in biscuits.

Duchess had delivered to half of his paper route customers. She had been very adept and smarter than some humans knew.

Brent eased himself back into his chair, careful to keep noise at a minimum. He pulled the brim of his baseball hat ever so slightly down to ease the glare of the sun rising higher in the sky. Brent made a big sigh—no more cold winters doing emergency work. This winter, he and Laura were off to Australia. This winter, after the hunt, he would be warm. Five months in Hervey Bay, located on the East Coast of Oz. He whispered to himself, "Let the hunt begin."

4

PHONE CALL TO LAURA

THE WEEK WAS progressing nicely, maybe a bit slow for Laura's liking, but she put it down to the excitement of their trip to Australia. Very soon, they would fly off to the land of Oz.

When she'd first approached her husband about possibly going on a trip of a lifetime to Australia, Brent had answered with an enthusiastic, "Count me in."

Laura had suggested a date that would be just a few days after he returned home from hunting.

Brent had mustered up a quick reply, "Just let me know when I'm supposed to be on the plane."

Laura had likened this situation to their wedding. Brent's responsibility was to show up while she took care of all the planning. This didn't mean that Brent was complacent; he knew from years of being married to her that two cooks in the kitchen didn't work. Laura could be very submissive in other areas of their marriage, but planning events wasn't one of them. She'd taken Brent's replies to mean that she was in full command of the trip to Australia. This had suited her, as she liked to research and felt pleased when a plan came together.

Laura had presented Brent with a file folder of documentation carefully placed in chronological order to simplify their discussions. Laura had told Brent that they would fly out of Toronto to Los Angeles. The duration of this flight would be five hours and fifteen minutes. Her voice had gone quieter when she'd told him the flight time from Los Angeles to Sydney, Australia, was fourteen hours and fifty minutes. Once they landed in Sydney they were booked on a domestic flight to Brisbane. This would be another hour and twenty minutes. Finally, the last leg of the journey would be from Brisbane to Hervey Bay. This final leg of the flight would be just less than one hour. This meant a total flight time of twenty-two hours and twenty-five minutes.

Brent had taken an exhausted exhale and resigned himself; these were just hoops they had to jump through to get to where they wanted to be. Laura had left it at that. She didn't have the nerve to tell him that, including the three-hour pre-check-in in Toronto and layover times in Los Angeles, Sydney, and Brisbane, it would take just over twenty-eight hours to get to their rented condo situated on the Pacific Ocean in the state of Queensland.

"Here we come, Hervey Bay," resonated in her mind.

They would be living in a place called the Riviera Resort, in a neighborhood called Torquay. The Pacific Ocean was just a hop, skip, and a jump away from the Riviera Resort. They would just have to exit their resort, hop across a two-lane road, and skip over pure white sands before they could jump and put their feet in the warm waters. The entire distance was about half the length of a football field. The condo was just shy of fifty-six square meters, but nobody would be coming to visit them that far away, and it would be easy to keep up with the cleaning.

Laura made herself a cup of tea and sat down in her favorite chair in the living room. She looked at the decor, which some would say dated the house. Laura had no problem with that because it spoke to the fondest memories she had. Also, if someone's purpose was to evaluate her interior decorating, then they weren't really friends anyway. Laura had plenty of friends, but because she had been with Brent for so many years, they were all somehow intertwined with the fire department. That was OK with her. Though all the men were unique and different, they seemed to marry women who were loving and very grounded.

A smile came to Laura's face as she acknowledged that her thinking might be outdated. There were also plenty of women who were firefighters, and rightly so. As for marriage, she only had to look at her oldest boy to understand that not everybody married the opposite sex.

Laura immediately thought of James and Daniel. They had been married eight years ago, and she would dare anyone to tell her that their love wasn't as real and as deep as anyone else's. Daniel was exactly what James needed in a partner. He was patient, gentle, and business savvy. Daniel could talk boardroom with the best of them but mostly left barroom speak to James. Daniel was the pure heart of the relationship and James the focused disciplinarian of the household. Everything ran like a train and was always on time.

Laura thought that, between the two of them, they were

raising a smart, loving child. Brady was nine, but he talked like a well-educated adult. He was tall, without an ounce of fat, and energetic to the point of being a handful, at times. This didn't bother Laura because his hugs were to die for. Brady didn't hug just anybody, and those he had no choice but to hug, he touched with indifference. But this all changed for Nana because Brady would lovingly squeeze her so that she felt the most special of anyone. Brady knew where his bread was buttered. Still, he loved Nana, and nothing Nana asked of him would ever be a burden. Brady loved her that much.

Laura's thoughts drifted to how well her younger boy did in the marriage department as well. Laura knew Michael had been floundering all through university and just after his graduation. He'd had no goal and no foundation in life on which to build upon. Laura had seen the armed forces as a place for Michael to hide—a place where others would dictate his life. Laura had honestly worried about Michael and what his future entailed.

That is, until he'd met and married Nicole. The Hudsons had soon adapted to her nickname, Niki. Laura couldn't help but close her eyes and visualize just how beautiful Niki was. Brent had, several times, told Laura that Niki reminded him of her in her youth. Secretly, Laura allowed herself to think, "I was a looker."

It warmed her heart to think that Brent had always thought she was the sexiest girl in the world

Being with Niki had allowed Michael to build his inner foundation block by block. Niki had obviously seen something that Laura had missed. Michael wasn't hiding anymore; he was thriving. Michael was leading men in the most elite special forces team that Canada had to offer.

Sometimes, Laura and Niki would talk about the misgivings Niki had each and every time Michael went on a mission. Niki had given birth to two children sired by Michael. The kids were as different as day and night. Henry (Hank), the oldest, was gentle and very loving. Whenever his dad came home from a mission, Hank showed him that he could also scrap. Michael and his son would horseplay daily, and only occasionally would Hank end up in tears. Niki would lovingly inquire as to why Michael had to make Hank cry. The reply was always the same: "To toughen him up." Laura knew Hank didn't need to be toughened up; he was plenty strong and dealing with his little sister, hurricane Catherine. Catherine was Daddy's girl. She could be wreaking havoc and raining destruction down on everything Hank was building but when Dad showed up, so did the princess. Both of Niki and Michael's children had two defining traits: they had their mother's warm hugs and their father's hard head.

Out of it all, Laura thanked her lucky stars that Niki had come into Michael's life. It was like Laura had prayed and the big guy upstairs had granted her wish. She had wanted a person strong enough to be with and guide Michael, yet gentle enough to teach his children to love and respect others. The timing had absolutely been correct to present Laura with her miracle: Nicole.

Laura was watching the sun go down. She had made herself a cup of tea and was sitting in her favorite chair. Right beside her was the phone. Laura knew Brent would call her right on the designated time. He was punctual to the point of being anal. After his long day in the woods, he would trek back to camp. Once back at base, he would have to scale a thirty-meter sand hill to make his traditional phone call to

Laura. Cell phone service was sketchy in those parts but, over the years, he'd found enough signal available at the top of what everyone called the Sandy's.

She went over in her mind the items she wanted to talk to Brent about. There were so many, and she had to prioritize them. Her husband would only be on the phone for a brief time before he would lose the signal due to bad cell service or a low battery.

Laura picked up the phone on the first ring. "Hello, dear."

"Hello," Brent replied. "And how are you, babe?"

Laura elected to go with their business first. She told her husband that his dress uniform was back from the cleaners. She wanted to know the whereabouts of his shoes so she could polish them. She informed him that the fire department wanted to know if, in the morning before his retirement party, he would address the rookie class. "Apparently, it's their very first day." On the same topic, Laura hinted that, with all that time alone in the bush, maybe he could work a little on his speech.

Brent was able to give two quick responses: yes to addressing the rookie class, and yes to working on his speech.

"Sweetheart, how's the hunt going? Nothing dead, I hope?" Laura further inquired.

Brent replied, "Nothing but my feet. It's hellishly cold up here. Don't you worry little lady, I will have my moose before the week is out."

Laura let out a big groan and dared to move on to a new topic. "Honey, you will never guess who called me and who came for a visit."

Brent answered, "Let me guess, an old boyfriend?"

Laura laughed. "Don't be silly; he's also a hunter. Niki called and came for a visit with Hank and Catherine."

"Great," Brent replied. "What's going on with everybody?"

Laura started into her report. "Hank is doing very well in hockey. Niki lamented that being a hockey mom is over-rated." Laura laughed and suggested to Brent that "Getting up to attend those godforsaken 5:00 a.m. practices are exacting its toll on her."

Brent broke in and refreshed Laura's memory. "When our kids were small and had an early morning practice, one of the parents would always bring a flask of rye so we could enjoy a coffee royal and take the chill off."

Laura joking replied, "That was why you were always so happy on Sunday mornings." Laura kept motoring on with what she wanted to say. "Hank and I were playing trucks, but not ordinary trucks. They were trucks that could talk. We have the most unusual conversations. One of these short chats was about how much he loves Papa."

Brent whispered "Aww" into his cell phone and inwardly, he felt warm with love.

Laura sensed that Brent was getting ready to get off the phone, and she still had one more topic of great importance that she wanted to discuss. Laura hurriedly said, "Catherine is really starting to develop into a beautiful young lady." Then she broke into the topic that was concerning her most. She informed her loving husband that "Niki worries about Mike when he is on assignment. She worries that one day he won't come home to her. She wishes he would just retire and take his pension and move back here around family."

Brent's reply was that "He would still have to find another

job because his pension won't be enough. He's too young to completely retire."

"Perhaps you could get him a position on the fire department?" Laura asked.

"I only have one bar left on my phone, so we have to wrap it up now," said Brent.

Laura knew her time communicating with the love of her life had come to an end. "Bye, baby. I love you. Be safe and come home to me. I miss you, Brent. We make good kids together."

"I love you too, honey," swooned Brent. "Keep the faith."

Then the phone went dead. Laura paused for just a minute to reflect upon how much she truly loved the father of her children.

5

LAST DAY OF THE HUNT

"TODAY IS THE day," Brent whispered. He stood outside and inhaled the crisp morning air. He was headed to the woods for the last day of the hunt. Brent wrestled with Sir Weighs-A-Lot the entire way until he reached his chair in the Trojan Horse.

Brent's hunting week was almost finished, and he had spent every daylight hour in the Trojan Horse. By midmorning on his last day, the time had arrived to stand up and stretch his legs. Even his throne, from time to time, needed relief from Brent's butt. The foam rubber pillow had become frail and weatherworn from its years of faithful service.

The last day of the hunt was a dilemma in itself. After the hunt, Brent would have personal traveling and family obligations. Tomorrow he would have to get an early start for home. Shooting a bull moose today would be labor intensive. If he were lucky enough to bag a moose at first light, it would be dusk before Brent would be able to process his kill enough for traveling.

And God forbid he shot a moose at dusk. It got cold at night in Northern Ontario. No matter how frigid the weather, Brent would have to gut his kill. No nimrod worth his salt would ever allow a moose that they had killed to deliberately spoil because it was inconvenient. He would have to employ a trick his Ojibwa companions had taught him. Cold as it might be, he would have to take off his coat and lay it over the carcass. This blanket would leave a human scent, both waffling in the night air and on the moose. This would scare off predatory animals during the night. Still, Brent would have to come back the next morning to finish the task of prepping the moose.

For this scenario, he simply would not have time. Brent kept his conscience clean. He had a prearranged agreement with his Ojibwa family that if this set of circumstances ever happened, the moose meat would fill the bellies of his northern companions.

Brent was scoping out the forest when something caught his attention. It was the audible mating call of a bull moose. He could feel his heart rate increase. The sound echoing through the woods indicated the moose was far away. Brent had his own enticements for this big bull. He had a tin can with a long hockey lace coming through the center bottom. He dampened the string with water and slid the pinched lace through his fingers. This created a sound that was eerily similar to a bull moose mating call.

He repeated the tin-can call, and the moose answered.

Brent tried part two of his enticements. He took out two small deer antlers and clacked them together, hopefully to sound like two bulls fighting. The rattling of the antlers fell on deaf ears, and Brent quickly gave up on this enticement. Once again, Brent called to the moose. He waited and got the response he was looking for. The only problem was that the sound was not getting closer to his location. Brent did not have all day to wait on this moose. He would have to get off his tree stand and hunt. He would have to find some way to lessen the space between himself and his prey.

Hunting on foot was an acquired skill.

Brent was so happy that his Ojibwa friends had taught him the concept and, most importantly, the physical act of stalking one's game. Most hunters when hunting big game on the forest floor are taught to walk one step and wait two, then repeat. His Ojibwa friends had said that animals have four legs, thus they move two of their legs in tandem at a time. Therefore, Brent walked two steps and waited three.

Brent was methodically still hunting through the woods. He stopped and did his tin-can call once more. Brent flinched as the moose called back, and he was close. He waited and scanned the bush in the direction of where the sound had come from. There, beyond the red twig dogwoods and up on the ridge ahead, stood a four hundred and fifty-four-kilogram bull moose.

Brent called the dogwoods slap grass because they were tall but relatively thin. If someone proceeded through the slap grass, it would bend to their will but, like an elastic band, it would snap back up and slap an unsuspecting hunter in the face. Brent knew this grass well, as he had the welts to prove it.

In the middle of the red twig dogwoods, Brent stopped

again and spotted his target. He couldn't shoot yet. He needed to get five meters closer to get a clear shot.

The experienced hunter took ten more steps and fell hard on his face. The crashing and banging sound that echoed through the forest was akin to a full-scale marching band. His face was bloodied, but still he managed to scurry back up to his feet. He saw the bull moose looking directly at him with nostrils flared. The moose gave a disrespectful snort, turned, and vanished into the forest.

The embarrassed hunter looked down and immediately spied the cause of his demise. It was a classic example of an unstoppable force meeting an immovable object. In this case, the base of a clump of dogwoods. Brent made his way back out of the red twig dogwoods and sat on a fallen tree. He laughed to himself. "You dumb fuck."

The hunt was over for another season. The shadows from the sun were long and ominous. Brent made his way back to the Trojan Horse and closed it up for another year. He descended his metal ladder and traversed the woods back to hunt camp. His Ojibwa family were there to greet him. It didn't bother Brent that he did not fill his tag for moose. Just having had solitude and peace with nature sufficed.

Brent's time was now limited to saying goodbye to his Ojibwa family, cleaning up camp, and making sure he got a decent night's sleep before his long trek home the next morning.

Brent laughed to himself. He knew that upon his return, Laura would be dressed to the nines in a very slinky dress. Truth be known, Brent suspected Laura, like himself, was counting the hours until he was back home and nestled in her charms. Brent had known he was the one when Laura had let him know early in their relationship that "I can see my babies in your eyes." Brent still remembered the first time he had laid eyes on Laura.

It had all begun when he'd been fresh out of high school and working his first full-time job. It had been for Canadian National Railways. He had been given the title of billing clerk, which amounted to nothing more than inputting data on a computer. Brent had gotten along fabulously with his immediate supervisor, Cody. He and Brent had had somewhat of a gentleman's agreement. The deal had been that when a good-looking, single girl was brought into the billing department, Cody would nonchalantly sit her next to Brent.

One day, as Brent had been plugging along on his computer, he'd gotten a visit from Cody. Accompanying him had been this beautiful creature, whom he'd introduced to Brent as Laura. One look at her and the young Casanova thought he had died and gone to heaven. She had been gorgeous and green eyed, with brown hair down to her ass and a body that just wouldn't quit. Brent had been selected to be her mentor and show her the ropes.

Truth be known, he had wanted to take her in his arms and fuck her right then and there.

They'd quickly become office buddies and had gotten to know each other well. Brent had found out that she was dating a guy named Pat, who was a first-year student at the University of Guelph, hundreds of kilometers from where Laura was living. Pat was living in residence, so this meant they would, at best, see each other once a week.

Brent, on the other hand, had been having casual dates with four different girls. He'd continuously enlightened Laura on his balancing act of successfully juggling his time between these four women.

A few months later, Laura had had her nineteenth birthday. Lover-boy Brent had given her a nice bouquet of roses and, since she had just become of legal drinking age, had asked her if she would like to go out on a date.

She'd replied, "I'm not going to join anyone's harem. If you truly want to go on a date with me, you are going to have to willingly get rid of those four bimbos." That completed, he could then ask her out again as a gentleman.

Brent had been wounded. He hadn't taken Laura's rejection well. He'd left work with his tail between his legs. Still, his curiosity had been piqued. "Who is this beautiful bitch anyway? Who is she to reject me, Mr. Casanova?"

He'd had to regroup. Brent had had to ask himself if taking a chance on losing the sure fucking coming his way for the off chance he may be lucky enough to foster the growth of a relationship with Laura was worth it. He'd looked at Laura from that point on in an entirely different way. He would conquer her. He would show her his charm, his wit, and shortly, maybe the end of Mr. Happy.

Over the next month, Brent had gotten rid of his girlfriends, one by one. Lover boy had become as single as single could be. Brent had then sucked up the courage to ask Laura out one more time.

Laura had known that Brent had been ridding himself of the ladies because she had been getting weekly progress reports. She had also been doing her best to screw with Brent's head. Laura had casually dropped the hint that she and her boyfriend, Pat, were drifting apart. Long-distance dating had been just too much for her to cope with. She'd also indicated that she was tired of being her boyfriend's Saturday night special under the pretense of a date.

Brent, with his heart in his throat, had asked her to go out on another date.

A shrug of her shoulders, a head nod, and an utterance of two words, "All right," and the deal had been sealed.

Brent and Laura would later fall in love. This had been the girl for Brent. Laura had been all he would ever want for the rest of his life.

Two significant events happened before he'd asked Laura to marry him. The first event had occurred on his first overnight stay at Laura's apartment. After an afternoon shift, he'd played late-night shinny hockey with the Canadian National crew. They'd rented the ice from one in the morning until two. Brent had played goal. After the scrimmage, he'd taken a particularly good shower because that night he was going to get in Laura's knickers, hopefully for the first time.

He'd arrived at her place around three. Laura had been in bed, but she'd gotten up to greet him at the door. They had just been supposed to visit, but both had felt that lightning was going to strike that night. And it did.

Brent had maneuvered his way into spending the night. Laura had made him promise that he would be a good boy. He'd agreed but, at the same time, lover boy had been lying through his teeth. Once under the sheets, he'd nestled into Laura's neck and found himself spooning her from behind.

Everything had been going great, but the big guy had not been cooperating. For the first time in Brent's life, he hadn't been able to pop a hard-on. There would be no marathon sex that night.

He had decided he was going to fuck her just like he had all the other women. His heart had said otherwise. Something had been different. He'd been in love. The treason in his heart had told his dick that this was not a conquest. Those days were over. His heart had wanted this relationship to be nurtured with patience so that this relationship would be everlasting. Yes, Brent had been in love for the first time in his life. Brent had left behind the world of fornicating and entered the universe of lovemaking.

Brent had asked Laura to marry him, and she'd graciously accepted. There had been one obstacle standing in the way. To make it official, Laura had demanded that Brent go through the formal process of asking her father for her hand in marriage. This had not been a problem for him, and they'd visited Laura's parents' house the following weekend.

Her parents lived in a small fishing village called Tobermory.

Brent had been able to separate her father from the rest of the family. The nervous suitor had had a big speech planned, that expressed his profound love for the man's daughter. Brent had gotten the first few words out when her father had stopped him midsentence.

Laura's father had said, "I know why you are here, and I'm not going to listen to a bunch of bullshit. Tell me in just one sentence what you can offer my daughter."

Brent had pondered for a moment and replied, "I offer her this: I will protect your daughter and love her every day of my life."

Laura's father had remarked, "Welcome to my family," and opened Brent a beer.

The drive home from the hunting camp would be long, and dusk would be settling in by the time he neared the city. Traffic would be getting thicker as the bright lights of the large city shone on the horizon. But Brent always caught his second wind knowing he would be home and back to Laura in a few more hours. Brent always loved when he got to see Laura for the first time after the hunt.

Brent played the part of a bull moose in rut.

Laura played the willing target.

6

HOMECOMING

LAURA WAS JUST stepping out of the shower. The clock read 11:05 p.m. She was drying herself in front of the mirror, which reflected her figure. Laura thought that soon her man would be home from hunting. She was now ready for any stalking and rutting her big stag had planned for her body. She smiled in appreciation of how well the body of a woman in her fifties was holding up. Her two girls weren't succumbing horribly to the evils of gravity. Her headlights shone brightly and stuck out way longer than the average woman's. As a teenager, this had bothered her and made her a tad self-conscious. But it had stopped the minute she married Brent.

Her husband loved the fact that he and every other man could see them poking out in every blouse she wore. Brent always liked it when she displayed her body, and now that the kids were grown and had families of their own, whenever they could get away on their own, her breasts were foreplay for their lovemaking later. She knew this, she liked this, and she discovered that she was a little bit of an exhibitionist herself.

Laura's hips and waistline were still attractive and could compete against any woman half her age. Just yesterday, Laura had gotten a Brazilian wax, but she'd made sure that a little strip of pussy hair was left. This was what Brent called his landing strip. Laura didn't really care what he called it as long as the big fella was a frequent flier.

Yes, she was ready. Ready for whatever was to happen when Brent returned home.

Laura heard Brent's truck in the driveway and, finally, silence as he turned the key to the off position. It was just after two in the morning; her Romeo would be tired and smelling of bush, a scent that sponge baths couldn't wash off. Laura listened and could hear the shower turn on. Either Brent smelled to high heaven, or he was being a good Boy Scout: always at the ready. Laura knew Brent would be kicking himself in the ass for not managing his time better. She knew he would not disturb her sleep just because he hadn't arrived home early enough to partake in their lovemaking rituals. Laura heard the shower turn off and Brent tiptoeing into their master bedroom. She felt the bed move as her husband eased himself ever so carefully under the covers.

In her best Mae West, Hollywood actress voice, Laura seductively whispered, "I smell a cleaned-up, lollipop big boy, and I want some."

Seeing that Laura was awake, Brent put himself in a position to allow his wife to lay her head on his chest. He could feel the warmth and smell the scents emitting from her body. This was when he felt most loved.

Laura loved this man with a heartbeat that sang out the song, "Love You, Love You, Love You."

When she lay her head on his chest, it meant she was home. It was where she belonged.

7

PREPARATIONS

IN THE MORNING, Laura got up early and sat in the breakfast nook, drinking coffee and reading the newspaper. When Brent finally got up, he greeted her as he always did, with a good morning kiss and a fondle. He always said it was a health checkup, but Laura knew differently.

"How are you feeling after your long drive?"

"I feel like a blocked punt."

"Brent, I'm so excited. We're off to Australia in the coming days."

Brent slowly replied, "Yes, babe, I know. I haven't forgotten and, in fact, I'm looking forward to it." Then he did a Groucho Marx with his eyebrows.

Laura quickly reminded Brent that two days before they left for Australia, he had to address the new recruits in the morning and that his own retirement party was later that evening. Laura suggested he keep working on his speeches so he would appear smart and articulate.

Brent smiled and told Laura, "I will be ready and as brilliant as ever."

They both laughed.

"Laura, I just want to let you know that I'm going to be busy, busy, busy. I have to get my truck washed. I need to get the mud off it from the hunt. Oh, and I still have to clean up the garage. I have to give my beautiful black beast the space it needs to hibernate for the winter."

Laura smiled and sarcastically replied, "Hey, Shakespeare. You only have two things to do. I hope there's enough time in a day to get it all done."

Brent didn't miss a beat when he said, "Doing nothing keeps me busy all day."

No matter, it would keep Brent out of Laura's way while she scurried around checking off last-minute chores from her list. "Brent, sweetheart, you need to listen to what I'm saying now. Focus, OK? Tomorrow is the last clothes washing day before we leave, so if you want any of the clothes you're wearing, make sure they are in the wash. Definitely, I repeat, definitely, you are not to wear fresh clothes tagged for Australia." That settled, she informed her hubby that "I'm going upstairs to the bedroom to continue packing and racking my brain about things I may have missed."

Brent smiled at his spouse. "OK, I'm going to finish my coffee and then proceed to my truck. I have to unload and stow away my hunting gear."

Laura took her last good-natured shot at her hubby. "Don't work too hard." Laura heard a voice call from the foyer.

"Hello? Is anybody home? Mom, Pop, it's me, Michael."

Sweeter words had never been spoken. Laura ran to greet her youngest son. She flew into Mike's arms and cried tears of joy that Michael was safe and back in her clutches. Brent was next and gave his son a hug and a kiss on the cheek. Brent always kissed both boys on the cheek. It was his way of regaining their scent after long absences and letting them know his love was unconditional.

Mike was not in uniform. He had learned years ago that his military colors caused his mother pain.

They resettled in the living room and partook in the pleasures of conversing about the well-being of other family members.

Mike found an opening in the dialogue to garner his parents' attention. "Guys, because of my mission obligations, I'm not going to be able to attend Dad's retirement party. Dad, I'm sorry. I feel terrible, but there's nothing I can do about it. On the upside, I'm here now, and I've missed both of you terribly."

There was a momentary silence before Laura asked her son, "How is your lovely wife doing? Wait," she interjected, "we'll get to Niki in a minute. How are our two adorable grandchildren doing?"

Mike put a quick stop to this chitchat when he asked, "Weren't they just here?"

Mama bear was quick off the mark when she again asked, "How is Niki doing?"

"Niki is a trooper and runs a tight ship when I'm away on business."

"Mike, how do you know she handles things like a trooper?" asked Laura. "I sense fear in Niki's voice whenever she talks to me when you're on a mission."

"Mom," Mike responded, "let's go back to James's and my childhood. Both of us were quite aware when Dad worked nights at the fire station. We knew because of the uneasiness that seeped through every pore in your body. Mom, kids are like dogs. They can feel the fear in others, especially loved ones." Then Mike added further, "Remember when we used to eat breakfast together before you helped us get ready for school? When the front doorknob turned and the door opened, you would drop whatever you were doing and rush to hug Pop."

Laura was deeply entrenched in what he was saying but tried to rationalize what her youngest son was implying. She raised her head and looked Michael in the eyes. She admitted to both Brent and her son that she had lived through it and sensed that Niki was every bit as strong as herself.

Mike, as gently as he could, continued to ease his mom's fears. "Niki married me, a military man, and knew what she was signing up for. Mom," he said, lowering is voice, "there is a stringent operational policy with our military's Special Operations Forces Command, and especially with my unit, JTF2. I cannot give Niki, you, or anyone else my deployment details. Mom, that doesn't mean I'm not given every opportunity to ensure adequate communication with my family. However, my activities are highly guarded."

Laura responded that "Yes, I know, but—"

"Mom, my unit is a scalpel not a hammer, which makes me faceless, shadowy, and part of a counter-terrorism force. So, if it's plastered on the news, it likely has nothing to do with me."

Laura replied, "Michael, I know you're trying to be kind,

but there is nothing you can say to alleviate a wife's or mother's worry."

Brent broke the ice to ease the tension in the room by saying, "Hey, what about those Toronto Maple Leafs?"

The three of them gravitated to discussing the Australia trip. Mike piped in with more information than his mom thought he should know. Laura was no shrinking violet and challenged how Michael could know such stuff.

Mike replied with just one word. "Mother!"

Brent again saved the day by asking Mike, "What brought you down this way?"

Mike answered, "I have business with the commander of Canadian Forces Base Camp Borden, just north of Toronto. But the number one reason I'm here is to see you guys."

Brent asked Mike if he was able to spend the night.

Mike replied, "Naturally."

Laura cooked up a meal that even kings would love. She loved her family. She lived for her family. She had a sense of pride in her three boys, as she called them.

Bedtime came early for Laura. She wondered where the day had gone. Time moved too quickly when her family came to visit.

Morning arrived, and the sun was welcomed as it shone through the windows, brightening an otherwise cold November day. Laura made it down to the kitchen to grab a coffee. It didn't surprise her that Michael and Brent were already sitting with cups of coffee in hand and dissecting the paper.

Two quick beeps of a horn from outside got everyone's attention. Mike rose and announced that his staff car and driver were waiting outside and that he had to be off to Camp Borden.

Laura's heart sank. Nobody had told her that Michael would have to leave at such an early hour. If she had known, she would have gotten up earlier to enjoy her baby boy's company.

Mike hugged his dad, and his mom was next. This was a bit of a love-hate time for Laura. She loved to have her son in her grasp but hated the fact that this could be the last time. Death could find him at any time on one of his deployments. With the hugs and kisses done, Mike left and got into a black Suburban. Brent and Laura waited at the front door until his vehicle vanished from their sight.

Laura started her last load of laundry before their trip to Australia. Laura sometimes did the washing when she was out of sorts or stressful events were crashing in on her. She felt like this was her therapy because doing the laundry put her back in charge. It wouldn't mean much to anyone else, but she was in charge of sorting and the order in which darks and lights were done. It was solitude from Brent, who wouldn't be found anywhere near this operation. Finally, it was a time to find solutions to problems that were causing her duress. The problems she had pondered in the laundry room may not have been earth-shattering to anyone else, but whatever the issues had happened to be, they had been in the way of Laura's peace of mind. Laura had come to terms about her son's deployment after doing the laundry

8

AFTERNOON TEA AND FAMILY

BRENT HAD RISEN early that morning and donned his dress uniform to go and tutor the new recruit class. When he got home, he hung up his suit and decided to take a bit of a nap because of the big night ahead of him.

Brent was awakened from his forty winks by the rambunctious activities of his grandkids. It was obvious to anyone with ears that Hank, Catherine, and Niki had arrived. Catherine was yelling at Hank, and Niki was trying to calm the situation with piercing threats to the both of them.

The turmoil and chaos were music to Brent's ears. He loved the sounds of children being children. A jolt from sleep was normally like the alarms going off in the fire station. This time, he welcomed the sounds of his grandchildren arriving. He loved them very much. It was not lost on him that this would likely be the last opportunity to hug and kiss them before they departed for their vacation.

"Hi, Papa," both of his grandkids said in unison.

In no time at all, he had Catherine on one knee and Hank on the other.

Niki came over and kissed her father-in-law. "It's nice to be here; I've missed you. Are you getting excited about your vacation?"

Before Brent could answer, Laura piped up and filled in his likely one-word reply. "Yes."

Brent laughed to himself and focused on his grandkids. He knew Laura and Niki could fill the afternoon with conversation all by themselves.

Catherine asked, "Papa, can you tell us a story?"

"Sure, I can. How about 'Jack and the Beanstalk'?" Papa replied.

Hank sang out, "Yes, Papa, that would be great. You tell such great stories."

Laura interjected, "Remember, Papa, they're just kids."

Brent started his tale. "There was this little boy, and his name was Jack. He was very talented and played a fiddle very well. One day, as he was playing for tips on a downtown sidewalk, a funny-looking man with bad breath dropped a bean into his fiddle case rather than money. At the end of the day, when Jack was counting his money, he found the bean. He thought it could be a magical bean, so he planted it in his backyard. Sure enough, the bean grew. The bean then split into three different parts. Most of it grew into corn, some of it grew into barley, and the rest grew into rye. Jack harvested these three plants and placed them into one big barrel. He added water and stomped it all down with his feet. Just like he was making wine."

"Ooh," said Catherine, "that's icky."

"Then he drank the juice, and it was good," Papa continued.

"What did he call this magical drink?" asked Hank.

"Well, he named it after himself," replied Papa. "Then he sold the drink to people and called it Jack-Daniel's."

The intoxicating fairy tale was finished. There was a knock on the door.

Hank and Catherine were the first to answer the door. It was Uncle Daniel, Uncle James, and their cousin Brady.

Daniel spoke first. "Hi, everybody. Nice to see you all." He then proceeded to give a round of hugs to everyone.

James spotted his father first and smiled. "Hi, Dad. It's good to see you. Mom! Give me a hug. Hi, Niki. How are things? How's Mike doing these days?" He spoke without expecting answers from anybody. James made the rounds with hugs and kisses and sat next to Daniel on the couch.

Brady had a computer game in his hands. He did his well-rehearsed greeting lines to all and then asked, "Can Hank and I go downstairs and play computer games on the TV?"

Daniel spoke up immediately, "Make sure you include Catherine as well!"

Brady obeyed. "Come on, guys. Let's go downstairs."

Laura got everyone's attention with the words, "I have breaking news." You could hear a pin drop, so Laura began her announcement. "Brent, when you were down for your nap, I got a phone call. It was from the mayor of Mississauga herself. She wanted to know how many members of our family are going to the retirement party tonight. I took a quick count in my head and said six. The mayor said that was perfect and that she would be sending a limo around to the house at 6:00 p.m. to take us all to this event. I thanked her and hung up the phone. I did a little jig around the house and could hardly wait until you all arrived to tell you."

It was heartwarming for the family to see the excitement in Laura. As the family proceeded to have coffee she was asked by James, "Why Australia?"

Laura reminisced out loud. "When I was a young girl, I remember my mom telling me stories of her fantasy, dream vacation in Australia. My mom would always end these conversations with the words, 'We could never afford to go anyway.' That always stuck with me.

"Now that your dad and I are both retired and money isn't too much of an issue, I approached your dad and used my womanly charms to plant the seed."

James, with comedic timing, added, "You mean Dad planted the seed."

"James!" barked Laura.

Momentary silence gave way to lighthearted laughter.

Laura stuck her tongue out at James, then told them all, "I did have to promise your dad sexual favors that complied with his wild imagination."

Again, everyone erupted into laughter.

James nodded, then smiled at his mom. "You are going to be a very busy girl."

Brent made sure Laura was finished weaving her tale before he asked his son, "James, what's new and exciting in your world?"

James was quick to reply. "Daniel, Brady, and I are doing really well."

Daniel interjected, "We're contemplating whether we should spend a week in St. Barts, probably in January."

Laura added, "Good for you guys. Brady could probably use a bit of a break from the cold winter."

Niki amusingly volunteered that "Daniel, with your pale skin, you could always use some sun for medicinal purposes."

Later in the afternoon, when the others had gone downstairs, Brent asked James, "How's your business going?"

Brent could see James's eyebrows perk up followed by a big inhale of breath that filled his lungs. Brent knew James was about to get on his soapbox and air out both his laurels and the grievances he had with the business. James looked at his father and said, "Dad, do you remember that fucking guy Rudolph Lidster, the big honcho from Meredith Reinsurance? Well, he gave me a telephone call last week. He went through all the pleasantries and then threw a goddamn fastball right at my fucking head. He told me that I had made quite a success of my company, and even the Initial Public Offering was better than anyone had expected. Rudolph informed me that I should be extremely proud of myself, and that he was proud of me too. Rudolph's voice then changed. He indicated that our conversation was a courtesy call to inform me that Meredith Reinsurance is planning to bring Hudson Reinsurance back into the fold. He said that within the next ten days Meredith, intends to float the shareholders of Hudson an offer to buy their positions at one dollar and fifty cents above the current market value."

Brent asked his son, "What did you say?"

James replied, "I told him to go fuck himself and hung up the phone."

Brent was alarmed by the nastiness of what Meredith was trying to perpetrate on his son's company.

James took Brent through the options of how he was going to defend against this hostile takeover of Hudson. James had been toying with a couple of options that he could enact. One was a poison pill defense. James explained that this defense, although very potent, could ruin him. It would reduce the share value of Meredith, but it could also greatly affect the assets of his own company, if he survived. The other was the golden parachute defense, and this was what he would go with. James adopted a phrase his father had used for years when he and Mike were growing up: "Save the last dance for the one that brung ya."

James opted to take care of himself and the senior management team. He felt obligated that if the takeover was successful, at least he owed them a payday. The golden parachute defense was designed to give additional compensations to top management in the case of termination of their employment following a successful hostile acquisition. The handsome payoff would greatly decrease his company's worth and thus make it unattractive to buy. James told his dad that this defense may harm his shareholder's value, but at least everyone important to him would leave Hudson's employ with a smile on their face. As for James, he would be set for life while still in his thirties—a good thing.

Brent tried to finalize their conversation by saying, "OK, if they try a hostile takeover of Hudson, then your entire senior staff gets a golden handshake that will significantly dilute the assets and stock value on the exchange, correct?"

James responded, "Yes, Pop. That's the layman's version."

9

THE GALA EVENT

BRENT STOOD IN front of the mirror and did a self-assessment. He liked what he saw. His dress uniform was freshly dry-cleaned, and his epaulets nicely adorned his shoulders. He affixed his medals over his heart: the twenty-five-year Provincial Exemplary Service decoration, the Ontario Medal of Bravery, and the thirty-year Federal Distinguished Service badge. Brent was proud of these medals, and rightly so, as they had come with a cost. He had seen more horror, death, and disfigurement than most.

The Hudsons were feeling excited, and the limo was shining like a new dime when they arrived at the reception. They entered the great hall with James and Daniel bookending for Niki and Brady. Everyone held hands. Following them were the guest of honor and his stunningly beautiful wife.

Missing was Hank and Catherine. Niki had deemed them too young to sit and behave for the duration of this festive event.

Brent and Laura entered the great hall to a standing ovation from everyone in attendance. It was a full house. Brent wore a smile of gratitude from ear to ear, and Laura's chest expanded with pride and love for her man. They were both overwhelmed by the admiration and respect shown to them as a couple.

Laura and the rest of the family were shown to a reserved table by a well-dressed and handsome rookie firefighter. Brent was escorted to the head table. There were four seats. The two outside seats were occupied by the fire chief and Captain Steve St. Louis. The two inside chairs were reserved for the mayor and Brent himself.

Brent engaged in small talk with the mayor and chief about his career and how proud they were of his service to the community and to the fire department. Brent spent a few minutes with Steve St. Louis and congratulated him on his promotion to the rank of captain.

The lights in the reception room darkened. It was now time for the moment Brent had anticipated most. But he also felt sheepish at all the kind words he received. The mayor spoke first, extolling the virtue of her fire department. Brent looked at the mayor with mixed emotions. At contract renewal time, Brent and his fellow firefighters had been painted as overpaid and draining the city of money it didn't have. Then, after the contract had been settled and the fire department had done a great job at some emergency, they had been heralded as the mayor's men and women, the best fire department in the world. The press had eaten this up. Brent remained courteous and respectful, and he thanked her for the kind words.

Steve St. Louis was next to speak. He said many kind words

about how Brent lived by the creed of leaving no man behind. He credited Brent with saving his life and told the firefighters in attendance that they could take it from him when he said, "I would follow Brent anywhere." These were simple words, but the respect behind them dictated that all fire personnel in the room give Brent a standing ovation.

Following Steve came the fire chief. The chief's speech was what Brent had feared it would be. The fire chief spoke exclusively about the rescue and the train derailment in 1979.

Brent looked to the heavens and thanked the big guy that he, his brothers, and the residents of Mississauga had all survived. Again, Brent was given a standing ovation for his heroics.

After the fire chief finished, the capacity crowd started to chant. "Speech. Speech. Speech."

Brent rose and headed for the podium.

The newbies in the room all rose to their feet and stood at attention. It was a sign of respect. Brent told them all to sit. He checked his microphone for volume and then proceeded. "I want to thank everyone for coming tonight to help celebrate this special night for Laura and myself. I also want to thank those at the head table for all their kind words. Steve, I, too, would follow you anywhere. You are my brother. Brothers don't leave brothers behind. You would have done the same for me. Chief, I want to thank you for your mentorship and sometimes looking the other way when I did things that weren't according to Hoyle."

"Who in the hell is Hoyle?"

The entire room broke into lighthearted laughter.

"I want to thank the mayor for the use of the limousine she supplied to transport my family to my retirement party. I hope that after my speech, the limo will still be available to take me and my family back home."

Again, there was a smattering of laughter throughout the hall. He waited for quiet to resume his speech. Brent looked directly at the new recruits in attendance. "This morning, I spoke to the rookie class. I warned you about the endless days of classroom instruction that lie ahead of you. I said your asses will be sore because of seemingly endless days learning about hydraulics, sprinkler systems, ventilation practices, and how to change the smoke plain in high-rise apartment buildings through physics. This profession is much more than just putting wet stuff on hot stuff. You new recruits will be instructed in hazardous material handling, auto extrication, medical aid, CPR, and how to tie specific knots. I impressed upon you that nothing can be done half-assed; people's lives depend on you. There is no sugarcoating the next words of advice I'm going to convey to you. It's not what you know that can kill you—it's what you don't know that can take your life. So listen to these wily old veterans you see around you in this room and take what they impart seriously. You are not playing a computer game. You can't lose your life and just hit restart again. That's not the way it works! You are fighting the dragon, and only one of you is going home. In the real world of firefighting, there are no do-overs!"

The entire room was hushed and absorbing the importance of the moment.

"I'll never forget my first call. The alarm went off, and it scared the shit out of me. I heard, 'Attention, Pumper Four, Pumper Two, Aerial Two, Squad One, and Car Four proceed to 1256 Creditview Ave. Vehicle explosion; one person injured.' I scrambled to put my gear on. My heart was leaping out of my chest. I assumed my position on the pumper. I knew this would be a tiered response. For some of the newer wives, this means that the fire, police, and ambulance services receive the alarm at the same time, and they all attend the call. The response to the incident seemed too short and too long all at the same time. My mind was working overtime. I was reciting my rookie thimble of knowledge in my head. 'Don't get off the pumper until it stops. Go to the side compartment and grab the first-aid bag and resuscitator. Get to the victim as quickly as you can but still look cool and professional.' I saw an adult male lying beside the car. He was on his belly, with his face turned to one side. When I got closer, I could see that he was breathing. My job was to keep him alive until we could hand him off to the paramedics, as per protocol. I remember seeing my crewmates buzzing around me. But I was so focused on my job that I couldn't make out who was who. I took a deep breath. Then I felt a reassuring hand on my shoulder. It was Dick, one of my crewmates. He said, 'You got this.' I asked the victim his name and at the same time surveyed his leg. It was hanging on by a tendon at midthigh. The guy told me his name was Doug."

Brent knew this was a ghastly story for some of the wives in the room. He was especially mindful that Brady was also hearing this. Brady was hanging off his grandfather's every word.

"I slipped the oxygen mask over Doug's nose and mouth. Protocol, for me, was then to check bleeding then bones. Dick had already applied a tourniquet on the remaining stump. I couldn't believe I didn't notice him do this. That just left bones to do. Yeah, bones, well, one part of the femur was entirely divorced from the rest of his body. Just a piece of tendon that hadn't given way kept the leg fragments relatively close. There wasn't much else I could do besides monitor his vital signs. I just kept Doug calm. Then Doug threw me a curveball. He asked me, 'How's my leg?' I looked to Dick to help me out. Nada, nothing, there wasn't a sound, just silence."

Brent's audience was intently following the story but snickered with the dark humor firefighters acquire when confronted with awkward dilemmas.

"I really didn't have an answer to this question. I was taught that caregivers are instructed never to lie to a patient. I took a deep breath and once again took a look at Doug's leg. How was I supposed to tell the guy that his leg was pretty much hamburger? It was never going to be salvaged. The leg was lost. Doug again asked, 'How is my leg?' In one of my more brainiac utterances, I said, 'Well, my legs are better than yours.'"

The audience erupted into a roar of laughter.

Brent carried on. "The paramedics arrived and took responsibility. I was thankful, thankful that they had arrived and relieved that I had done my job. I remember thinking that this was the first time I was clearly able to see and recognize my crewmates. I will never forget driving back to the station and looking out the windows of our five-man cab. I spotted little boys and girls waving at our shiny red beast as we drove past. The vehicles around our pumper seemed to give our truck a wide birth of respect. I was feeling proud of how I handled my first call and proud that I chose the right profession."

Brent carried on, telling his audience that, back at the hall, the entire crew had attended to putting the pumper back in running shape. He and his crew, with extreme care, had gotten the dirt off the vehicle with specially treated dust rags. Every nook and cranny had been seen to and treated. In no time, the pumper had been back in tip-top shape. After all, no one from the public should see a dirty fire truck.

Just as the last dust rag had hit the pail, two police officers had entered the bay doors. They'd requested a word with the captain. Captain Don Strait had come down the stairs. He'd conversed with the two police officers, then called for his crew to gather around. Captain Strait had then let them know that the response they had just been on had been an organized crime hit. He hadn't known the motive because the officers had withheld that information. What they had told the captain was that if any of his crew had opened or even jarred the trunk of the victim's car, another bomb had been rigged to explode."

Those attending Brent's retirement party had their mouths agape with shock and horror.

"Not to worry," Brent told them. "We all lived to fight another day. I would like to conclude this night by saying that in this profession, it's tough to be new. New to being a firefighter. New to being married. New to more responsibility than you have ever had. It can be done. Especially with a loving partner. In my case, my loving partner's name is Laura. Laura, could you please stand up? I want to thank you for completing my life. Without you, I am not."

Brent blew Laura a kiss and put the microphone down. He closed his eyes and relished the tremendous standing ovation reserved for a hero. Tonight, that hero was him. He left the podium with a straight back, eyes ahead, and a chest bursting with pride.

10

OFF TO OZ

BRENT AND LAURA hustled their luggage to the front door. They were running late, and Laura was concerned because the limo James had sent to take them to the airport was already waiting outside. Nonetheless, whenever they traveled, there was always a last-minute check of documentation: they had their passports and all other necessary papers. To complete the check, Brent asked Laura if she had her credit card.

"Yes."

"Good. We can throw money at whatever else we need."

Outside and safely sitting in the posh back seat of the limo, Laura's eyes took in the nice-looking young man who was to be their driver. She couldn't help but see the Hudson Reinsurance insignia on his suit coat. She was impressed and silently mused that both her boys had drivers at their disposal. Somewhere in there, Laura thought, was at least an element of proof that her sons were both quite successful. Laura did not consider money to be the ultimate validation of achievement. She was also not naive in her understanding that there was a world of difference between what James earned and the money Michael was paid. Laura's measurement of success was down-to-earth, simple, and only applicable to her three boys: "Be good at what you do, and never lose the boy inside the man."

At long last, Laura and Brent made it to the designated gate for their flight to Los Angeles. Pedestrian traffic around them was a hive of activity, but they felt somewhat less stressed securing an empty row of seats at the airport to accommodate them and their carry-ons. Brent decided that a washroom visit might be in order before they were called through the gate to their seats.

Laura and Brent got seated on the plane. This was when Brent realized he would have to spend over four hours on an aircraft that was not going to serve him food unless, of course, he was willing to pay inflated prices. He was just about to complain to Laura when Laura cut him off at the pass.

Laura informed him that his favorite sandwiches were packed, and she was ready to feed her bear at a moment's notice.

The flight didn't seem that long because both of them knew the next leg was going to be a marathon. Their plane landed at LAX, and the first thing that struck the two of them was that this airport was huge. As they had a three-hour layover in front of them, Laura and Brent took a relaxed pace finding the proper terminal for the next leg of their continuing flight.

Again, as the departure time neared, Brent decided that it would be a good time to take a leak. He found the bathroom signs, but to get there, Brent had to travel a long way. Once inside, he tucked his boarding card into his passport and put it on top of the urinal he was using. Feeling relieved, he then took a leisurely stroll back to where Laura was sitting.

Laura said, "We will be boarding in five minutes."

Brent replied, "That's great. Do you have our passports and boarding cards ready?"

"I have mine. Where are yours?" Laura asked.

"You have it," Brent barked.

Laura's eyes went round as saucers. "No, I don't. You took them with you when you went to the washroom."

Laura was right. Brent panicked and hustled back to the washroom—specifically to the urinal where he had relieved himself.

Another man was in the process of doing a one-handed pee, with his other hand on Brent's passport so he could read it. As Brent neared this stranger, he looked at Brent and said, "Yep, it looks like you."

As Brent took his passport and boarding card from the stranger's hand, he couldn't help but notice that the guy's body was in an awkward position. He was in real fear that this person might piss on his shoes. He thanked the stranger and made a mad dash back to his boarding gate.

Laura was waiting nervously until she spied Brent jogging toward her. Then a smile as big as the moon became evident on her face. They could now board the plane.

Brent was glad that the rest of the trip would be with Qantas Airways. Neither he nor Laura had ever heard a bad word spoken about this airline. Judging from the width of their seats, they would at least enjoy wiggle room, unlike North American airlines that made passengers feel like they were stuffed into a sardine can. As Brent surveyed the inside of the plane, he came to the realization that this particular plane was huge. He noticed a stairway up to the second floor of the aircraft. This was a sure indication to him that there was an entire floor of first-class patrons on board.

Brent was then greeted by a flight attendant who pointed out their seats. Brent had a window seat, Laura had the middle seat, and a cute, young American woman had the aisle seat. The row configuration in economy was alternating rows of three and four seats.

As the plane lifted off the runway, the young woman in the aisle seat was already asleep. This made sense, as it was damn near midnight. Brent got this wild idea that perhaps this would be an opportune time to join the mile high club. The only obstacles hindering his scheme were Laura's elbows slicing into his arms and ribs as he attempted to be amorous. Brent eventually gave up and settled in for the thirteen-hour flight to Sydney.

What Laura and Brent hadn't counted on was that the young lady in the aisle seat had a bladder the size of a basketball. Laura tried the best she could to hold it but, over time, she had to tap the young lady to wake her up. Laura apologized for the intrusion and blamed it on old people having tiny bladders.

The interior design of the plane allowed Brent to get up and walk the aisles. He wasn't one to get a lot of sleep while flying, so by the time they arrived in Sydney, he was not only tired but exhausted by kilometers of walking. Ahead of them were still two connecting flights. One from Sydney to Brisbane and another from Brisbane to Hervey Bay.

Finally, both Laura and Brent noticed that when their

final connecting flight was nearing touchdown in Hervey Bay, they somehow got a second wind. They put it down to the excitement of reaching their final destination.

A small propeller aircraft took them on their last leg of the marathon journey. When its doors opened to let the passengers disembark, Laura felt a warm burst of air cocoon her body. She was in heaven. This was the vacation she had dreamed of, and now she was living it. Bright daylight blinded her eyes when she walked down the portable stairway that the ground crew had positioned at the front exit. She traversed the tarmac and reminded herself to get out of her travel clothes as soon as it was possible. She had a smile on her face and if no one else had been present, she would have jumped high in the air and clicked her heels together, just like an elated little girl might have done.

Brent's head seemed to be on a 360-degree swivel. He was looking everywhere. The biggest thing to register with him were the vivid colors that seemed to dance upon the landscape of rhythmic heat waves. The terminal was just steps away, but Brent still had time to check out the fine shape of the woman ahead of him. Yes, Laura still turned his crank; she had a sweet-looking butt.

Entering the terminal, it struck both Laura and Brent how small it was. It seemed that it was a two-door operation. The entrance door at the front meant you were departing, and the exit door meant you had arrived. A single luggage conveyor belt had been activated, and their luggage was going in circles. There were no customs to go through, as they'd cleared that hurdle in Sydney. Brent thought Hervey Bay Airport had to be for domestic flights only, as international flights would need a longer runway to land.

They hailed a taxi and gave the driver their new address: the Riviera Resort. Brent went to tip the driver, and the man refused to take their money.

Brent inquired as to why, and the gentleman replied, "Mate, you don't tip anyone in Australia; further, mate, there is no goods and services tax. So when you buy anything, you only pay the sticker price."

Brent thought, "Nice."

11

BRENT AND LAURA'S
NEW HOME

LAURA LOVED HER new digs. The condo was only fifty-six square meters, but it was everything she needed: colorful, clean, and it had a good view of the resort grounds. It had two ceiling fans but no air-conditioning. She thought this might rear its ugly head as far as Brent was concerned. Laura opened the sliding balcony doors at the front of the condo and then the sliding balcony doors at the rear. The sea breeze that motored through their unit was more than enough to substitute for air-conditioning.

Being so close to the ocean and white sand, Laura was happy to find that she had ceramic tile floors. This meant that a quick clean with a damp mop would cure any problem with any white gold that found its way into their rental. She saw two pristine brick barbecues outside that were available for use. Last, the pool, which was to die for. Laura loved being on the ocean, but she had to confess that being in the ocean was, at best, a necessary evil. Laura much preferred the pool. Her footing was always secure on the concrete bottom. The water was always pristine, and little sea creatures weren't nipping at the exposed skin on her body. Yes, she preferred the pool over the ocean.

Brent's first ritual on vacations was to check out the workbench, as he called it. It was a queen-size bed and firm; he enjoyed that aspect of it. Then he would bounce around on the couch to see if it was comfortable. This particular sofa wasn't. It seemed very Posturepedic, which meant your back would be always straight, and nowhere would the classic Brent slouch be welcomed. The seat cushions were hard. "Who makes a couch with ass-breaking padding?" Brent knew right then and there that he would purchase his own chair. As Laura well knew, Brent's comfort was always number one in his books.

It was time to get showered and changed and, for the first time, submerge their toes in the ocean. Laura laid out her wardrobe on the bed. She smirked. "I hope Brent's truly not a jealous man. Some of these outfits show more skin than even I'm used to." She shrugged this off, knowing Brent always wanted her to dress as a more sexual creature.

Secretly, she didn't mind. Laura even recalled one of Brent's favorite sayings: "Better to be looked at than overlooked." To round off her secret thoughts, Laura knew she would be away from anyone she knew. No one who mattered would judge her, and Brent certainly would remain aroused for the next five months. That, Laura decided, was a good thing. Laura had learned years ago that a horny man was never angry. Laura popped in and out of the shower and was then ready to explore their surrounding area.

Brent held Laura's hand as they crossed the two-lane road in front of their resort. A few steps farther was a boardwalk that meandered the entire length of the town. Tomorrow they would investigate the boardwalk further.

Laura felt her feet sink in the white sand. She immediately removed her thongs and handed them to Brent to put in their beach bag. Laura was able to look up and down the beach. As far as her eyes could see were diamonds of white sand shining in the sunlight. The gentle sea breeze was enough to cut into the heat of the day. It must have been 30°C already.

The big moment had arrived. Brent took Laura's hand, and they looked into each other's eyes. Brent gave Laura a nod, and they simultaneously dipped their right feet into the clear, clean water of the Pacific Ocean. Brent gave Laura a celebratory pat on the ass, then his vision found two women strolling the beach—topless. He thought to himself that this vacation may even be better than he'd first thought.

Laura saw this as well. Unbeknownst to Brent, Laura was having a meeting with herself in her mind. She was truly happy about Brent's appreciation of the female form. Laura thought she should also contribute to this philosophy. Behind Brent's back, she quietly removed the top of her two-piece suit. She tapped Brent on the shoulder and asked him if he wouldn't mind putting this article of clothing into the beach bag.

Brent ogled Laura's breasts, looked Laura in the eyes, and gleefully responded, "It will be my pleasure."

Outwardly, Laura blushed. Inwardly, she felt liberated. She felt naughty and loved because Brent was on her team.

The next day was a day of logistics. They had to shop for food. They asked the front desk for directions to the neighborhood grocery store. They found out it was about four kilometers along the ocean. That meant the esplanade would take them right there. Laura and Brent decided to walk as the day was perfect, and it would give them a chance to explore along the way.

They first noticed that there were exercise stops at designated areas along the route. They came upon a large picnic area complete with barbecue pits and steel grills. What astonished Laura and Brent was the cleanliness of the area. Not a piece of garbage anywhere but in its proper place: a trash can. It was nice to see public barbecues and the immediate area being respected.

Laura noticed along the way that there were no touristy, three-for-twenty-dollar T-shirt hustlers, but neither were there name-brand stores like Old Navy. There were just storefronts of mom-and-pop operations, each separated by a restaurant. Their neighborhood of Torquay was loaded with restaurants.

Finally, they came across the grocery store. They did a big shop and flagged a taxi for the ride home.

Just before bedtime, and while Brent was lounging on their front balcony overlooking the pool, he reflected on a humorous event of the day. While they'd been walking on the esplanade to shop for groceries, they had spied a suntanned male almost 2m tall, rippling with muscle, running at them. As he'd neared them to pass, Brent had noticed just how handsome this Australian specimen happened to be. "What a treat the love of his life would get to enjoy," Brents thought to himself.

The runner passed. Laura tried but she couldn't keep quiet. She turned to Brent with her eyes just sparkling and her face a little flushed. Laura smiled the biggest grin, and out of her mouth came the words, "Hoochie mama."

They both had a giggle, and Brent sucked in his belly. He knew the night ahead would likely be very frisky.

12

FRASER ISLAND

LAURA WAS TRYING to get Brent to understand her sense of urgency. She stated that they had to go to River Heads to catch the ferry to Fraser Island. They talked on the bus, and it was then that Laura broached the possibility of seeing a dingo or a kangaroo, and maybe even a koala, in the wild. They arrived at River Heads, got off the bus, and headed for the ferry.

The ferry was packed with a few cars and passengers right up to the upper two levels. They lucked out and got two seats by the railing and right by the narrow steel steps. Laura now got to watch for dolphins while Brent enjoyed a great strategic place for cleavage watching. It didn't take long for Laura to spot her first dolphin. Brent mumbled something about flippers and fins and went back to doing his thing.

The ferry took about thirty-five minutes to arrive at Wanggoolba Creek. The ferry dock was two metal plates laid on the sand. The ferry lowered its ramp, and everyone disembarked. Nothing else was at this site except for specially equipped buses. These buses had twenty forward gears and four reverse gears. People's names were read out, and they got on the bus with a tour guide named John.

The first stop was the rain forest in Central Station. Here, they learned about the flora and the distinct trees growing on the sand island. They learned that the rain forest had been logged, causing devastation to the ecosystem. They gleaned knowledge about the dog tree, whose name came from the fact that it had no bark.

There was a creek that flowed all the way through the rain forest. It didn't make a sound, and it was crystal clear. Why? There were no rocks or impediments to create enough turbulence to make noise. It was called Silent Creek.

They got back on the bus and began to traverse the sand-rutted road leading to Eli Creek. The road was very bumpy, and their backs felt every bounce. They finally got out of the rain forest and came to 75 Mile Beach Road. It was really just a part of the beach where traffic went both ways. The speed limit was eighty kilometers per hour. There were no definite lanes, as the tide dictated where the road was.

Laura believed that the southbound lane skirted the surf, and the northbound drivers were in charge of avoiding head-on crashes. The best way to picture this highway was to think of driving on Daytona Beach. The view driving on this highway was amazing. The surf and colors of the ocean were breathtaking.

What happened next just blew their minds. Here they were, traveling at eighty kilometers, and their guide, John, came on the PA system and announced that if they looked out the front window, they would see an airplane land. Sure enough, the plane landed right in front of them and took its place ahead of the bus in the flow of traffic. It had to be said that 75 Mile Beach Road was only ninety-three kilometers, or fifty-eight miles, long. Go figure.

They arrived at Eli Creek. Eli Creek was another freshwater body that originated in the rain forest. The best way to describe this creek was to say it was like a lazy river at a water theme park. It was not deep, but after a rain, the flow was such that one's body could be propelled down to the ocean. The Hudsons learned that when freshwater met saltwater, a distinct and visual line in the water was evident.

Back on the bus, they continued up the beach until they came upon a shipwreck by the name of Maheno. This was another good photo opportunity. Apparently, a Japanese ship had been towing the cruise liner back to home base for scrap. Somehow, the Maheno had run aground, and the Japanese crew had just left it there. The Royal Australian Air Force had even used it for target practice during World War II.

Laura and Brent played a game: who could spot the first koala, dingo, or kangaroo in the wild? Whenever Laura introduced a competition, it was never optional. If Brent ever wanted to get laid again, it was in his best interests to play.

She remembered the tour guide saying, "Dingoes are a rare sighting, but you never know."

The surf and the ocean turned her crank with its roar and pastel colors. Eli Creek found her dipping her toes into the clean, pure water, and her eyes beamed at the sand dunes that surrounded them. The shipwreck was just another photo op. Off the bus, she hustled to take her shots. It was impossible to take a picture without a multitude of tourists milling about.

The next stop was Coloured Sands, which were huge sand

dunes with over seventy different colors in them. These dunes were ancient, and Laura suspected the different colors were the product of time passing, such as the Ice Age and Iron Age.

They went back down 75 Mile Beach Road and headed for lunch at Eurlong, which had the only resort on the island. The resort was very nice, and the smorgasbord lunch was great. Laura remembered they had been informed that Fraser Island was the largest sand island in the world. Surprisingly, Laura found it funny that, even with all this sand, they had to import sand from the mainland to build the block buildings. Wrong type of sand, she surmised.

After lunch, they spent the afternoon at the jewel of the island, Lake McKenzie. This had the second purest water on the planet. In order for the fresh water to see the light of day, it had been purified by going through sand for over one hundred years. The visual of the lake was breathtaking, with the whitest sand that Laura and Brent had ever seen in their lives, and the only color in the water came from the reflection of cloud spots when they blocked the sun.

Laura emphasized to Brent, "I'm talking pure."

Brent was feeling sore and tired from always tensing up on the bus rides.

Laura was exhilarated. Her mind and eyes drank in the scenery. She then pulled one of her mom's tricks. She went behind a bush and changed into her swimsuit. She walked on the bleached sand and stopped just short of the water. She inched ever so slowly until her next step would bathe her toes.

Brent suspected she had her eyes closed so she could just enjoy the moment using her other senses.

In she stepped. A big breath of air filled her lungs, and she looked back at Brent and smiled.

Her smile would live on in Brent's heart.

Time passed, and Brent had a blissful snooze on the beach. A familiar voice woke Brent up. Laura was calling his name from the water, loudly, and pointing behind him. Brent looked up, and there stood a dingo about two meters away. It took him a minute to realize this was not just a dog but a true-blue, wild dingo. Another flash in his head said that if he hadn't heard Laura, and hadn't moved rather suddenly, the dingo would very likely have pissed on his head. Brent composed himself, grabbed the camera, and shot a picture.

Laura had spotted the first dingo and now led their little game. It was time to depart the beach. They got on the bus, and the tour guide was truly agog at their dingo sighting. They were the only ones who had gotten pictures. The spectacular lake and the sighting of the dingo had made their day.

The ferry came, and they departed for the mainland. Brent looked at the water but didn't see any dolphins. He sat down and Laura spied dolphins.

They got back to the dock at River Heads and boarded their double-decker bus. On the trip home, they conversed about the day's events.

Laura yelled, "Look!"

Brent panicked. "Where?"

"You missed them."

"Missed what?"

Two kangaroos had been hopping about in a field.

She gave him a big, shit-ass grin and sarcastically asked, "Just what kind of hunter are you?" She now led their little game 2–0.

Brent would have to see a koala first or there would be no living with this girl.

13

FIRESTORM

THE NEXT DAY was a down day for the both of them. They were tired out from Fraser Island. They were both sitting down watching the Australian news. The big story for Brent was the bush fires in the state of Victoria. As they sat there, sipping their wine, the news reported that approximately two hundred people had lost their lives. There were still twenty-four fires burning out of control, and the winds were due to pick up again later that day and the next. Entire towns in the mountains and foothills had been ravaged. The reports coming out of towns such as Marysville and Kinglake would make even the most hardened person tear up.

In order for him to adequately absorb what was taking place, he revisited his own career as a firefighter. Brent had been a structural firefighter, tackling residential houses, commercial buildings, and industrial buildings. There was a world of difference between what he had done and the specially trained firefighters who battled those freaks of nature.

Brent started a conversation with Laura. Brent needed Laura to understand what was taking place. He wanted Laura to picture herself in the position of those mountain people, who, for the most part, had seen a fire or two while living in the mountains, and understand the false sense of security they had that they could handle this fire.

The fire itself was in the Melbourne area, in the mountains and foothills. Brent smiled and told Laura that it was hard to call anything mountains after having seen the Canadian Rockies. Australians were a hardy, outdoor breed. They preferred country life to employment in cities, yet Australian urbanites and Australian rural folk were not that far apart. Brent had a sense that the infrastructure differed widely between these two areas. Paved roads versus dirt roads. Options of travel were greatly diminished. Instead of hydrants, they had wells and ponds and so on. Brent asked Laura if she was getting the picture he was trying to draw.

Brent got up from his chair and walked over to the balcony railing before he sat down and faced Laura. He said to Laura in a serious voice, "All that babble was necessary because I want to put you in the typical scenario that most of these people are caught in." Brent decided to personalize his tale. "Imagine that we are married with two kids and live in the foothills north of Melbourne. We built our homestead at the top of a mountain, and we see smoke over the next mountain. Decisions have to be made."

He told Laura that it was human nature when confronted with immediate danger to do one of two things: fight or flight. Brent asked Laura to think of their friends back home in Canada. Brent believed they would use this thought process: the men would stay and fight the fire to protect their worldly possessions. Brent asked Laura to keep in mind that no one knew at that point just how bad things truly were. It was impossible to recognize that there was a firestorm over the next mountain.

"We think the fire is far away and it won't impact us but, just in case, I will protect my family. We have a conversation and decide it would be best for you to get the kids in the car and head away from the fire. In five minutes, you, my precious, and our kids are moving out in the car, heading downwind and ahead of the fire.

"I then protect our house and wet the roof with water from a water hose. We, like the rest of the mountain population, have a water source and a generator pump to power a thirty-eight-millimeter hose stream. I look at the progress of the fire and am alarmed to realize embers are everywhere, starting little fires. The blazing heat from the 40°C weather is scorching hot. Ashes are dropping on my clothes and leaving burn marks. The wall of fire itself is now climbing our ridge at a rate of speed that even I have never seen before.

"My ears are telling me that it sounds like a freight train. My head tells me that the likelihood of escaping with my life has greatly diminished. The house that I was trying to save is the only thing that might be able to save me. The firestorm is traveling about one hundred kilometers per hour. Therefore, it will consume everything and pass very quickly. Our house will burn, but I know it will burn at a slower rate than other consumables. This may allow me to weather this beast and then escape the house before it's too late.

"I go into the house to the safest place possible. I hear the awful wind, and the last thing I notice is the house filling up with hot air before it explodes. I have been killed, but I can take solace in the fact that you and the kids are safe."

Laura looked at Brent and shook her head. After a nice day, she thought they would talk about kumbaya moments, not Alfred Hitchcock horror shows.

Brent gave Laura a wry smile and said that his horror show, as she called it, was about to continue. His demise happened just five minutes after she had left with the boys. "You, Laura, put the car in gear and pull away. You worry about me, but you know that I'm a practical and self-reliant guy. The smoke seems to be catching up to you. You look down at your speedometer and are amazed that you're traveling about eighty kilometers per hour. You are on a winding dirt road where you can safely go about sixty.

"You turn on your windshield wipers, hoping to get a better sight line. This doesn't work. Looking out your rear window, you see flames coming faster than you are driving. Our young kids in the back seat are starting to panic. You step on the accelerator, and now control of your vehicle is an issue. Rocks fly at every turn, and embers are flying ahead of you and starting spot fires in the trees. You realize that this monster is gaining on you.

"You take solace that a crossroad is ahead, and you can turn left or right to get out of the way of the heat and flames. You slam on your brakes at the four corners. You become aware that the fire has outflanked you, and your options are limited to straight ahead. You try and outrun this fire on a winding dirt road. You feel the radiant heat, and you hear sounds mimicking a freight train.

"You floor the gas pedal and are now driving in a speedy,

reckless manner. The kids are in full panic. You are in full panic. On the next bend, you lose control of the car and spin out into a ditch. The fire overtakes and consumes the vehicle, and you and the kids perish. If this scenario sounds gory, it is, but it's what these people face." Fire, in Brent's mind, was the worst way to die. Again, human nature, when confronted with imminent danger, was fight or flight. Sometimes, either way, you were just fucked.

The newscaster reported that the fires were a result of arson.

"My God, how do these people live with themselves?" an exasperated Brent exclaimed. Brent rose and stretched after his long-winded scenario. He approached Laura and poured himself another glass of wine. He sat down beside his wife.

Laura looked at Brent with misty eyes. She was horrified with the matter-of-fact tone of voice that Brent had used to tell his story.

Brent and Laura continued to watch the Australian news coverage of the fires. They were witnessing something right out of a Hollywood movie, except it was real. There was no ducking the impact it had on each and every person who was privy to witness it in this time of extreme sadness. A television news station interviewed an elderly man about the fire and what he had lost.

This gentleman was having nothing to do with his lost material things in life. He told the reporter that the only thing he wanted was to hold his wife. This must have struck a nerve with the young reporter because he searched and was able to find the man's missing wife at another evacuation site. He interviewed the elderly woman who also was having nothing to do with her lost material things in life. She told the reporter she just wanted to be in her husband's arms.

The reporter put her in the company news helicopter, and they flew to her husband's location. She spied her husband, and tears started streaming down her face. She called his name out several times, but her voice was too feeble. The elderly woman then ran the best she could. It seemed to be a struggle for her to move toward her husband. The husband became visible in the camera shot, and he was not running but was shuffling his feet as fast as he could toward his wife. His legs would no longer allow him to run. It ended like a Hollywood movie, except it was real and the emotions were raw. The couple embraced and both sobbed in each other's arms. The deeply loving elderly couple were oblivious to anything or anyone around them.

"Wow, what a powerful emotional experience," Brent quietly stated to end this significant emotional event.

Laura reached over and took Brent's hand in hers. Neither one of them wanted eye contact, as they preferred to keep secret the entire range of emotions that both chilled and warmed their hearts. Laura excused herself for a bathroom break.

Once she was out of sight, Brent wiped his tears on his sleeve.

When Laura returned from the bathroom, she noticed that the afternoon sun was beginning to lower itself against the backdrop of a crystal-blue sky. Dinner would be late.

When Laura poured herself another glass of wine, Brent sensed that his love had a pretty good buzz going. Brent thought to cure the problem when he asked, "Takeout?"

Laura responded, "Pizza?"

14

WICKED ON THE EAST COAST

WEEKS WENT BY before Laura and Brent had another adventure. The day had finally arrived. They flew from Hervey Bay to Sydney to pick up their rental to explore the East Coast while going back up to their home base. Their mode of transportation was to be a Wicked van. Even before they picked up their vehicle, they spied the Sydney Opera House.

Laura demanded that the taxi stop and park so they could get out and physically touch this famous landmark. After which, Laura looked at Brent and stated, "How can you say you were in Australia and not touch the Opera House?"

The Wicked Van Company owned a fleet of vans complete with clever and also nasty sayings on them. Laura was thankful they got a newer van that was an automatic. Their van had a drawing of a big iguana on each side panel.

They drove the van off the lot and immediately headed to

Bondi Beach. Laura saw that this beach was something out of a fairy tale. The surfers were ripped and being encouraged by bikini-clad girls with hourglass figures. Both thought that this beach wasn't the largest that they had seen, as it was easily walked from end to end. After they dipped their toes into the ocean, they had to move on to find a caravan park before dark. They'd already mapped out the stops they were going to make on their travels back up to Hervey Bay.

Brent shouted out, "North Narrabeen Beach."

Laura laughed and opined about how Brent was still learning about driving on the opposite side of the road.

The landscape was rugged with many twists and turns, but the vistas were breathtaking.

The next day, they headed to Budgewai. They drove the beach roads and went through several small towns. They noticed that Australia seemed to be one big beach. The white sands and pristine waters were ahead and behind them as far as they could see. Budgewai was a one-horse town with no real business section. They did have a pizza store and that was where they decided to have dinner. Brent piped in that Budgewai did have an ocean swimming pool. This pool had been built a long time ago. The locals spent days meticulously piling boulders in the ocean, to form the pool walls. It was a place where locals could go for a swim and not have to fear being eaten by sharks.

Laura quizzed Brent on these pools being about fifty meters in the ocean. "What about shark attacks before people even get to the safety of the swimming pool?"

Brent replied that "The sharks and the townsfolk have an agreement."

Laura laughed.

Holiday Point, just above Forster, was the next stop. Laura spied a sign on the road for a place named Toronto. They just had to go. The town was small and nondescript but, for nostalgia's sake, they were still glad they'd investigated. They finally reached their destination for the day. It was a nice town. So nice that Laura spent the afternoon in the discount mall shopping for bargains. Brent didn't mind, as the 32-degree weather outside was becoming unbearable.

The Wicked van had run its course as a way to bed down at night. The bed was hard, the sleeping space cramped, and nighttime pit stops inconvenient. The park where they were staying for the night had cabins with running water and showers.

Laura, secretly, had also had enough of the sleeping arrangements in the Wicked van. She looked at Brent, smiled, and said, "Get us a cabin, and I'll love you a long time."

Brent chuckled and that was the last night they slept in the van.

The next morning, they went down to the beach and decided to while away the day by just enjoying the sun and conversing with the Australian people. The locals always asked Brent and Laura about how they were enjoying their vacation in Australia. They both loved Australia and everything about it. Brent and Laura told the locals this and could see their chests inflate with pride.

Coffs Harbour was the next destination on the Hudsons' list. Coffs Harbour was where they found out that the iguanas on the sides of their Wicked van were tiny compared to what they walked into at a sports field. The locals informed them that the iguanas found in this area were some of the world's largest.

Brent became an interested spectator of some old fellows playing lawn bowling. They allowed the couple to join, with Brent on one team and Laura on the other. This was a nice use of an afternoon.

Back at their rented cabin, Brent teased Laura about the old birds wanting to play with her so they could look down her top.

Mischievously, Laura replied, "Can you blame them?"

Byron Bay was a landmark stop for Brent and Laura. It was an entire town made up of hippies. The town itself seemed stuck in time, with period buildings and, of course, locals dressed in the garb of days gone by. It didn't take long for Laura to realize that the people there might be living in the past, but the prices of goods seemed to be futuristic. They strolled away the afternoon at multiple flea markets and at dusk, they looked for yet another soft bed to lay their heads on.

A cabin was rented, and a bottle of wine was opened. Dinner was a bag of chips and another drink. They talked about the sayings written on the Wicked vans, and Brent's favorite was, "Pussy Power."

Laura's happened to be, "Save the Planet...Get off it."

15

Fantasies and Fiji

BACK IN HERVEY Bay, Laura was hot. She wasn't sure if it was the night air or the amount of wine she had consumed. Futuristic stories of swimming on the Great Barrier Reef and an excursion to Ayers Rock would have to wait. Their trip to Fiji all arranged as a surprise for Laura by Brent, was just around the corner, but sunset with her babe was most pressing. She told Brent to grab a beer and come with her to the ocean. It was a sunset that was more than beautiful on this particular night. Laura grabbed a beach blanket and walked hand in hand with her lover across the road.

Brent thought they could see the sunset just fine from their balcony but gave no resistance.

The sun seemed to drop out of the sky as Laura smoothed the blanket on the sand. They both sat down, and Laura fiddled with Brent's fly.

Brent asked Laura what she was doing.

She remarked, "Remember all those fantasies that swim around in your head? Well, right now, I'm going to eliminate one of them." With that, she lowered her head, but it was not in prayer.

~

It was another perfect morning at the Riviera Resort. The morning sun shone brilliantly in the cloudless sky. Laura was sunning herself in the privacy of their front balcony. She was determined to get some of her white bits tanned before their plane left from Brisbane for Fiji later that day. Brent had just finished his morning coffee. It was time for him to peruse the flyers that Laura had accumulated from the travel agency.

The first brochure he picked up to read had paragraphs such as, "With cobalt-blue water, colorful coral life, and white, sandy beaches, the South Pacific feels like a picture-perfect postcard. You can do everything, including snorkeling and kayaking to diving and surfing—or do nothing at all. The best resorts in the South Pacific give you plenty of options."

Brent tossed this brochure back on the table and picked up another one. This leaflet was less flowery and more statistical. Fiji consisted of 330 islands, with many of them uninhabited. Suva was the capital of Fiji and also their biggest and most populated city. This was all fine to Brent, but he didn't really care too much about Suva and the islands. He and Laura were going to only one destination called Treasure Island and would be taking only one single trip to the mainland, which in fact was just a bigger island. It would be for a night of dancing and merriment at the Hard Rock Cafe in a tourist town called Nadi.

Brent liked to frequent Hard Rock Cafes, as their merchandise stores allowed him to add to his collection of golf style visors. Brent liked these visors because they were reminders of all the diversified places he had been in the world. He also liked the fact that he would receive brownie points from Laura, as she liked both the music and the loudness at which the music was played.

He picked up his coffee cup and returned to the kitchen for a refill. He had the knowledge that Laura had previously dissected all the pamphlets, and she would serve as his go-to for any information he might need.

16

MIKE CALLS HIS PARENTS

BRENT HAD JUST finished putting the milk back in the refrigerator when the telephone rang. He picked it up and heard the words, "Hi, Pop," on the other end. It was Mike.

Laura was just coming in from the balcony, still topless, with her breasts swaying hypnotically before Brent's eyes. Laura yelled out, "Hi, Michael!" and hurried into the bedroom to get dressed.

Brent didn't know whether he should be concerned or happy, so the first words out of his mouth were, "Everything all right?"

Mike assured his dad that everything was fine with him, Niki, and the kids.

Brent told Mike that "You are a hard person to get a hold of."

Mike replied, "Yes, I know. I was on deployment. I heard

from James that you and Mom are going to Fiji for a week's vacation." Then he added sarcastically, "While on vacation."

Brent laughed and asked Mike, "What did we do to deserve this phone call?"

Mike went on to tell his father that Fiji was undergoing a military coup. Mike had no intentions of educating his dad on the detailed background of how this had come about. He thought it would be no good to clutter his father's mind with these sticking points. Instead, he elected to say that the coup was a peaceful event resulting from a previous coup that apparently hadn't been handled correctly, with due consideration to the Fijian constitution.

Mike read from a public bulletin. He wanted his father to hear that Fiji had been placed under Public Emergency Regulations, putting the country under emergency rule for thirty days. This regulation gave the police the right to control the movement of people and to stop any broadcast or publication it deemed could cause disorder, promote disaffection or public alarm, or undermine the government or state of Fiji. "So, Dad," Mike said, "this means there is no freedom of the press, and the military and police have additional powers. Remember that Fiji is a conservative country. Bathing suits and skimpy clothes are fine at the resorts and smaller islands, but on the mainland, you're going to have to make sure that crazy wife of yours dresses accordingly."

Laura exited the bedroom and hurried over to Brent. She told him it was her turn to talk to Michael. Once on the telephone, Laura started into a barrage of questions. She wanted to know about Michael, his wife, and his kids.

Michael offered up that he was going to be home for the foreseeable future, which would allow him to burrow deeper into the hearts of his family. He told his mom how well Hank was doing in hockey, and that he was one of the best players on the team. "The other day, Hank had a practice at five o'clock in the morning. Immediately, Niki came to me and said she doesn't do five o'clock practices. That's a time for dad and son to bond."

Laura laughed, and Mike carried on telling his mother that Catherine also loved hockey and played every weekend in a girls hockey league. He mentioned that Niki, while he was away on deployment, would never miss any game or practice with the two of them. Mike boasted that he believed Niki was just as much a sports fan as he was. Laura told Michael all about their approaching trip to Fiji and how she was so looking forward to it. Michael had to hang up the telephone and told his mom that he loved her and to enjoy herself. Mike heard the dial tone and took solace in the fact that his dad knew the potential perils of Fiji and would protect his mom from harm.

The time to vacate the Riviera Resort was drawing near. Laura had previously laid out Brent's clothing on the bed so that he could see what would be going to Fiji. Brent, as per his nature when Laura was packing, smiled and nodded and agreed to everything. Then, when Laura's back was turned, he snuck in his old, blue-jean shorts, which were a staple of his because they fit like they were a part of him. Laura and her packing would be an entirely different matter. She would lay out ten days of clothing even though they were just going away for seven days. Phase two of her packing would entail Laura circling the bed numerous times, matching and re-matching different outfits to see what pleased her fashion sense the most. Finally, a decision would be made, mostly driven by the fact that her back was up against the clock.

The taxi ride to Hervey Bay Airport was uneventful. They flew from Hervey Bay to Brisbane Airport. By now, the multitude of kangaroos seen along the way was commonplace. The palm trees doubled as umbrellas for the countless days of cloudless skies. Yes, what was commonplace in Australia was a far cry from a Canadian winter. Laura and Brent disembarked the prop plane and went to Fiji Air check-in wicket. Boarding cards in hand, they went to the proper gate and waited to embark to Fiji.

Laura and Brent were safely seated inside the cabin area of the plane. Brent looked around and was astonished by how few passengers were going to Fiji.

Laura had a different take. She loved that there were very few people on the plane. Laura could inhabit her own row of three seats and stretch out for the four-hour flight ahead of them. That was what she did.

Brent was more pensive. It didn't take long for him to establish that the coup in Fiji had to be the reason why this aircraft was flying four hours without any hope of breaking even on the finances. The telephone call with Mike began to deeply resonate with Brent. He was keenly aware of the possible perils that might await them on the Fiji Islands paradise.

Brent sat across from Laura in the adjacent row of seats. He looked at his Laura with love and devotion. He reminisced about their early days when his friends had boldly chastised him and said he had been punching way above his weight class.

Yes, Laura had been a beautiful, young woman and homecoming queen in her senior year of secondary school. That didn't matter to Brent; he knew what was in Laura's heart. She was always kind and gentle with a North Star that guided her to family first. When they had been starting out as a young married couple and money had been tight, it had been Laura who went without. She would suffer before her boys did.

Brent would often ask, "Are you my girl?"

Laura would never answer with a pre-rehearsed, monotone, disinterested verbal reply. Laura would stop everything she was doing. She would face her love and, in a gentle, heartfelt voice, answer, "I'm your girl."

Brent perpetually bathed in the love that manifested from within Laura's heart and soul. In the middle years of their marriage now, they were in the prime of their lives. They were fit, they were attractive, and they were flirts. Their marriage was fun; it was like two soulmates playing on a stage of love and laughter. They would always joke around about who had changed who the most. Brent would tease Laura about the exhibitionist she had become, and Laura would reciprocate with how she had shaved off the rough edges of a redneck and turned him into a fine gentleman.

She'd then snicker and say, "A gentleman is what your friends call a pussy."

Then they would both laugh. What had always remained unsaid between the two of them was that both statements were true. Laura had become a bit of an exhibitionist, but it was her way to keep the marriage alive and vibrant. She knew her man. Most of Brent's fantasies would forever remain in the bedroom, but she didn't mind dressing showier and presenting more cleavage if it would help her lover with his foreplay. Truth be known, Laura didn't mind men's eyes being entertained by her body.

Now in their early retirement, the spark was still there.

Laura's body held up more than anyone deserved, and her beauty was still deserving of a crown. Brent's fitness and good looks made him as handsome as ever.

Yes, looking back, he had made all the right choices, and perhaps he was punching above his weight class.

Their airplane touched down like one's head hitting a pillow: soft and gentle. Kudos to the professionalism of the pilot who had landed the aircraft safely. The Hudsons walked through customs with a wave of a hand. Then it was outside to look for their transportation to Treasure Island. Both of them took the time to take deep breaths of unadulterated, pure Fijian air. Their twenty-seater, shiny white bus arrived, and everyone was seated. The goodwill ambassador from Treasure Island was on board and, with the use of a microphone, welcomed all the tourists. He asked them a series of questions and one, in particular, stood out.

"Do we have any newlyweds aboard?"

The timid arm and hand of a Japanese groom rose on high.

Laura looked at the newlyweds and thought fondly of the journey that lay ahead of them.

As they were driving the road toward Nadi, they passed a green signboard that simply read "Fiji   Ah Beautiful Fiji."

Nadi itself wasn't all that big or sprawling, but that wasn't a major concern to either Laura or Brent as they both spied the massive Hard Rock Cafe sign rising high above the landscape of the downtown core of Nadi. They drove through Nadi, comfortably conversing with others on the bus shuttle until they reached the boat dock at Port Denarau Marina. From there they rode forty-five minutes on a luxury catamaran to Treasure Island.

Laura informed Brent that she felt like she was riding on

a big, old house that was floating on water. While she had Brent's undivided attention, Laura went on to educate him from the brochures that she had previously read.

Treasure Island was involved in the protection of endangered species, which included hawksbill turtles and crested iguanas.

Brent wanted to say, "I need to know this why?" He was a little more attentive when Laura spoke about the reintroduction of marine species and cultivations of the coral reef. Still, his mind was more focused on docking the luxury catamaran at the 5.86 hectares Treasure Island Resort.

Feet firmly on the ground, Laura and Brent took a 360-degree look around. They were both very impressed with what they saw. Over the following week, they both snorkeled on the reef every day, and each day was different. The fish in the tropics were beautiful and all in technicolor.

Brent thought he witnessed an octopus capture a good-sized fish, complete with a blue dye attack. He thought it was fascinating to see. His education was further broadened when a resort guide informed him that the blue dye was a defense mechanism to probably protect the octopus from the rather large fish.

Laura loved the three-tiered infinity pools and swam in them daily, but mostly she liked to sit around the pools, read a book, and work on her suntan. The entire island only took twenty minutes to walk around. This became a daily ritual for them, and in the late afternoon, they strolled hand in hand like lovers during mating season. They also ate entire authentic Fijian suppers. Laura learned to cook a Fijian dish and was quite impressed by the way it was made. Brent ate three different kinds of fish and a multitude of other Fijian food that he hadn't even known existed. It was all good. So, in keeping with his tradition, he added Fiji to his list of authentic cuisine.

Every night, there was a traditional Fijian show. The performers played instruments made from nature and did classic dances. The costumes they wore were very colorful and always meant something culturally. One night, they had a pretty impressive war dance going. One slip of their weapons and heads would roll, though no one in the show would receive injuries. Some of the children who watched with their parents were affected. They were scared and cried in terror.

Laura mused to Brent, "Why aren't they leaving with their children?"

All the shows would finish by nine thirty each night. Brent and Laura would then go to the pool area and enjoy the ambiance of the live band and the warm, summer night breezes. The Hudsons would strike up conversations with the other guests, who mainly were from Australia, but they also met others from New Caledonia, Japan, Croatia, and Copenhagen.

Laura had been taken by surprise by some Copenhagen children, girls about four and six years old. The first few days, the kids had swum nude. On about day three, they'd started coming to the pool wearing swim bottoms. Laura remarked, "I betcha their parents were told to get those kids attired properly for the pool."

Brent inquired, "Why would they do that?"

Laura was correct in what she said next. "The pool area also has male children under ten, and it can be awkward for them because of cultural differences."

Brent replied, "A parent got fed up and bitched."

"Think about it," she replied.

Laura described their housing, what the Fijians called bures.

Their particular bure was very spacious, complete with air-conditioning and bona fide Fijian furnishings. The design of these bures was similar to a semi-detached dwelling back home.

Brent liked the Japanese newlyweds who were honeymooning on the other side of their bure. The wall that separated them was not very thick, so any sound could easily be heard. Laura and Brent couldn't understand them, and the newlyweds couldn't understand the Hudsons, but the sounds of love were universal and needed no interpreters. During one of their pillow talks at the end of the day, Brent would broadcast that the young groom was definitely a sprinter. Brent whispered to Laura that he felt this Japanese husband needed his assistance.

Laura said, "I don't think so! You've got business to take care of in your own bure."

Brent was told about the staff and their working hours. They worked twenty-four days on and five off. Brent and Laura bonded with one of these workers; his name was Mark, and he was a porter from the boat to the room and, when you leave, the reverse. The occupancy on the island was about half, or maybe even a little less full. Mark was a very nice young man whose girlfriend also worked the same hours as he did. He slept four to a room because he was not married. He made three dollars and fifteen cents per hour, with room and board included.

Mark invited the Hudsons to a kava ceremony one night. Kava was a Fijian drink. It was made from the root of a plant grown in Fiji. Mark said to them that "You can't say you were in Fiji without having this drink." The root was pulverized with a rock. The kava bits were put into a bag and mixed with water. This was poured into a round bowl to represent the earth. Two half coconut shells completed the tools.

An appointed Fijian dipped the shells into the kava. He specifically offered it to one person. That person executed a deep clap to signal their acceptance. They got handed the shell and chugged the contents. While doing this, the server and everyone else clapped three times. When the person was done, they clapped three more times. This was a respectful thing. It tasted like dirty water. In about one minute, one's tongue went numb, just like with Novocain at the dentist. It was not an alcoholic or an addictive drug.

Brent was offered another. He clapped. One minute after he drank it, his tongue and now his jaw went numb.

Laura asked Brent if he thought he had had enough of this kava.

Brent answered no and drank more and then more again. Brent's jaw was a little hard to shut, but other than that he felt fine.

At long last, it was time to go. Laura asked Brent how he felt. There was no slurring of words nor a craven desire for munchies on his way to their bure.

Brent said, "Good, except I feel very bloated."

The Hudsons got back to their bure, and Brent sat on the bed and immediately fell fast asleep.

Their last day on Treasure Island at the resort came way too early. The next day they would be on an airplane back to their other vacation, so Brent and Laura could continue with their dream of a lifetime. But tonight, Laura was preparing for an epic date with her husband. She was going to wow her man; she was going to be the climax event of a fireworks display. Another mixed drink was consumed, and it was off to the Hard Rock Cafe.

17

LAST DANCE

ETAK HAD CROSSED Laura's red line. Laura pulled away and shouted at Etak, "Fuck off, and leave me alone!" With that, Laura bolted across the dance floor in search of Brent.

Etak caught her and spun Laura around so hard she temporarily lost her balance and ended up grabbing back onto him for stability. The pressure Etak's fingers exerted on Laura's arms made her flinch with pain.

Heard next was the gut-wrenching sound that only a fist makes when it smashes into the unsuspecting flesh of another. All eyes in the bar darted to the dance floor. Brent knew that sound only too well, both on the giving and receiving side. In a nanosecond, he was up, and the fire in his eyes told everyone this panther was on the move. Behind Brent, also stirring, were the three other men from the military. Laura was lying on the floor, and blood was pooling around her head.

Etak, with his fist stilled cocked, was staring down at her. He had a fuck-you smirk on his face.

Brent couldn't get to Laura fast enough. His entire world seemed to be in slow motion. His target lay right ahead of him, and with all the inner strength he could muster, he threw the best haymaker of his life. Down went the piece of shit. Before he could tend to his Laura, he heard the sound of a gunshot, and his world went black.

18

NOTIFICATION

JAMES WAS IN his office working through the vast number of items he had to deal with. He looked at the wall clock and saw it was almost time to take a coffee break. This was a routine demanded by Daniel, who wanted to make sure that even the CEO of a company took time to just decompress and enjoy a few precious minutes to himself.

The intercom in his office sounded, and James picked up the phone. It was his secretary with information that some immigration official from Fiji was waiting to talk to him.

James said, "Hello" and he carried on with the phrase, "What can I do for you?"

The immigration official introduced himself and told James that he was listed as the emergency contact on his parents' immigration papers.

There was a moment of silence as James tried to mentally

work through what the hell had happened and what kind of trouble his parents were in. James then asked, "What kind of emergency would precipitate this call from you?"

The immigration official, in somewhat of a robotic voice, stated, "Sir, your parents have been involved in a tragic incident."

James interrupted the bureaucrat. His voice was in a full-blown panic. "What's wrong? What happened? Are Mom and Dad OK?"

The public servant, in a calm and straightforward utterance, informed James that his task was just to tell the emergency contact that a serious event had taken place and to inform James of the avenues he could use to pursue answers.

James raised his voice. "What happened?"

The civil servant explained that he had no more information and that his responsibilities had been satisfied. If James wanted any more details, he was to call the Nadi coroner's office. He furnished James with a phone number and the coroner's name. The immigration official ended the call with an abrupt goodbye.

James hung up the phone and stared at absolutely nothing. He was numb. He was scared. What paralyzed his emotions the most was the phrase, "Call the coroner." James informed his secretary that he would be unavailable for the rest of the day. He put his head down on his desk and let out a loud wail that alerted all that something was amiss with the boss.

James gathered himself and dialed the Nadi coroner's office. There was no answer. He tried several more times in the next hour with no better results. He decided to telephone the Nadi Police Department. He explained everything up to this point and asked the duty officer if he could fill in more of the details.

The blunt report back to him was, "No information is available as the investigation is still ongoing."

Brent's oldest son slammed down the phone in frustration. James made a call to his husband, Daniel, and explained the situation to him. No one had to tell them that something terribly wrong had happened. Together, Daniel and James quietly cried and consoled each other. James said he loved Daniel but had to hang up so he could get in touch with Mike and Niki. Daniel told James to do whatever he had to do and that he and Brady would abide by any decisions necessary to reunite the Hudson family.

The cell phone rang as Niki was opening the car door to let her kids into the car. She had just picked them up from school. James was on the other end and wanted Niki to get in touch with Mike to inform him of these stressful events.

It didn't take long before James's private phone line lit up. Mike was on the other end spewing a thousand questions at once. James was at a loss to answer any of them. The fact was nobody really knew anything. The omen of bad news was just floating around the Hudson family like a dense fog. Two questions dogged the Hudson brothers: what had happened, and why was no one furnishing them with information, good or bad?

James said it first. "I have a company jet. This is our parents."

In unison the boys blasted out, "Fuck it. Let's go!"

19

INITIAL HOSPITAL VISIT

THERE COULD BE nothing more chilling than sitting in a hospital room looking at one's father struggling for life. This was what confronted James and Mike on their arrival at Nadi Hospital in Fiji. Before them, their father reclined in a semi-seated position, his eyes closed, with a chest tube inserted between his ribs and a breathing tube in his throat to create an airway. Here resided the wounded, lion-hearted monarch of their family. Their Superman was being force-fed from plastic tubes containing fluids from plastic bags hanging nonchalantly on an IV pole. Both the boys sat in utter silence. The situation was rather ironic between viewing the sedate, generic hospital room and then looking out the hospital room window to beautifully manicured lawns and palm trees swaying in the breeze.

It had been two days since their initial visit to their father's hospital room. This morning, in their rented condo, they prepared for a tête-à-tête with the doctors; they also secured a meeting with the investigating police detective. James and Mike decided to split responsibilities, with Mike conversing with the hospital doctors and James probing Nadi law enforcement for answers into what was being called a happenstance at the Hard Rock Cafe.

James thought that Mike's military training, and the probability of him having seen gunshot wounds while on deployment, would help him understand what all the medical terminology meant. James would carry on to the police station, knowing that, so far, they had been stonewalled in finding out any information about their parents' case. James would put his negotiating skills to good use.

20

MIKE GETS A DIAGNOSIS

MIKE, ON HIS return to the hospital, hustled right to his father's room. Immediately, he saw that the chest tube had been taken out, along with the air tube that had been invading his father's mouth. Silent, happy tears rolled down his cheeks as he realized that this was a good sign. Behind him entered a nurse and the surgeon in charge of his dad's care. Mike sat down in the visitor chair, the nurse checked the IV tubes then left, and the surgeon faced Mike to begin his consultation concerning his father's diagnosis.

"Hello, my name is Dr. Zayn Leba, head of surgery. First, let me tell you how sorry I am for the loss of your mother. I know she must have been a fine lady. Your father was shot twice in the back. The first bullet was shot from a distance, and the second was shot from close range.

"The bullet came from a low-velocity handgun. I'm not a

forensic scientist, but I've seen enough of this type of wound to tell me it probably came from an old military pistol. This is probably why your dad is still alive. The actual bullet came from a 9 mm, soft-point shell. This bullet, coming from an older, low-velocity handgun, caused the soft nose to expand on impact with the flesh and more so with bones. If he had been shot with a newer revolver housing a hollow-point shell, it would have been far worse.

"Immediately after your parents were shot, the blood from your dad's wounds was stopped by a Good Samaritan. There was nothing anyone could do for your mother. The ambulance arrived within minutes and your father was given oxygen and immediately transported to this hospital. Your father's wounds were serious, as both bullets passed through the right side of his back and exited through his right lung. We took him straightaway to the operating room. Your father had a collapsed right lung. We inserted a chest tube to drain and alleviate the pressure in his chest cavity. This was to assist in expanding his right lung. We did a CT scan of his entire torso. We were able to surgically remove the bullet fragments that were contained in his torso. Unfortunately, we found a small reoccurring air leak from his lung. We were able to surgically seal the leak.

"The first bullet hit and broke ribs. This caused bone fragments to act as spears and shred everything in their path. It was just luck that no other vital organs were hit. Still, a high degree of damage to soft tissue was sustained. Therefore, you can imagine the damage to muscles, tendons, and ligaments.

"The second bullet was shot at close range and fortunately for your dad, the bullet went between his ribs. No bone fragments were propelled. Instead, the bullet passed right through the soft tissue of his body, again hitting the lung but no other vital organs. After three days, the chest tube greatly increased his lung function, to the point where the chest tube and the endotracheal tube were removed. Your father's lung expansions remain stable but will be monitored.

"Up until this point, he has been heavily sedated to keep him inactive as much as possible. Today all sedatives have been discontinued. The remaining intravenous drug going into your dad is for pain management because of the trauma caused to his body. The other bag on the IV pole is saline, which keeps your father hydrated. We will monitor him for at least a week. If all goes well, we will release him."

Mike asked Dr. Leba, "If all goes well, as you say, will my father have a complete recovery?"

The doctor replied, "Medicine is not an exact science, but his prognosis is very positive." Dr. Leba told Mike, "Right now your father is heavily sedated, but in the next few hours, as the sedative wears off, he will become conscious but still be very groggy."

Mike shook the doctor's hand and walked outside to get a breath of fresh air. He cried quiet tears of joy for his father and mournful tears of rage for the mother he'd lost and loved so much.

21

JAMES AT THE POLICE STATION

JAMES LEFT MIKE to the doctors, and he walked out of Nadi Hospital. He sat in the back of a limo and headed to the Nadi Police Department. The distance between the two locations was one kilometer but, for stress-filled James, it seemed to take a lifetime. James didn't know which officer was assigned to his mother and father's case. He hoped for a detective with years of experience and investigations under their belt. What he did know, was that he needed answers.

The limo came to rest outside of the front doors of the police department. James jumped out and proceeded to the front desk, which was attended by a smartly dressed, uniformed officer. James introduced himself and observed that his purpose for being there appeared to be known.

The officer introduced himself as Sergeant Ratu Cama.

He instructed James to wait and that Detective Isaac Roko would be out presently to show him to his office.

James waited thirty minutes before Detective Roko finally met with him, and they proceeded to his office. Detective Roko started their conversation by consoling James about the critical injuries to his father and the death of his mother. James thanked him and got right to the point. He wanted to know where the investigation stood at this point and time. Detective Roko opened the case file and began scanning the report.

"Brent and Laura Hudson arrived at the Hard Rock Cafe at approximately 8 p.m. They were observed to be heavily under the influence of alcohol." Detective Roko went on to say, "Laura Hudson was dressed and acting in a very provocative manner."

James interrupted him, "What do you mean a very provocative manner?"

"Well, James, your mother was dressed rather scantily, dancing and moving her body with sexually deliberate movements."

"How does that get her killed?" countered James.

Detective Roko continued, "Your father was also very intoxicated and was belligerent toward the other patrons who were in attendance. He started arguing with four partygoers and a fight ensued. Your mother joined in to assist your father and, unfortunately, they were both shot. Your father sustained two gunshot wounds to his back, and your mother was shot in the head and died immediately."

"Bullshit," retorted James. "My father, belligerent? He's the most measured and calculating person there is. What's the name of this witness? How reliable—"

James was cut off by the detective. "We are still investigating but, as of this time, we are unable to secure any reliable eyewitnesses," stated Detective Roko. The detective went on to say, "When the gunshots rang out, all the patrons ran and scattered in all directions. When the police arrived, absolutely no one remained at the Hard Rock Cafe except one waiter."

James burst back into the conversation. "What is this waiter's name?"

Detective Roko was losing patience with James. Abruptly he stated, "The waiter was trying to piece together what he thought probably happened. He was not an eyewitness. He was inside the Hard Rock Cafe, and your parents were outside in the patio section."

James was just about to lose it. "You're telling me that there are no eyewitnesses to this crime. You're telling me, that of all the patrons and tourists that frequent the cafe, no one saw what happened? How can that be? Either your police department is hiding something, or your department is completely incompetent. Whoever murdered my mom and shot my dad has to have put the fear of God in the police, the staff, and the patrons of the Hard Rock Cafe."

Detective Roko slammed the file shut. He took a deep breath, then stared right into James's eyes. He said, "Sir, this investigation is still open, and facts remain to be gathered. It is insulting for you to cast aspersions on me and my fellow police officers. Please lower the temperature of your words and the insinuations in their meanings."

James took a page out of his father's book: "One can catch more bees with honey than you do with shit." He apologized to Detective Roko and blamed it on his mourning for his mother's death and father's injuries. He asked Detective Roko,

"Sir, could I have a copy of the police investigation, and could it include a copy of the coroner's report?"

Detective Roko apologized and recited that "The investigation is still ongoing, and the coroner's report is not available to you."

James shot back, "Not available or being withheld from me?"

Detective Roko had had enough. He rose from his chair and opened the office door. He indicated to James that he had been given his cell number and that if the police found out more information on his parents, they would be in touch with him.

Inside James was fuming, but he was smart enough to know that in any negotiations, one needed to step back and funnel all pertinent information through the proper channels. In this case, the proper channels would be a lawyer and an investigator. James didn't bother to thank or shake the hand of Detective Roko. He exited the police station and hotfooted it right to the waiting limo and jumped in the back seat. James was off to rejoin his brother at the hospital.

22

THE PLAN

JAMES FOUND MIKE in the well-groomed courtyard of the hospital, sitting on a bench underneath a palm tree. James was convinced that the investigation into the death of their mom and the attempted murder of their dad was an out-and-out cover-up. He suggested to Mike, "We have to hire a lawyer and an investigator."

Mike listened intently before he gave his thoughtful analysis. Mike replied, "James, I know where you're coming from. Let me offer you another alternative. You're thinking that we need a lawyer for the legal haggling ahead of us. Well, I'm here to fucking tell you that our kids will grow old and die before you get any information from the police or the Nadi Office of the Coroner. As for the investigator, I can't delve too deeply, but let me inform you that investigations are a huge part of what I've used in my operations. Now let's revisit the lawyer.

Lawyers ask questions and shuffle paper. If things don't go their way, lawyers get subpoenas, then the courts get involved. James, please consider me a middleman. I don't ask questions like a lawyer, I interrogate." Mike smiled and added, "Your part is to find me $9,000, which I will need for seed money."

James laughed and simply said the word, "Done." James completed telling his half of the story. He then asked Mike about what he had found out from the doctor.

Mike told James about the detailed report Dr. Leba had given to him. Mike made James aware that their dad was breathing completely on his own and might be awake. Mike and James went back into the hospital to their father's room.

23

THE FULL PICTURE
STARTS TO EMERGE

IT WAS EERILY silent as Brent looked up at the ceiling. He was groggy but alert. He was trying to piece together the events that led up to him being situated in this hospital room. He looked for another bed in his room. He didn't really know why, but he knew that if Laura had been able to, she would have been sitting on it, waiting for him to awaken. Immediately, his spirits lifted when he saw his two boys enter his hospital room.

James was the first to rush over to his dad and give him a gentle hug.

Brent witnessed tears falling from his oldest son's eyes.

An apprehensive Mike was next to hug his dad.

Brent sensed something was wrong. The process of elimination drew his thinking to Laura.

Mike sat back down on the foot of the bed and was about to ask his dad how he was feeling.

This was all interrupted when Brent blurted out, "Where's your mother?"

Both his boys covered their faces with their hands in hopes of muffling their sobs of pain, along with their tears that could fill a bathtub.

Brent raised his voice. "Where the fuck is your mother?"

It was James who was first able to utter any words. His voice breaking, he replied, "She's gone."

"What do you mean she's gone? Where the fuck did she go?" cringed Brent.

Mike answered with a cracking voice, "Pop, she's dead. Some son of a bitch shot her in the head."

For a man who had been shot twice in the back and who had a hoarse voice due to his throat having been invaded by a breathing tube, a sorrowfully awful scream of "No!" escaped Brent's mouth. This was the pain of a man who had just suffered an irreparable loss.

The doctor hastily entered Brent's hospital room and informed the two sons that perhaps it would be better to leave because of their father's agitated state. The two boys turned and headed to the door when they heard the fragile voice of the father. "I want names! Do you hear me? I want fucking names!"

The last sound they heard was the wailing of a man, completely broken.

Back at the penthouse condo that James had rented, the two boys decided it was time for a serious meeting of the minds. They knew their dad. He had spent his entire life trying to help others in times of need. They were also privy to stories of the rare occasions when his red line in the sand had been crossed. Brent would take all the bullshit one could give, but a time would come when he would have enough. Brent would calmly utter the words, "Humor me." The person's actions after that point would dictate the degree of pain they would suffer. Most of their dad's friends called him One Shot. In his younger, barroom days, his fights had ended quickly with one shot. Brent had spent his share of time in the woods, hunting over the years. He had such a successful game-to-kill ratio that his Ojibwa friends had carried on the name of One Shot.

James and Mike were on a mission to find out about the identity of everyone who'd crossed the Hudson family line!

24

THE INVESTIGATION IS EDITED

JAMES RECAPPED IN conversation what they knew to Mike. He ended with, "We know fuck all."

Truth be known, Mike was a lot more proficient in the conversation that James was trying to lead. The younger brother asserted that although they knew only a limited number of the facts, they were both suited to getting to the truth better than anyone.

James looked puzzled when he inquired, "How's that?"

Mike smiled at his older brother then spoke, "Shut the fuck up and I'll tell you." Mike went on with his plan. He told James that they should divide up the responsibilities. While in Fiji James would be the caregiver, for their father. Mike cited the information gleaned from Dr. Leba and explained that their dad would be probably another two or three days under hospital care. James was to secure a way home for their mother's remains, whether that be in casket or urn. James was to front this entire mission with cold, hard cash. Mike told James that the Hudson Reinsurance jet would probably take them all home, including building special supports for their mom's casket if Dad preferred a casket over an urn.

James looked up and answered, "I'll make it happen and, if needed, I'll buy a bigger jet."

The younger brother carried on. "If possible, James, could you ask Dr. Leba if he can get his hands on the autopsy report on our mother? Please, James. Just ask once and don't beg. Make it sound like an afterthought. I don't want Dr. Leba to become suspicious of what we're up to."

25

MIKE WEARS NO WHITE HAT!

IT WAS MIKE'S turn to tell his older brother what his part would be in this covert operation. Mike looked at James eye to eye. In a firm voice, he said, "James, the less you know about how I attempt to obtain the police report, the better for you. You need to have plausible deniability in case things don't go the way I'm planning."

James answered, "What are you talking about?"

Mike accentuated his reply, "Think about it, bro." He then went on with the rest of his plan.

This would be the last time they discussed anything until they were in international airspace. James was alerted to the fact that Mike might not be at the rented condo for the next few days. James, in turn, told Mike that he would keep him abreast on the progress of his responsibilities. James wondered just how far Mike would go to fulfill his side of the plan. Finally, to end this one-time conversation, James informed Mike that he would cover for him with their dad. It was getting late. They embraced each other and went off to their respective bedrooms.

The last words of the night were uttered by James. "Your $9,000 will be here at the condo by noon tomorrow."

James went to the hospital the following morning. He was prepared to care for his father but also hardening himself to face his father.

26

THEIR DAD WANTS ANSWERS!

THE LIMO DROPPED James off, and he entered the hospital. As he closed in on his father's room, he heard talking and the familiar voice of his brother. James entered the room, smiled, and said hello to his dad and then immediately shot Mike a glaring look. He bit his tongue and said, "Nice plan."

Mike responded that he'd just arrived and then asked a question of their father. "Dad, when you and Mom went to Treasure Island, Mom wrote me an email that said you guys had met a very nice young man. Do you remember the guy's name?"

His dad took his stare off the ceiling and looked at Mike and said, "I believe his name is Mark."

Mike told his father he had to go do some banking.

James just shook his head and did a quick mental rehearsal of the conversation he was about to have with his father.

It didn't take James long to understand that his father was sedated only enough to dull the piercing edges of his pain. Yet he was still coherent and fully remembered the significant emotional events that had changed his life forever.

Brent recited in chronological order the circumstances that had ended up with him shot and his wife murdered.

James could only listen in silence and wipe the tears from his eyes as he came to understand how different the police report was from what was coming out of his father's mouth. James told his dad that Mike was looking into who the attackers were and what charges were filed against them. James told his father that his job was to get better so that they could get him and Mom back home.

Brent ended the conversation with the words, "OK, son."

Their talking morphed into silence as they both let the tears in their eyes flow like rivers down their cheeks.

27

DAY ONE TREASURE ISLAND

MIKE WENT INTO stealth mode. He knew he had to cover a lot of ground to get the intel on what exactly had happened with his parents. He treated this as a covert deployment to secure real intel on just what had happened to two of the highest valued assets in his life. Mike was fighting against the rage inside himself, against letting the rule of law prevail. He would complete his part of the bargain with due consideration for those who would stand in his way.

Mike left James by their father's bedside and immediately started to execute his plan of action. He returned to the rented condo to pick up the $9,000 that James had secured for him. Mike silently unlocked and entered the door to the luxurious penthouse condo that James had rented. The absolute vastness, the smell of leather, and the sight of gold fixtures exuded wealth. Mike thought this was a far cry from the sand dunes, swamps, and farmers' fields that he called home while deployed on missions. He sat down on the sofa and rested his feet up on the coffee table. He put his head back, shut his eyes, and reflected on the past few days.

He then proceeded to Port Denarau shopping mall and secured a burner cell phone. Mike called the Treasure Island Resort and booked several nights in a bure. He told the receptionist he would pay the $2,000 in cash when he arrived. He then made his way to the marina to catch a water taxi that took him to Treasure Island. On arrival, he could see why his mom and dad had liked the place so much. The resort was beautiful.

Mike played the tourist role to the hilt. He blended in perfectly with the other foreigners. He very discreetly investigated and tracked down the young man his mom had held in such high praise. Mike was able to secure time with Mark after his shift ended for the day.

Mark visited Mike and they shared a drink or two in his rented bure. Once the introductions were made, Mike began to interrogate Mark. He was looking for an angle to elicit the young man's assistance. He found two prime areas worth pursuing: drugs and the political climate. Mike found that Mark liked his cocaine. Mark complained that being paid poor wages resulted in poor-quality coke. Politically, Mark was pissed off about another military coup and his human rights being trampled on. It troubled him that the freedom of the press was all but gone. He hated that the transparency of truth had morphed into military propaganda. This meant he was unable to keep abreast of what was truly happening in Fiji.

Mike said to Mark, "I guess you didn't hear about the Canadian couple killed at the Hard Rock Cafe?"

Mark replied, "Actually, I heard they were murdered by four members of the military."

This was the opening that Mike had hoped for. He loosened his new friend's tongue with another drink. Mike asked, "Would you be able to find out who those men are, and possibly where they are stationed?"

Mark laughed. "Why? Are you looking to kill them?"

Mike smiled. "No. Actually, I am a private investigator hired by the family to find out what actually happened to their loved ones." Mike then showed the young Fijian a picture of his mom and dad.

Mark stood up from the chair he was sitting on and uttered, "I know these people. They were really nice. He was a cool guy, and his wife had a booty to die for."

Mike let that comment pass and steered the conversation toward his ultimate goal. He told Mark, "I can pay a finder's fee for any information you can gather for me."

Mark smiled and informed Mike that he had a good cop friend who worked at the Nadi Police Department. He was sure that he could get the names and whereabouts of the military murderers.

Mike pressed on and asked, "If I could get a copy of the police report, I could up the ante on the finder's fee."

His Fijian friend asked Mike, "How much is this finder's fee?"

Mike didn't answer directly. He went on to explain to Mark that there were conditions to this deal. Mark would have to furnish him with the name of his police buddy. He would have to be very discrete and not tell anyone what they were up to. Mike went on to say that the names and whereabouts of the military personnel would garner Mark $2,000.

If he could secure a copy of the police report, Mike would add an additional $1,000. He then asked Mark, "What's the name of your police friend?"

Mark didn't have to think long or ponder much about doing this deal. He told Mike the name he wanted to hear. "Venasio Tubuna."

Mike, feigning bad manners, asked Mark for his last name. Mark replied, "Volau. Mark Volau."

Mike had set the hook, and the bait was swallowed. Now he needed an exit. He let Mark know that once his mission was accomplished, he should bring Venasio back to Treasure Island for a night of good nose candy. It would be his treat.

Mike smiled and said, "I'm tired, and it is time to get some shut-eye."

28

DAY 2 TREASURE ISLAND

THE NEXT MORNING, Mike took the time to really explore Treasure Island. It surprised him that he could walk its entire circumference, on the white sand, in approximately half an hour. He fueled his body with authentic Fijian cuisine. Mike took the time to dip his toes into the infinity pool.

When an employee strolled by, Mike asked him, "Have you seen Mark?"

The worker stated that "Mark asked for a few days off, and the boss approved it."

Mike said, "Thank you," and the employee proceeded along his merry way.

It was time for Mike to take a water taxi into the underbelly areas of the Port Denarau tourist area. Once he arrived at Port Denarau, it didn't take long for him to secure a gram of good-quality blow. This would create about twenty typical lines that could be snuffed up a person's nose. The effects of each line would last about thirty minutes. He thought $110 of James's money seemed a fair price to pay.

His next stop took him to a hardware store to pick up some magic ingredients to bolster the potency of the cocaine he'd bought for his newfound friends. Afterward, Mike had business at the Office of the Coroner before retiring and spending the rest of the night at James's condo.

29

DAY 3 TREASURE ISLAND

DAWN WAS BREAKING, and Mike had to shift positions on James's sofa to avoid the bright rays of the sun. He could hear James in bed, still snoring. Mike's special forces training allowed him to put his tiredness aside and focus on the analysis of his mission. He closed his eyes as he visualized his break-in at the Office of the Coroner.

Yesterday, in the daylight, he had cased the place for signs of cameras or alarms. It had gone smoothly, with no hiccups. It did not surprise him that neither alarms nor cameras had been installed. Fiji wasn't a very wealthy country and, therefore, like all governments, budget cuts were the order of the day. Mike had waited until after dark to do the actual break-in. Once inside and in the file room, he had been able to use the light built into his burner cell phone. He'd searched in the file cabinets until he'd found the Hudson file. A closer look had brought him to his mom's autopsy. He'd used his cell phone once more to take pictures of all the pages contained within the file. He'd left as stealthily as he'd arrived.

Mike departed James's condo and spent the entire day doing a detailed recon of Port Denarau and Nadi for possible future needs.

Mike caught a late-night water taxi back to Treasure Island. The tourists were partying heavily, and the alcohol was being poured liberally to all partygoers at the island bar. Mike made himself stop in for a beer and partake in the foolishness that abounded. Shortly after, he took his leave and returned to his bure. He laid his head on the pillow, but sleep evaded him. Memories of his mom came flooding in. The pain he felt for her loss was overwhelming, even for a well-trained, special forces veteran. That night he cried himself to sleep.

30

DAY 4 TREASURE ISLAND

THE NEXT MORNING, Mike awakened with the feeling that he had been through a game of rugby. His body ached everywhere. It wasn't because of the bed; it was because of the continued stress his body had been under, even in sleep. He never became relaxed.

He spent the day on the island. Mike lazed around and played friendly with anyone who came his way. He wanted to be seen by the transient tourist traffic. He was also smart enough to remain as incognito to the staff as possible. Mike did, however, elicit intel that Mark was again off work that day but would be back the next night, as he had to work the following day.

The day went well, his plan was in progress, and the shit hadn't hit the fan.

31

DAY 5 TREASURE ISLAND

ON THE MORNING of his last full day at the resort, Mike's body felt much better. He felt somewhat refreshed and ready for the day's business. He did a recon of the island for anything or anyone that might be out of place. Finding nothing suspicious, he returned to his bure, sat down on a chair, and pulled out his cell phone. He took the time to have his coffee to prepare himself to read his mother's autopsy report.

Mike re-read the entire autopsy report before slamming the cell phone onto his chest. He was even more angry then when he read it the first time. But, as he reflected upon what he just read, he became enraged. He stormed out the door. He walked to the sandy beach, prepared to do another lap of the island. Mike found himself a desolate section of the beach and sat down on a piece of driftwood shaped nicely to act as a seat.

All his emotions came flooding back. The dams in his eyes

broke, and an uncontrolled current of tears cascaded down his face. These were not the tears of a son grieving for his mother. These, for Mike, were tears of fury. Mike visualized what must have happened according to the tale the medical examiner had woven.

His mother had been knocked unconscious as a result of a punch from a strong person, likely male. The punch had broken her nose and chipped one of her front teeth. When she'd hit the floor, a 10 cm gash had opened up on her forehead. Mike knew his mom would have bled heavily from her face. The examiner had written that the victim had regained consciousness. He'd gone on to write that, as proven by the blood trail found at the scene, the victim had crawled across the floor to protect a male gunshot victim from further harm. Mike knew his mom would have done whatever she could to protect the love of her life. It was no surprise to Mike that she'd covered his body with her own. Mike's tears stopped immediately. He looked to the heavens with disgust. The medical examiner had recorded the cause of death as a single gunshot wound to the back of the head.

The last thing Mike read was, "The victim was executed."

It was a somber walk back to the bure. Once inside, he opened the bag he'd purchased at the hardware store. The printed label read Rodent Poison. Mike knew it as strychnine. This product was not new to him. He'd needed it while on deployment with the special forces. He knew all about it being a white powder, colorless, and odorless, but most of all he knew it was deadly. Yes, he had mixed this lethal drug with cocaine more than once. Today he would combine the two drugs and tonight treat Mark and Venasio to a chemical cocktail causing death. Their deaths would be nothing more than collateral damage. Mike had no feelings of remorse. He was simply a special forces soldier completing his covert mission. The leaving of witnesses, more often than not, caused operational failures.

32

NOSE CANDY

THE OCEAN AIR blew through the curtains of the bure. Mike heard the voices of Mark and Venasio coming up the walkway. Mike rose and shut the windows to contain the conversation to the inside of his Bure. Mike greeted them at the door. They both had been drinking but were still well within their wits. Mark formally introduced his police friend to Mike. Pleasantries were discussed, then it was time to get on to the business at hand.

Mike asked Mark, "Do you have the names of the four men and a copy of the police report?"

Mark smiled like the Cheshire cat and showed Mike what his eyes wanted to see. They had completed their side of the deal. Mike did see one flaw. The police report was the original. He asked Venasio, "Why the original?"

Venasio barked, "You wanted the police report. So, what's the problem?"

Mike left it at that.

Venasio asked Mike, "How did you know the names of the military guys wouldn't be in the police report?"

Mike knew from his conversation with his brother, James, that there would be no way that the police would ever commit to putting anything incriminating on paper.

He answered Venasio with, "Just lucky I guess." Mike quickly changed the subject and brought out the bag of cocaine. He cleared off the kitchen table and formed two long lines of blow. The lines were each longer than anyone could hope to snuff at one time. Mike turned it into a game. He told both Mark and Venasio that "There will be an extra $500 for the one who can inhale the most." He would put them in competition with each other.

Both of the Fijians smiled and took their places at each end of the table. Before the start of this deadly game, Mike gave Mark $3,000. Mike presumed that half would go to Venasio.

Mike informed the both of them that "Right after you do the nose candy, you should take the rest of the bag and retire to a secluded spot. A place where you can enjoy the fruits of your labor."

Mark piped up that he knew of a place on the beach that would keep them out of sight. Just as importantly, he would remain hidden from his bosses. "One, two, three, go," said Mike, and the contest started.

The two of them were young, healthy, and in good shape, with nice, large lungs. They both actually caused Mike to worry that they might get to the end of their lines. The two of them did well, and after they exhausted the capacity of their lungs, they sat down immediately on chairs to regain their faculties.

Mike divided the $500 evenly between the two of them. Mike tucked the remaining contents of the cocaine bag into Mark's pocket and assisted them in their hasty exit from his bure.

Mike just had a few more pieces to fit into the puzzle. He knew he had about fifteen minutes before the painful contractions of their muscles would start. Five minutes after the onset of contractions, Mark's and Venasio's deaths would come by respiratory arrest. He used this time wisely. He cleaned and disinfected the table. He bleached the chairs and anything else either one of them might have put their hands on. Mike opened the windows, opened the door, and off he went to see the results of his actions.

It didn't take long until he spotted a grown man curled up in the fetal position, lying on the pure-white sands of Treasure Island. He found some broad palm tree fronds and laid them carefully on the sand. He made sure to step only on them. He did not want to leave footprints. Mike made a positive ID and established it was Mark. Mike checked his carotid pulse and satisfied himself that Mark was deceased. Mike looked around for Venasio. He wasn't that concerned, as he knew Venasio had to be somewhere close. He didn't have time to search the entire island, but he was secure in the knowledge that the young police officer was also dead.

He hurried back to his bure and made a cell call for a water-taxi pickup for 4:00 a.m. Mike was headed towards James's condo. The water taxi arrived right on time. Halfway between Treasure Island and Port Denarau, his cell phone went to its watery grave. Mike saw no sense in showing either his father or his brother the contents of the medical examiner's report. He would try to spare them the knowledge that their loved one had been executed.

Mike arrived back at the rented condo and heard his brother pissing in the toilet. Mike was laying down on the posh couch. He stood up and took a soothing morning stretch.

His brother proceeded to the kitchen and put on a pot of coffee.

Mike snuck up behind James and yelled, "Hey, fuckhead!"

James almost hit the roof with fright. He looked at Mike with panicked eyes. When he recognized Mike, he immediately punched him in the shoulder. A smile came over their faces and then both brothers embraced in a loving hug.

Sitting comfortably in the living room of the condo, Mike asked James how their father was making out.

James informed his brother that Dad was doing really well. He would be in rehab for months getting his body back to normal. The doctor had said there was severe muscle damage, but his lungs were healing fine. James carried on by telling Mike that he had retrofitted the jet to carry their mother's casket. Tracks had been installed on the floor to keep the casket stable during takeoff and landing. James said he'd had to give a bribe to find an attending doctor and nurse to accompany them on their flight home.

Mike paused and cocked his head.

James had the floor, and he was going to keep going. The doctor he'd secured was Dr. Leba. The negotiations, when finally completed, would have the doctor and nurse holidaying in Hawaii on Maui and Oahu with all their expenses paid for a week. They would then be flown back to Fiji on James's ticket. James looked at Mike and smiled. "I only had to book one room, as the nurse happens to be the doctor's wife." He told Mike that he'd tried to be really smooth with Dr. Leba about trying to secure the autopsy report. "There was no way the doctor would go anywhere near the medical examiner's report," lamented James. He asked Mike how he had done with his responsibilities.

Mike was short and curt. "Mission complete." Going through Mike's head was the possibility of two more witnesses. Mike was absolutely sure that he had the same information as the authorities. He was also sure that his mom's murderers would not be brought to justice.

James broke into his thoughts by indicating that it would soon be time to leave to pick up their father. They would then leave in a convoy from the hospital with Dad and the medical staff in the ambulance and Mike and James in the limo.

Customs was problem free, which was a relief to both Mike and James. Once in the plane, and after both the stretcher for their dad and the coffin for their mother had been secured, it was wheels up for James's Bombardier Challenger 650 aircraft. Once they were in international airspace, the stress level diminished for the two boys. Now, the gravity of the moment settled in. Their father was severely injured, and their mother was dead.

Brent temporarily dismissed his medical staff and requested a visit from his boys. Once the doctor and nurse were out of earshot, Brent opened the conversation. He was looking for answers. He looked to James for those answers. Brent wanted to know, "Have the police apprehended your mother's murderers?"

James told his dad, "Not yet, but the investigation continues."

Brent, with a louder voice, inquired, "Just what are we going to do about this? What's the plan?"

James had this answer rehearsed and informed his father that once the plane landed, he would hire a lawyer and a private investigator.

Brent pondered this information for a short moment and, with a frustrated voice, said, "What the fuck do we know?"

The boys looked at each other and decided to come clean. James reiterated that it was a police cover-up, and Mike had the names of the four military men involved.

Brent looked at Mike and asked, "Do you have the names with you now?"

Mike replied, "Yes."

Brent looked at both the boys. The pain on his face was evident. Not from his wounds but from his broken heart. He asked no one in particular, "Was your mother raped?"

Mike soberly answered, "No, Pop. I read the autopsy report. It said cause of death was a gunshot wound to the back of the head."

Brent shifted to a more comfortable position before he gave his two boys his additional thoughts. He told them that he knew Laura had been punched in the face. Brent wanted to be furnished with the names and addresses of the motherfuckers who had killed his wife. He looked at James and said that "Your investigator should get photos of these bastards." Brent wished James' lawyer well but stated that "No way in hell is a lawyer going to ever solve this case." Brent's eyes went cold just before he stated his threat. "You boys have one month to get this solved. After that, I will solve it my way." Brent closed his eyes, and Dr. Leba returned to his bedside to administer pain relief. Nothing could numb the pain that Brent felt over the loss of his Laura.

33

VENASIO TUBUNA

VENASIO LEFT MIKE'S bure in a state of euphoria. He was high and feeling no pain. The police officer stared into the night but couldn't see his friend Mark. He did however notice that his mouth seemed full of saliva. Venasio spit. It was blood he was spewing. He had seen this before.

In Fiji, the majority of the population was far from wealthy and living with rodents was just a fact of life. As a young lad growing up on this island paradise, he had seen rodent poison being used by many households as a measure to control these vermin. Every family had at some time witnessed a household pet that had digested the poison. In a situation like this, it wouldn't take long before the animal would start bleeding, either from its nose or mouth. Not long after this started, the pet would wince in pain and what followed would be an anguishing death. On rare occasions, a toddler of the household would also digest this rodent poison. Before even emergency assistance was called, the parents would induce the child to vomit. They would do so by making the child drink coconut oil.

Venasio knew he was in trouble and that time was of the essence. He headed right for the kitchen where the chefs prepared meals for the vacationers on Treasure Island. Venasio pounded on the door and, luckily for him, the baker was hard at work producing pastries for the morning's breakfast. The baker took one look at Venasio and seemed to know exactly what the issue was.

The baker said, "Poison."

Venasio, still high on cocaine, could only nod his head.

The baker immediately made Venasio drink as much coconut oil as he could. The poison victim had enough sense to know that the more he could drink the better. The result was almost immediate. Venasio was expelling the last of his stomach contents.

The night baker called security, and the Treasure Island utility boat was used to transport the sick police officer to the Nadi shore where he was transferred immediately to a waiting ambulance.

Venasio arrived at Nadi Hospital in critical condition. The hospital had been forewarned that a poison victim was en route. The doctors knew there wasn't really any antidote for rodent poison. All they could do was neutralize the deadly poison the best they could. They knew this poison was similar to the blood thinner warfarin but many times more potent. Control of the severe internal bleeding would be the paramount factor in determining the young police officer's chance of survival. They would only be able to feed him vitamin K, which would work to counteract the effects of blood thinner. Then they would employ a regime of 50–100 g of activated charcoal per dose for several days. The activated charcoal would absorb the active ingredient in the rodent poison called brodifacoum.

The rest of the treatment would all hinge on the victim's age, health, and, most importantly, the grace of God.

34

HOME AND REHAB

THE NUMEROUS FLIGHTS to get from Nadi to Toronto
took their toll on Brent. Brent made it home. He was definitely
stiff and sore. Yet he thanked his lucky stars that Dr. Leba wasn't
skimping on the pain medication. Brent didn't realize that his
nurse was the doctor's wife until they were on the last leg of
their flight home. He was happy to make her acquaintance.
Her name was Naomi. She had a gentle nature that was a nice
departure from Dr. Leba's bluntness.

The plan was for Brent to return to his house to begin
his recuperation. Rehab would commence on the advice of a
specialist, handpicked by James. Before rehab, James would
get his dad re-examined by an elite surgeon. This would be a
second opinion on the quality of Dr. Leba's work. For now,
Brent would get his TLC from the Hudson family. Niki would

reside in Brent's home and put her culinary skills on display, and Hank and Catherine would dote on Papa's every need.

There was a final meeting of the minds in Brent's bedroom between him and his two boys. One of the agenda items was to discuss what would happen from here. Brent opened the meeting with a shocker. He instructed James to get his investigator to furnish him with photographs of the four fuckers who had killed his wife. Brent wanted to make sure the names, addresses, and photos matched up. He wanted to be kept up to date on the progression of the investigation. He looked at both his sons and stated, "This is going to cost money; I want to pay for all the expenses."

James thought for a moment, then took to the soapbox. He said, "If you and Mike put every cent you have together, you would already be out of money." James realized he had just belittled his father and his brother. In the momentary silence, he laid down a hypothetical blueprint that let everyone save face. He told his father and brother that "This is also my mother. There will be no expense spared to make sure these murderers get the justice they deserve." He continued to tell them that they should not spend one red cent to complete this operation. James said, "I'm not going to use my personal money either." He puffed his chest and said, "Hudson Reinsurance will be more than happy to fund this mission."

Mike piped up, "Can you do that?"

James, speaking to no one in particular, said, "I own the fucking company, and if I can't throw money at catching the bastards who killed my mother, then what kind of son does that make me? Besides, the more it costs, the more stocks I'll just float on the market."

The three of them debated more about the merits of

who would supply the money but, ultimately, James's way of thinking ruled the day.

Money issues settled, Brent wanted the Canadian embassy involved in the investigation by contacting and working with the Fijian government.

Mike shut this suggestion down. He argued, "That is a dead-end road." The military, because of the coup, was the government. There would be no chance that they would bring to justice any of their commissioned officers for a couple of tourists.

As Brent's frustrations slowly surfaced, he reluctantly agreed. Brent spit out that at least he wanted a newspaper subscription to the Fiji Times. This was in hope of maybe gathering any information about his wife's murder.

James said, "That can be done."

The words had just gotten got out of James's mouth when Brent, in a loud voice, said, "What's your guys' plan?"

James suggested that they give his highly recommended lawyer and the private investigator time to see what they could come up with.

Brent's patience was done. "You've got one fucking month!"

There was an eerie silence. Individually, they all had an independent theory of what justice should look like for their mother. James thought his lawyer and investigator would be instrumental in resolving the issue and would see that these murderers faced trial.

Brent was hostile. If his boys couldn't solve this horror show, then he would take matters into his own hands.

Mike compartmentalized his thinking. James was naive. Mike loved his brother but knew there was no way in hell James could play by the rules and be successful. James's life had been full of obeying regulations, declaring his intentions, and thinking justice works for everybody. Mike thought about his father. He could visualize his dad wanting revenge, but nowhere in his thinking could he envision how Brent would accomplish such an endeavor.

Brent broke into the stillness when he said that "I love you boys, but right now I need to rest and get my head together."

The boys left the bedroom with the agreement that they would meet in another couple of weeks. By then, a clearer picture of what was happening should appear.

Outside on Brent's front yard, the boys dealt with the unpleasant task of dealing with their mother's remains. It was still the dead of winter, and the ground was frozen. They decided to put her in a deadhouse at the neighborhood cemetery for the time being. This would give their father a chance to think about what he wanted done with their mother's body. It surprised the boys that they didn't know whether their dad wanted to bury or cremate their loved one.

35

STORM CLOUDS

THE TWO-WEEK HIATUS found the three of them juggling emotions and trying to get back to normality. Brent
would not put Laura in the ground nor contemplate anything
to do with a service. He received a sympathy telephone call
from one of his many Ojibwa friends. He offered Brent, as a
sign of respect, a place of honor for the love of his life in their
death house. Brent never even hesitated to accept this gracious
offer. The care and admiration given to deceased loved ones in
the First Nations communities far outweighed the cold slabs of
shelving that reminded him of a big-box store. He immediately
reclaimed his wife's body and had it transported to his hunting
grounds. Continuously running through his mind was his right
to pursue justice for his spouse.

He suspected what Mike thought but wouldn't say: nothing was going to happen unless they took it upon themselves

to mete out their own justice. The one thing Brent was not going to do was involve either of his boys in anything outside the law. He would formulate and carry out his action plan on his own.

James spent the time getting reacquainted with his business. Hudson Reinsurance was running like a clock. The money in the corporate and personal bank accounts was still flowing in like a cascading waterfall.

He received a concession phone call from his one-time mentor: the student had beaten the teacher. Rudolph Lidster of Meredith Reinsurance hoped there were no hard feelings and said it was just business. James's golden parachute defense scheme had worked and saved his company and cost Meredith millions of dollars.

James threw a softball and informed Rudolph that he knew it was just business. He ended with a fastball when he said, "Rudolph, you taught me fuck all and your business profited greatly from my abilities. You were lucky to have me."

Rudolph laughed and James's point was made.

James had a son's concern about his father. Brent was at home and participating in his rehab. That was a good thing. In fact, his spies had told him that his father was doing very well and could expect a full recovery. He wasn't exactly sure if their reports were legit or if it was the money James was stuffing into their pockets that was speaking. His dad's back and chest muscles were loosening, and his body was becoming more flexible every day. James did have one pressing event that he had to talk over with Mike.

36

DIFFICULT POINTS OF VIEW

MIKE, SITTING AT home, predicted what the eventual outcomes would be to the problems that lay ahead of the Hudson family. Their mother was dead. There would be no help from the law or government agencies. The cover-up would succeed. His father would take matters into his own hands, and he would die. The cover-up would still succeed. He and James would be left with no parents. Their children had already lost their nana; he didn't want them to lose their papa too. Somewhere along the way, he would have to insert himself and try to turn this gloom-and-doom scenario into something salvageable. Mike's cell phone rang.

James had dialed Mike from his cell phone. There was a pressing matter that had to be discussed. When Mike answered, James went right into his monologue. He told Mike he had a story to tell him, and he was afraid of the ending. James told

Mike that he had received a phone call from the travel agency he had used to supply Dr. Leba and his wife Naomi with their all-expenses-paid week in Maui and Oahu. The travel agent had passed on to James that Mr. and Mrs. Leba from Fiji had drowned in a snorkeling accident. The agency had said that they had not been able to find the next of kin but had noticed the vacation had been paid for by Hudson Reinsurance. They had wanted to know if James could help find the next of kin so that they would have a contact to ship the remains to. James had told the agent that he didn't know any next of kin but would pay to have the remains flown and delivered to Nadi Hospital. From there, a person at the hospital should be able to sort things out.

Mike, to this point, had remained silent.

James, through his dread, mustered the courage to ask Mike, "Did you know anything about this incident."

Mike did not hesitate to answer. He asked James, "Are you good at math?" Mike reminded James that the latter had floated him $9,000. He had spent $7,630. With $1,370 left, Mike informed James that he'd bought a plane ticket to Hawaii.

James screamed, "Who the hell are you?" At that moment, James felt he didn't know his brother. He couldn't believe that this family man, a man in service of his country, was a cold-hearted killer.

Mike finally calmed his older brother. He informed James that he should listen to what he had to say, as it was now his turn to climb on the soapbox. He explained, "In special forces, you learn two things. The first is how to kill. The second is how to eliminate your tracks." He left no room for James to interrupt. Mike asked James, "Who had the ability to uncover our tracks and point the authorities in our direction? Whether you think it or not, we are on a mission. James, you have a head for figures, so figure this out. The minute Mom was murdered, you should have realized we are on our own. I love you, brother, but you're fucking naive to think the people behind the Fiji coup give two shits about a dead tourist. It's beyond the pale." Mike went on to say, "Do you think Dad is going to let this rest? He's not."

James saw his opportunity to regain control of the conversation. James countered, "Don't you see? This makes us no better than the guys who murdered Mom."

Mike fired back. "Meredith Reinsurance tried to exterminate your company. What did you do? You took the golden parachute defense to retaliate. You may not have thought too much about it, but you did cause collateral damage." Mike went on, "A country puts an unfair tariff on another country's products. What does the injured country do? They retaliate, knowing that their own citizens will be collateral damage." Mike got to the point. "Mom was murdered. Something priceless was taken away from us. We know, or should know, that we are the only ones who are going to solve this problem." Then Mike asked James, "Are we going to solve this problem?" Mike went on to corner James on how his lawyer and private investigator were progressing.

James had to admit that his lawyer was caught up in red tape, and his private investigator had been put on a plane and exiled back to Canada.

Mike educated his brother on the fact that "If we are to get justice for our mother, collateral damage is just the price of doing business. James, to avenge our mother, we are going to have to manufacture our own journey for justice. Brother, do you really think I'm a coldhearted, merciless son of a bitch who feels nothing?"

James could sense the anguish on his brother's face.

"I had a difficult decision to make," Mike said somberly. "The doctor and nurse heard our conversations on the plane. They knew we would, in some shape or form, return to Fiji. I had to weigh silencing them against letting them live to possibly tell the authorities in Fiji about our plan to eventually return. James, if the Fijian military discovers our plan, every one of us who returns to Fiji is doomed to be killed."

James let the cold, ugly truth sink in. Nobody would be wearing the white hat. There would be no hero in this scenario, only villains and victims. Their journey would be messy, but the cards of justice would be dealt.

37

REHAB AND DECISIONS

ONE MONTH AFTER they landed back home, the three of them met again at Brent's house. Mike's family had done a great job of caring for Brent, but Brent decided it was time for Niki and the kids to go back home. He wanted to be left alone with his memories of Laura. The two boys had no idea what they were going to discuss or how wide the scope of the conversation was going to be. They didn't have to wait too long, as Brent started the communication with what amounted to a question period for James.

Brent asked James, "Do you have the private investigator's report?"

The answers he received were alarming. The only useful documents were the photos of the four men. After shaking his head in disappointment, Brent asked for the profiles of all these men. He wanted names, addresses, and ages. Mike was able to immediately furnish all the information on Laura's killers. Brent looked at Mike and took him through some interesting articles he had read in the Fiji Times. He thought it was a tragic coincidence that the doctor and nurse had drowned, and that Mark from Treasure Island had died because of a drug overdose. There was no mention of Mark's police friend, Venasio.

Mike bowed his head and said, "God bless them all." Inside, Mike felt sick. A footprint not taken care of could come back to haunt all of the Hudsons.

This was Brent's way of letting his boys know that he knew. Brent's next topic was to inform his sons that he was feeling much better, and rehab consisted mostly of stretching and walking to help maintain the expansion in his lungs. Therefore, he was going to go back to his hunting camp to regain his endurance and do weight training by carrying Sir Weighs-A-Lot.

James was going to interrupt, but his father waved him off.

Brent said further, "I'm going to sell the house. There is no need to live in such a big dwelling. I'm going to downsize and get something smaller. The only thing I'll miss is the presence of your mother in every room."

Mike couldn't get past the fact that his childhood home was going to be on the market.

James understood the practicality of it and asked his father, "Is that why you had Mom transferred to a deadhouse around your hunting camp?"

The quick answer from Brent, and not necessarily the truth, was a simple, "Yes."

Mike sat observing his father. He did not concentrate on what Brent was saying but on how he looked and held himself.

Niki had said that "Brent spends every waking hour doing his exercises and stretching."

Mike had taken it upon himself to get in touch with his dad's physiotherapist. The report he'd received had left him stunned.

The physiotherapist had told Mike that "Your father is a man possessed. It is us who continuously have to tell your dad to slow down." They'd agreed that Brent's time with them could well be shortened. The patient was a self-starter and very motivated.

James asked the million-dollar question, "Where do we go from here?"

Brent took the reins. He told his boys that "I'm going to go to my hunting camp to clear my head."

James and Mike just nodded. Once outside, James asked Mike what he thought.

Mike spoke matter-of-factly when he stated, "I'm going to monitor our father. You should be ready at a moment's notice."

"For what?" inquired James.

Mike also indicated that James should start a Hudson Justice bank account.

Again, James asked, "For what?"

Mike knew James was very business savvy. He was just not an expert in the seedy underbelly of society. Mike, with a look of concern, wasn't waiting for an answer when he said, "They killed his wife. What do you think Pop is going to do?"

Brent left the selling of the house in James's capable hands. He gathered the clothing he would need as well as the equipment needed to run his hunting camp. He did all his survival grocery shopping, hooked up the trailer, grabbed his trusty Sir Weighs-A-Lot, and headed out.

It was a long and tedious drive to camp. Brent had to stop several times to give his poor, aching body a stretch. On his arrival, one would think that the tom-toms had danced a jig on the sound waves of travel. The hunting camp was already lit up and, on further examination, a foreign generator was gassed up and pumping electricity and warmth into the cold, railway car. Brent was thankful. He was tired and knew the word had gone out that he was on his way. What he hadn't foreseen was the foresight of his youngest son.

Mike had taken it upon himself to go to his parents' house and locate his mother's phone book. He'd looked up "hunting camp" and found an emergency contact number. It belonged to Clinton Strathroy, an Ojibwa elder. Mike had answered every question Clinton had about the circumstances of his mother's death, and he'd told him that his father was on his way to rehab out there and to get his head straight.

Clinton had told Mike, "Your dad is a dear friend, and his Ojibwa family will see to the welfare of both his body and spirit." Mike thanked him, said goodbye and hung up the phone.

After Brent settled in and changed over the generators, Clinton Strathroy came calling. After they greeted each other and Clinton expressed his condolences, Brent dropped a bombshell. He wanted Clinton to teach him how to track humans. Brent went on to tell Clinton that he knew plenty about the physical components of stalking, but what he wanted to learn were the idiosyncrasies of tracking a target who possessed intelligence equal to his own.

Clinton understood completely what his friend Brent had meant. Clinton agreed to share his generations of knowledge about tracking. The first kernel of education that Clinton provided to Brent was to study the pictures and bios of the four men whom Brent had posted on a cupboard. He told his friend to commit to memory these images and bios. They must become second nature in his new world of hunting down these animals.

Over the summer months, Brent acclimatized himself to life in the bush. Clinton put him through exercises in the dense forest that would assist him in capturing his targets. He brought Brent many films of wolves on the hunt. He also brought books about how their patience and stealth paid off. Clinton reversed the process of pheasants scaring the hell out of unsuspecting hunters when they took flight. Instead, Clinton had Brent quietly intrude in the pheasants' space without alarming them. Clinton taught Brent not to focus on the many norms of a target but rather home in on one specific norm that the target consistently partakes in.

"Remember," said Clinton, "we are all creatures of habit. Find the prey's Achilles' heel, and you will be able to systematically eliminate the target." Clinton understood what others could not. "If you take away everything a man loves and lives for, you have created a dangerous man."

Brent, because of all this training, was the most focused he had ever been. His only distraction was his home. It was with mixed emotions that he heard from James that it had been sold. His body was healed as good as it was going to get. Still, he was grateful that he felt capable and strong. Brent's mind was altered the most. He no longer thought like a fine, upstanding citizen of the world; he was closer to thinking like a lone wolf. He was cloaked in darkness, and his season of hunting was about to begin. He would wait until the snow fell in Canada before he flew to his new hunting grounds: Fiji.

38

VENASIO'S SUMMER

VENASIO STOOD ON the steps of Nadi Police Department headquarters. He had just finished a lengthy and grueling questioning at the hands of internal affairs. They had wanted to know in-depth details about how his friend Mark had died from an overdose of cocaine and rodent poison, and how he himself had almost died from poisoning.

Venasio had woven a tale of probable occurrences. He had gone to Treasure Island to visit with his friend Mark, whom he had grown up with. They had sat around and drunk kava. Venasio told them this had likely been the source of the poison. Rats and rodents liked to nibble on the roots of kava plants, and oftentimes poison was placed on the roots to deter this. Venasio had looked across at the three-man board and said, "Perhaps the kava root was not washed before it was pulverized, and so the poison got into our drinks that way."

Among a myriad of probing questions, the board had asked him, "Why is the report from the hospital lacking a blood test?"

Venasio had replied, "You will have to ask the doctor."

Everyone in the room had known the truth. Venasio was thankful he'd had the foresight to give the doctor a bribe to lose the blood test. The blood test would have shown that he had also been high on cocaine. That in itself would have led to a criminal charge and instant dismissal from the police department. He knew the board suspected. Proving it was another thing.

Venasio drove home from his interview and immediately opened a cold beer from the icebox. He sat on the front porch in his favorite chair. It was time to rationalize all the events happening to him.

Why had he been poisoned?

He could only come up with one viable reason. It had been to silence him about what he'd furnished to the Hudsons. Venasio couldn't tell the Nadi police or the Fijian military that he'd stolen the official police report and furnished the Hudson investigator with the names of four high-ranking military officers along with the report. There would be no investigation or imprisonment as punishment if he were ever caught.

"No," he spoke out loud. "There would be very little fanfare. The military would, in short order and without ceremony, murder me, and no one would be the wiser."

Venasio was a smart man and wasn't prone to making the same mistake twice. He had mistaken the Hudson investigator as an outside entity. He processed that he had actually talked to and been poisoned by a Hudson. Which Hudson he didn't know. He would find out.

Venasio also had a set of facts. He had the names of the injured parties: Brent and Laura Hudson. He knew who had paid for and flown one injured party and one deceased party back to Canada: Hudson Reinsurance. This was where Venasio would start his investigation.

He put the search engine on the Internet to work looking for Hudson Reinsurance. The amateur sleuth got a hit. He had his first Hudson. The CEO of this organization was James Hudson. Another search of James Hudson confirmed that he was indeed a wealthy man. He was gay and happily married to his husband, Daniel. James's bio went on to explain that he credited his success to his father and mother. This confirmed to Venasio the identity of at least one more of the Hudsons.

James credited his father with his love for nature, be it in the woods or human tendency's. James had the ability to know what was apt to happen, whether it was hunting game or sealing a deal in negotiations. One had to know what an adversary was most likely to do. James went on to say in the bio that his father had taught him how important it was to focus. Stalking game required the ultimate focus, not to mention that in the boardroom, it allowed him to stay ahead of conventional thinking. For that matter, it applied to all facets of life.

James's bio followed up with his mother. His mother, Laura, had been a very compassionate person who'd shown empathy to all living beings. She had cried at sad movies, cried at happy movies, and cried when any of her boys had gotten hurt. Laura had been the matriarch of the Hudson family. For her, it had been family first. Business and all the wealth in the world might make someone happy but, for her, wealth had never been able to make her feel as happy or important as her family did.

Venasio picked out enough tidbits of information to seek out the Fiji Immigration Office. The next day, he walked into their office garbed in his full dress uniform. He wanted to look official. He was on an information-gathering expedition.

Venasio cornered an immigration case officer and told him he wanted red flags on any commercial or private aircraft with the names Brent or James Hudson on the manifest. He thought further and added, "Anyone with the name Hudson." The last thing he instructed the case officer to do was to inform him of any aircraft rented or owned by Hudson Reinsurance that had landed at Nadi.

Satisfied that his wishes would be followed, he proceeded to the Ministry of Housing and Community Development. Venasio felt more comfortable at this ministry because he had another childhood friend who was employed with them. The two friends separated themselves from the rest of the office population by settling into a remote office. Venasio told his friend just as much as he could without giving away classified information that could spell danger for him. Venasio clearly told his friend that any information was to come only to him, to keep it on the hush-hush.

Venasio got his childhood buddy to keep vigilant for any rentals leased under a Hudson name. After further discussion, it was decided that, for any rentals leased by numbered companies, his friend would contact the owner of the rental about whose name had been on the check at payment time. The only flaw in Venasio's plan, which he was aware of, was if the rental had been paid for in cash. Still, he held out hope that this avenue of investigation would prove profitable. He thanked his childhood friend and left.

Venasio was finally ready. He knew his plan wasn't foolproof, but it was a good recipe for success. If the Hudsons ever put their feet on Fijian soil again, he would know. They would pay handsomely through their bank accounts for his silence or through the stoppage of their hearts. Venasio preferred option one but didn't care if option two had to be invoked. In the end, either option would suffice. The young police officer took specific joy in the fact that he was alive and that the Hudsons, with all their money, didn't know this.

39

SUMMER MONTHS

OVER THE SUMMER and into the fall, the younger brother stayed in contact with James but a lot less so with his dad. Winter was closing in, and things weren't adding up.

"Why hasn't Pop even bothered to look for a new house?"

It wasn't like his father not to visit his grandkids for this length of time. The last time Papa had had a visit to dote on his grandchildren had been just before they'd gone back to school last Easter.

"Why hasn't Dad had a service and burial for Mom? What are his health and state of mind like at present?"

Mike had these conversations from time to time with James, but this time his brother seemed to fluff him off. James never tried to avoid the topic, but he just didn't seem to know the answers requested of him. Mike had had enough.

He visited James as soon as feasible to inquire about their father.

James informed him not to worry because he was in touch with their father once a week. James said, "Dad has only missed phoning the last two weeks, but I believe he is scoping out his hunting area before the actual hunting season begins." When asked about their mother, James answered, "Dad is in a wait-and-see mode because he's still not sure about burial versus cremation." James had no answer for why Papa hadn't visited the grandkids. James, like Mike, knew their father was in the best shape of his life. His Ojibwa family were making sure he did his rehab and stretching.

"What about buying a new house?" Mike chimed in. He could sense that James was pondering over what he was going to say next.

James reluctantly uttered, "About that, I have no fucking idea."

The brothers looked at each other. They could each see the wheels turning within the other. Self-doubt was starting to creep into both of them.

The younger sibling halted the negative thoughts and excused himself for a moment to make a cell call to the elder of the Ojibwa community, Clinton Strathroy. "Hello, Clinton. This is Mike Hudson, Brent's son."

"Yes, I know. How are you?" Clinton answered.

For a short time, they discussed pleasantries until Mike could get to the meat of the matter. The young man asked the same questions that he and James had already asked themselves. The answers he was presented with were alarming. Clinton began to weave a tale that this special forces soldier found worrisome.

Clinton said, "Brent bought himself a small house with the money he received from the sale of your family home." Clinton informed Mike that "This small house is in the Oakville area." About their mother, the story went that their father had paid a great deal of money to have their mom put in a refrigerated trailer. Currently, the trailer was parked at the hunting camp. "Your father gave us more than enough money to keep the generator fed with diesel fuel." Clinton went on to say, "Brent isn't at the hunting camp as of now."

The youngest Hudson's heart began to sink.

Clinton said, "He has gone home to visit with all the Hudson family before returning for hunting season."

Mike didn't try to question what Clinton had said. He sensed the elder was confident in the details and that his story was true. Clinton was just repeating the lie he had been told by their father. The last thing Mike asked Clinton had to do with his father's health. Clinton let him in on the fact that his father had spent many moons in the woods sharpening his tracking skills, so his strength and endurance had never been better. There it was; Now it all made sense. Mike Hudson thanked the Ojibwa elder and hung up his cell phone.

Mike was usually a pacer when he was on his cell. At this moment, he was still and standing in one spot trying to figure out how he was going to tell his brother that they had been taken in. The sale of their family home was part of a living will. The reason for the refrigeration of their mother had become evident. There would be no service or burial because there were some outstanding issues: four of them. Mike's stomach filled with nervous butterflies. His father was ill-equipped, as an army of one, to go up against the firepower of the Fijian military. Mike steeled himself into military mode before confronting his brother with this sordid turn of events. Mike rejoined James, who was sitting on the chesterfield in his living room. He reiterated the tale that Clinton had told him.

James went absolutely white as a ghost. The gravity of what he had just been told hit hard.

Mike thought his brother was going to pass out.

Two deep breaths later, James's face went from being white as a ghost to bloodred.

The young brother felt like he was looking into the eyes of the devil.

James rose to his feet and, in anger, threw the glass that held his water directly at his fireplace. The glass broke into a thousand pieces. James turned to his younger brother and told him that he needed time to absorb what just happened. James needed guidance. James did what Mike had previously done; he left the room and made a cell call, this one to his husband, Daniel. Daniel's whole existence was wrapped around solving problems. He was an immigration lawyer. James told Daniel his tale, and Daniel told him a partial solution. Before James went back in to continue with Mike, he was told to wait for a return call from Daniel. In minutes, James's cell rang. Daniel had additional pertinent information for the brothers. Brent had cleared immigration three days earlier in Nadi, Fiji.

James returned to his brother and sat down beside him. He was about to give Mike instructions about what they were going to do next.

Mike knew that, even in childhood, when James got like this, he was in business mode. The world of what-if scenarios was over; it was pay-attention time.

The solution rolled off James's tongue. Hudson

Reinsurance would front the entire operation. Mike would have sole access to the company's private jet. He would go to Fiji to locate their father and protect him. Mike went to interrupt James but that was quickly stopped. James explained that to rescue their dad and evacuate him back home would be fruitless.

The younger sibling nodded his head in agreement.

The JTF2 warrior was to ghost his father and let him take out his targets. If the time came when Dad was in danger from a target, Mike was to eliminate the target. James would now entertain additional discussions that his brother had to offer.

Mike started by indicating that the leave from JTF2 that he was currently enjoying was coming to an end.

James fired back that "It is time for you to retire."

What never needed to be said was that this was family: nothing else mattered.

Without missing a beat, James said, "Hudson Reinsurance will hire you as the chief of security." Hudson Reinsurance would pay him multiple times higher than the military. As a bonus, Mike would be furnished with lucrative stock options. If anything happened to him in defense of their father, his family would be taken care of for the rest of their lives.

Mike briefed James on the fact that there were four targets; therefore, he would need an additional three retired, JTF2 veterans. To protect Brent, they would form four pillars. The purpose was to surround him and act as perimeter protection. He let his brother know that protection of this degree was going to be very expensive.

James listened and quietly retreated within himself. He told his brother that he had to make another phone call first before he agreed to Mike's way of thinking. He left and had a short talk with Daniel. Once back in the room with his younger brother, James started a new conversation. He said, "I've talked to Daniel, and I have a few amendments to the plan. First, the four pillars are out. I don't know of any paid bodyguards who would lay down their lives, if that's what it came to, for money. Family will take a bullet for family. You and I are bush savvy and handy with rifles, handguns, and even knives. Daniel is a whiz at high tech and will accompany us for logistic support. That's the deal. Are you in?"

40

ONE MORE MISSION

MIKE HAD A mission to plan. Immediately, he took a short-haul flight from Toronto to Ottawa. Rather than going straight home, he went to his base at Dwyer Hill. Mike was lucky enough to get a sit-down with the base commander. He asked for additional leave to take care of an urgent family matter. The commander sympathized and showed a great degree of empathy for Team Leader Hudson's dilemma. In the end, the Dwyer Hill base commander had to deny one of his most valued Team Leaders extended leave. The commander told Mike that he would have to get another family member to take care of his fatally ill father. Mike immediately, with respect to his commander, gave his resignation. His fable about his father's demise didn't cut muster. That was OK with Mike, as James's offer of employment would put him immediately into a six-figure salary. Besides, with all that was taking place, Mike was ready for something new. His time in JTF2 was over.

Mike hurried home. Niki, Hank, and Catherine were glad to see their husband and father. Mike sat them all down and broke the news. Niki felt that the world was being lifted off her shoulders. She knew what she had signed up for with a husband in the special forces, but living with the anguish of never knowing if her husband would always return had been making her a nervous wreck. The two kids were understandingly somber. They had reservations about leaving their friends.

Mike maneuvered Niki aside and whispered in her ear a secret surprise about where they were moving to. Now that they had to move off the base.

Niki was able to put a positive spin on the problem when she said the people they were leaving behind would always be their friends, and they would get to make new friends in their new neighborhood. This explanation seemed to settle the two children.

Mike was pleased his entire brood was in favor of moving and starting a new adventure. Mike excused himself and moved to a secure, quiet area to call his older brother. When James answered the call, Mike told him that he needed a job.

James laughed, "Welcome aboard, little brother."

Mike requested that James have the jet ready to go in twenty-four hours.

James felt unsettled. He revisited with Mike the fact that their father had a three-day head start. James worried that their father could be dead even before he and his brother had put their plan into effect.

Mike explained that mission readiness took time. He assured James that their father was a very smart man. He would still be in the recon phase of his quest to retaliate against the perpetrators who'd killed his wife.

Reluctantly, James went with what Mike was saying.

Mike ended the call by letting his brother know that he would be taking the next short-haul flight back to Toronto, he would need the Hudson Justice bank account to be full of money.

Mike heard his front door open and close. His two children were heading out to the backyard to play. This meant Niki would be alone, and he would have the opportunity to talk to her. He found Niki in the kitchen, at the stove, stirring a stew. Mike crept up behind her, placed "his business" against her ass, and moved his hands up her sides and under her arms to reach their final goal. He was mildly amused when he was met with absolutely no resistance.

Niki loved her man, but the kids were just outside and about to come back in. She moved away from Mike but signaled that a continuation could resume later on that night.

This gave Mike his opening. He told Niki that he had just delayed his retirement to complete one last mission as a special favor for his base commander. Mike let Niki know that he had to leave immediately but promised that this would be his last deployment. Mike just had time to hug his wife and children before heading out. Mike never liked lying to Niki, but he knew that if he were caught in this lie, Niki would understand.

His flight to Toronto was uneventful. Mike was sitting at the working desk inside his suite at the Hilton Toronto Airport He opened his computer, loaded the required hardware, and proceeded to go directly to a link on the dark web. The dark web was perfectly legal, and Mike was seeking out all three clear benefits from its use: user anonymity, virtually untraceable services, and dark web sites. Even though Mike was on the Internet, he enjoyed the solace that came from knowing that he was virtually undetectable. The way into this specific rabbit hole was known only to some special forces personnel.

The password to obtain web functionality was "missionsoffthemarket."

Mike knew who was on his team; now it was time to arm his squad. He highlighted an icon called Pro Shop. This brought him to a page where he could buy weaponry. After Mike purchased the weapons he needed, the Internet options guided him through all the trick stuff and gadgets that Daniel could possibly need. Mike thought about possible errors and omissions. His military training had taught him to calculate possible worst-case scenarios. Mike ordered up a special forces field doctor from Australia. The doctor would be responsible for his own medical supplies. The process did not end there. He was prompted to file his flight plan. Mike entered Toronto, Vancouver, Honolulu, and Nadi.

His computer thought for a moment, then informed Mike that the pro shop he wanted was in Port Moresby in Papua New Guinea.

Port Moresby was the safest place to receive his weaponry and ammunition. Papua New Guinea was selected after a multitude of factors were considered by the internal artificial intelligence of the computer. Port Moresby was deemed the best place to secure contraband and avoid customs and immigration. There was nothing left to do now but gather up his brother and brother-in-law. It was wheels up on the Hudson Reinsurance jet.

41

STALKING 101

BRENT HUDSON HAD returned to Nadi, Fiji. This time, he had a far different feeling and purpose than the first time when he had vacationed with Laura. He remembered the excitement of visiting a different country and the intrigue of exploring their customs and beauty. All these feelings had been replaced with a steely resolve to rebalance the scales of justice. The first thing he did was rent himself a detached dwelling in a secluded area just on the outskirts of Nadi. The house had a small pool and was surrounded by tropical jungle, but the 30 meters on every side of the rustic dwelling had been cleared and served as an unobstructed, spacious perimeter. This left a great sight line and would lessen the chance of being surprised by anyone in opposition. His nearest neighbor owned a dog that seemed to bark at its own shadow. This finicky dog's larynx added an additional layer of security.

Brent designated one of the rooms as the war room. It was here that he posted on the wall, pictures of the men who'd murdered his wife. Their biographies and addresses were underneath each of their mug shots. Brent surveyed the war room and knew it would grow substantially with additional intel as this mission progressed. The flight time and the layovers to get to Fiji weren't any more relaxing than when he'd first traveled to Fiji. He thought he had done extremely well to find accommodations on the first day. But for now, he needed rest and retired to the comfort of his bed for the night.

The next morning, Brent established that logistics would be the first order of the day. It hadn't escaped Brent that if he wanted to eat, he had to become a grocery shopper. Shopping for food was another trigger that saddened him in the wake of Laura's death. He needed a car. He didn't want to go through the regular channels of a car rental agency. Instead, he looked in the classifieds of the Fiji Times for a car for sale by the owner.

The vehicle he purchased wasn't a junker, but it also wasn't pristine. Instead, it was an economical, compact Ford designed not to stand out from the other vehicles in the area. Brent had to seek out the shadier side of Nadi. He required a gun. The most important matter about purchasing a weapon in the underworld was to know who to approach. Brent didn't truly know who that might be, so he looked in the seedier parts of town. He was able to purchase a revolver. He was charged twice as much as the market rate but that was of no worry to Brent. If the gun lasted as long as his heartbeat, that would suffice.

It was another hot, dusty day in Nadi but, at sunset, Brent could be found doing laps in the swimming pool. This was his way to clear his mind from all the noise of the day. This allowed Brent to stop thinking about multiple chores and focus exclusively on his mission. He spent the next hours committing to memory the intelligence he had posted in the war room.

The morning of the third day found all of Fiji under a storm cloud. It was to be an all-day rain. Brent welcomed this weather; it allowed him to drive and sketch the Nadi area while under the cloak of puddles and mud. Brent wasted no time investigating Black Rock Camp in Nadi. This camp was not the personal residence of the perpetrators of Laura's death, but it was where they all spent most of their working days. This would be the starting point for developing profiles on his targets.

It surprised Brent that Black Rock Camp wasn't very well fortified. There were two guards posted at the access point and a railroad-crossing type of barrier arm that went up and down manually to let personnel and visitors into the compound. Brent suspected that once in the heart of Black Rock Camp, the military's strength would be more evident.

Part two of this plan was to find his way to all four of the targets' home addresses. Brent would record what cars they drove and take down license numbers. The last thing Brent wanted to do was tail the wrong car that wasn't owned by one of his targets. Brent assumed that these four Fijians were like most adults. They would go to work and then return to their respective houses. Tomorrow morning Brent would be in a position to observe each of these monsters as they reported to work at Black Rock Camp. The four targets worked the day shift and were released from their work responsibilities at 1600 hours.

Brent remembered a wise adage instilled in him by his

Ojibwa friends. It was a phrase of wisdom that stated, "No one can hunt the whole bush, so what you can hunt, hunt well."

Brent tallied the time it should take for each of his targets to get from Black Rock Camp to their own dwelling. He would let that actual driving time elapse and add ten more minutes to see if the target's vehicle was parked in the driveway. The first one of these scumbags to break this established routine would become more vulnerable and undoubtedly less in their comfort zone. They will be Brent's first installment in finding justice for Laura's death.

42

FIJI ARRIVAL OF TEAM HUDSON

MIKE HELD A briefing on the jet between Australia and Papua New Guinea. The first order of business was to formally introduce the field doctor, Alec Sumner, to Team Hudson. Alec was a veteran of many covert operations around the world. He had saved many of his military brothers with his skills and ingenuity. His location would be a safe house recommended by the Australian special forces.

Mike handed the team all the available intel. This included pictures and addresses of the four targets. Still unknown was the whereabouts of their father. Mike let his family members know that when talking about their dad on radio, he would be called the Golden Goose.

Daniel asked, "Why?"

Mike retorted, "It's an added layer of security and may never be needed. I'm just covering all the angles." Mike relayed further information to his charges. James was to rent a condo in Nadi and Daniel was to rent a yacht, complete with a speedboat, to anchor out at sea. When that was accomplished, they were to get back to Mike and furnish him with the pertinent details.

James furnished each of his teammates with a credit card that would eventually be billed to Hudson Reinsurance through various numbered accounts.

Mike had made connections through his fourteen years of working with other countries' special forces. He borrowed on his friendship with members of the Australian Special Air Service Regiment (SASR or SAS). Consequently, he was furnished with a safe house to use in Nadi, no questions asked.

The flight to Papua New Guinea was coming to an end, but not before the fax machine spit out data relevant to the mission.

Daniel was able to work his connections, and he came up with both the make and model of the car their dad had paid for and his Nadi address.

Mike thought that, in the world of secret agents, this might very well have been his dad's first mistake. He sarcastically thought that if Daniel could find their father, the Fijian military could as well.

As much intel as possible was now known.

The Hudson Reinsurance jet was parked temporarily at Port Moresby International Airport. The Hudson team continued by taxi to the address of the pro shop. Once inside, they checked out and approved the hardware for the operation.

Daniel was able to persuade Mike to upgrade their communications system. He went with a new state-of-the-art arrangement. The receiver and microphone were virtually undetectable to the naked eye. All that was left to do was get the weaponry to the safe house and distribute the killing machines to the crew. Mike put James and Daniel on Fiji Airways, while he flew on to Nadi with the Hudson jet. This kept the precious cargo with him and wouldn't expose the others to any possible immigration problems. Mike was sure that Daniel, through his circle of business associates, had greased the palms of an immigration official or two. Mike knew his brother-in-law. He did confirm with Daniel and was correct on his assumptions.

Landing in Nadi and getting through customs was a breeze. The safe house was comfortable but by no means opulent. The suitcases of clothing and guns were safely tucked away in the back bedroom. The others on his team entered Fiji without a problem. The Hudson clan hooked up at Mike's house to go over, for one last time, the faces of the targets. Mike held up a photo.

In unison, they said, "Captain Etak Wainiqolo." Mike showed another and the team remarked, "Lieutenant Josefa Gavidi." Then the next photo was shown. "Major Lala Tavai." Finally, the last picture. "Captain Tui Nacola."

The three of them checked out two last items: their earbuds and collar mikes.

Mike declared everything was in good working order. "By tomorrow night you two guys make sure you're settled in and ready for anything, good or bad. Choose what weapons you prefer and have them in good working order at all times. It will take me a couple of days to track down the Golden Goose. I want to also get a lay of the land."

"You mean Dad," smirked James.

43

CAPTAIN TUI NACOLA
GOES FISHING

DAY AFTER DAY, Brent religiously kept up his surveillance on the entrance gate to Black Rock Camp. Nothing seemed out of place, just normal operations. He suspected that the four murderers acted the same way as the guys back at the fire department. They worked a shared shift and were part of a team, just like his own crews. Therefore, they should be tight with each other. Brent surmised that they were friends.

Mike knew his father was calculating and that he would continually revisit his action plan. His father was not a dumb man. Mike had faith that his dad would be able to merge what he had learned while tracking game animals and apply it to tracking humans.

Brent was going over his observations of these military

men. As a group, whenever they left the house in uniform, they went to Black Rock Camp. Three of them drove their own automobiles to and from base. Major Lala Tavai had a driver and a black, shiny SUV with the Fijian emblem on the rear doors. Brent had seen this car before. So far, everyone had not deviated from their natural routines. Brent decided to abandon his original plan. Instead, he would exclusively do surveillance of their homes. He wanted to find out who was on the move after they had eaten their final meal. Brent would also spot-check some early mornings to catch anyone going out early, before their duty time at Black Rock Camp.

Two days later, Brent finally hit pay dirt. Captain Tui Nacola caught Brent's eye when under surveillance. He got into his car and left his home at 9 p.m. It was a dark and pleasant night. Brent followed Captain Tui Nacola down a dirt road at a safe distance. Brent shut off his car headlights and was careful so as not to let him hear the engine. Brent parked his car in an out-of-the-way spot and, in stealth mode, crept down to observe Captain Tu Nacola. Brent drew his gun and quietly closed the distance on his target.

Brent could see that Captain Tui Nacola was preparing a small fishing boat to enter the water. Captain Tui Nacola was securing the twenty-five-horsepower Johnson to the back of the boat. Camouflaged behind a bush, Brent observed that the beachfront was not well maintained. It was obviously shoreline for local fishermen to launch their boats into the pristine waters of the Pacific Ocean. Brent watched Captain Tui Nacola give two hard shoves and jump in the boat. He started his motor and, guided by moonlight, set out into the night. Brent put his gun back in his waistband. He knew that trying to mete out justice on Captain Tui Nacola by using a gun in the dark wasn't the best plan. It would be hard to see his target, and the noise would alert anyone in their proximity. Brent would wait in a secluded place for Captain Tui Nacola to return from the ocean.

Brent sat down on the hull of another seemingly abused but seaworthy fishing boat. He remembered hunting moose back in Canada; specifically, he recalled the time he'd had need of a tin boat to traverse a lake. When the boat had been secured on shore, it had been too far to jostle the motor back to camp, so they'd just looked for an adequate place to hide it. Perhaps Fijian fishermen did the same.

Brent had nothing to do until he again heard the sound of Captain Tui Nacola's motor, so he decided to do some investigating in the scrub grass and trees. Sure enough, one dumb fuck had hidden his motor in some thatch only a few meters past the first clusters of trees. Now Brent also possessed a means of transportation on the ocean. The wheels started to turn in Brent's mind. He spent the rest of his time, before he heard the drone of a motorboat, formulating a plan. As the boat got closer to shore, Brent secured himself a hiding spot.

Captain Tui Nacola headed back on shore at 11:15 p.m. Brent detected that his target was unloading several pails of fish and housing them in the trunk of his car. Undetected was anything resembling a fishing rod. Captain Tui Nacola had a fishing net somewhere out in the darkness. Brent didn't know if net fishing was legal in Fiji or not. He shook his head. Brent didn't care; he wasn't here to give out tickets. Brent thought that wherever Captain Tui Nacola's net was, the fishing seemed plentiful.

Captain Tui Nacola secured his boat, then he hoisted his motor into the car and left. Brent saw no need to follow him, as it was reasonable to infer he was going home to gut and clean his catch. Brent would go home and further hone his plan to eliminate Captain Tui Nacola.

44

THE HUDSONS MEET UP

MIKE WAITED A few days before he proceeded to his dad's rented house. When he arrived, there was no vehicle present. There was no way he was going to park in the driveway, so Mike took up a position off the property in a secluded spot.

The youngest son knew his father well. The house was a bit more weatherworn than he had expected, but the rest of this location was pretty much as expected. The yard had great sight lines to detect the arrival of unwanted guests. The pool in the backyard was probably medicinal as well; Brent likely used it to continue his rehab and keep in shape by swimming laps. His dad's doorbell was a finicky, small dog that would bark at the hint of anything out of place. The final piece of the puzzle was the rear door, which had almost immediate access to the Fijian jungle.

Surveillance was sometimes a long and very tedious job.

Being in the military, it had been drummed into his head that patience was everything. Mike had already been watching his father's house and the surrounding area for over six hours. This gave the youngest son a chance to revisit the testy conversation he'd had with his older brother about accusing Mike of being callous and without remorse.

Mike thought long and hard about his years in the elite Joint Task Force Two. The physical training and intensive mind play he'd received over the years were entrenched in his psyche. He'd had a career of doing rewarding and sometimes nasty tasks for the security of his country. Somewhere along the line, it had become mission over all else. Mike had never given too much thought to collateral damage. He hadn't been able to afford to because the security of his men had always come first. The retired team leader wavered from his hard-core thinking and realized his older brother may have a justifiable point of view.

Mike knew he was now a civilian. His country no longer depended on him to rectify a situation at all costs. He would have to re-educate himself about the meaning of empathy and the understanding that all traces or footprints did not have to be swept away like a grain of sand at tide change. Still, he hoped that being decent to his fellow non-combatants wouldn't bite his ass.

It was close to midnight when Mike saw headlights coming up the road. Sure enough, the yapping alarm clock activated as his dad pulled into the driveway. Mike wanted to make sure his presence was known before his father entered the house. The son pulled into and parked in his dad's driveway. He smiled because he could see his dad's right hand poised on his pistol, Mike got out of the car and yelled at his father, "Dad, it's me, Mike!"

His father, in a calm, measured voice, simply said, "Get your ass in here."

They both proceeded to enter the house.

45

DIFFERENCE IN AGREEMENT

BRENT HUGGED HIS son and kissed his cheek. He then turned his back to retrieve a bottle of rum. He told Mike to sit down so they could discuss why he had followed him to Fiji. Brent slid Mike over a glass and poured a healthy shot, straight up. There would be no mix, just pure spirits and conversation.

Mike recounted to his dad the conversations he'd had with James and Daniel. After much discussion they'd all agreed to come to Fiji so they could take part in seeking justice for their mom. Mike relayed the assets that were in place, which included guns, ammo, and a communications network. Mike carried on and told him of the approximate locations of the others and that they even had a special forces field doctor.

Brent downed his first glass of rum and poured himself another. Mike passed, as he admittedly was not much of a drinker. Brent looked into his son's eyes with love and sadness. His wheels in his mind were churning to comprehend what had just been said. Then the realization of the danger his children had placed themselves in came to the forefront of his thoughts. "How could I justify to Laura the death of her children in the pursuit of justice?"

This question allowed Brent to change the direction of the conversation. He told Mike that he wanted him, his brother, and his brother-in-law to go home. This was a solo mission. Brent was not going to endanger his children. Brent's voice was becoming louder and his facial expressions fixed. Brent looked into Mike's eyes and now saw defiance.

Mike took a strategic page out of the military playbook, to outman your opponent. His father was not willing to debate the matter, so no progress would be forthcoming. He told his father that he was going to get in touch with James and Daniel, and they were going to have an immediate family meeting. Daniel would take the speedboat and dock it in Nadi. James would pick him up there and then proceed to their dad's location. They would be at the rental house as soon as possible.

The next hour was quite between Brent and his son. The stillness was broken up once again by the twenty-four-seven, four-legged alarm clock. James and Daniel entered the house and embraced Brent. In the phone calls, Mike had informed them of Brent's resolve.

Brent poured more rum into everyone's glasses and started to detail his conversation with Mike.

He was interrupted by a terse response from James. "How dare you, you self-centered son of a bitch! You think this is your calling and no one else's. She was our mother, not just your wife. We have already discussed the perils of this mission and yes, we are fully aware we all could die if we fail. We have seen to it that Mike's family and Brady will be taken care of for the rest of their lives, if needed. Personally, I think Brady will understand that if his fathers don't come home, it means they died for a noble cause. This is the only option, Dad. We are staying here to carry out justice for Mom. The only thing left for you to do is join us or go home." James took a sip of his drink and could see his brother and his own husband nodding their heads in approval.

One could cut the next moments with a knife.

Brent stood up and went to his war room.

The moments turned into minutes.

The silence was broken when Brent yelled out, "If we're going to work as a team, you'd better come in here and I'll tell you my plan for Tui."

The meeting now over and bruised feelings put aside, the family went their separate ways. James went back to the luxury penthouse condo he had rented previously. Daniel hitched a ride with James to the Nadi docks. They hugged and said their goodbyes at the moored speedboat that was Daniel's ride to get aboard the posh, million-dollar yacht. The field doctor's safe house was still unknown to Mike and the rest of the Hudsons. This was because the best safe houses followed one golden rule, they were only known to the occupant; If everybody knew, a safe house wouldn't be safe.

Mike's safe house was close to Brent's modest bungalow. He took the opportunity after the others had left to have a frank conversation with his father about the pros and cons of this newly formed mission squad. They decided that Brent would know the entire scheme, and the others would only know their responsibilities and locations. This was to safeguard the others in case of capture and interrogation. The oldest and the youngest of the family also agreed that if any of them did get captured, the mission would change from offense to the recovery of the Hudson in trouble.

Brent and Mike concluded that any witnesses who got in the way of them executing their mission would not be classified as collateral damage and eliminated. Mike would put Dr. Alec Sumner in charge of finding and securing a makeshift jail cell. His new, temporary assignment would be to act as the jailer of witnesses but not as a full-time guard.

Dr. Sumner indicated that, at his dwelling, he could secure and monitor multiple persons at the same time.

Mike would try it James's way and hope it wouldn't come back to bite him in the ass. In the end, Mike had to smile to himself. He would let all the witnesses live, feed them three square meals a day, and pay them handsomely at the end of the mission for their silence. He told his father that before they got paid with his brother's money, he would give them a veiled threat: if they talked to the authorities, they should expect a return visit. Both Brent and his youngest son chuckled, and Mike got up to leave.

As Mike stood at the front door hugging his father goodbye, he whispered into his ear, "I'm special forces, and I will take veto power if I need to."

His dad just laughed. "I think we're going to make a good team. Good night."

46

MONITORING THE SITUATION

THE NEXT DAY started early, as Brent went into Port Denarau. He had thought very carefully about the way Captain Tui Nacola's life would end. Brent did all his shopping in the hardware store. He spent a fair amount of time in this one store.

Mike was shadowing his father to make sure he didn't get into any trouble. The family knew some of the details for the attack on Captain Tui Nacola. He knew the where and when. It was to be at sea, and it was still two days away. Mike used his state-of-the-art satellite portable radio to get in contact with Daniel. He wanted to make sure Daniel's speedboat would be adequate for his part in the Tui plan.

Daniel surprised Mike with his reply. He said no because his speedboat would look out of place, which could cause Tui to become suspicious. Instead, he was putting a rented Bayliner 742 Cuddy Key through its paces on the water. Daniel knew they could not afford a breakdown or an untimely malfunction at any time during a critical point in the mission. Mike's brother-in-law had decided that this particular vessel would blend in and help him look like a wealthy tourist out fishing.

Daniel had set up his satellite computer in the bedroom area below the deck. From the Hudson team meeting, he knew what boats were going to be used to complete the Tui scenario. He double-checked the tracking device on the target's boat. The tracking device was working well. The signal from the other tracker, which was secured to the boat that Brent would probably use, was intermittent.

James was assigned to replace the tracking device. Once that was completed, he rejoined Daniel on the Bayliner.

Daniel radioed back that everything was on track, and he was in the process of transferring the scuba diving gear, complete with spare air bottles and an underwater spear gun, to the Bayliner. He reported to Mike that all his bases were covered.

Brent decided to ease the stress of the day by partaking in a few libations at a tourist bar. He knew that tomorrow was still not the day to execute one of the bastards who had killed Laura. Brent wished the timing was right to kill Captain Tui Nacola, but because he still had to do some reconnaissance on the other three, Tui would get a reprieve. Another piece of the puzzle was still unknown. Where and when was Captain Tui Nacola selling his fish? Important or not, the sale of the fish had to become known.

After Brent left the tourist bar, he proceeded to a local liquor store. Once inside, he was shown to the Canadian whiskey section. He marveled at the fact that of the eight original, imported Canadian whiskey brands, he didn't recognize any of them.

His day in Port Denarau had come to a completion. Brent was careful not to exceed the speed limit on the way home. Being picked up by the local police was not in his game plan. Once at home, he cracked open his original Canadian whiskey plus the hardware bags and began to play with the toys of justice that would help end Captain Tui Nacola's life.

Mike sat down in his living room and switched on the television for background noise. His puzzle to solve included the purpose of the supplies his father had bought at the hardware store. So far, Mike knew that Captain Tui Nacola was a fisherman who owned a boat. His dad had access to a boat and motor. Brent had access to the same water as his target. The purchases that his dad had made both troubled and befuddled him. It bothered Mike that he wasn't able to figure out his father's complete plan. He knew that his dad took particular pride in knowing the whole story while just letting the others know dribs and drabs. This wasn't the deal that Mike had entered into.

47

CONFESSIONS
IN THE DARKNESS

THE BROTHERS HAD always been close and could tell each other anything. As Mike settled in for the night in his own place, he had time to reflect and think about family. "Who the fuck are you?" were the harshest words Mike had ever endured from any man whom he loved and respected. His conversation with James over the poisoning of Mark Volau and Venasio Tubuna, and the Hawaiian holiday drownings of the doctor and his wife had resonated with him. The younger brother hated to see anger and disappointment on his sibling's face. Mike could justify Mark Volau and Venasio Tubuna's poisoning, but he would die with a secret he couldn't tell his brother or anyone else. Mike had let the doctor and his wife live.

On the marathon flight from Nadi to Toronto months

ago, the hours had passed very slowly. The cabin area of the Hudson Reinsurance jet had been darkened. Every once in a while, Mike had found himself the only one awake. He had been painfully aware that sustaining the loss of a loved one was permanent. Mike had been deep in thought when he'd gotten a tap on the shoulder. It had been Dr. Leba.

Mike had moved over a seat and let the doctor sit. Mike had listened to every word that Dr. Leba had quietly spoken, in order not to wake anybody else.

Dr. Leba hadn't been happy with the military coup in his Fijian homeland. It was untenable for many aspects of life. There was no free press. Medical facilities were not being properly staffed, and medical supplies were being hoarded or impounded to be used on only the elite.

Mike had taken that to mean military officers and their influential friends.

The good doctor revealed that the military had encouraged him and his wife to dismiss the Hudsons' request for in flight medical aid.

Mike had stopped the conversation and asked Dr. Leba to go and get his wife, Naomi. He had not wanted to formulate a plan for them unless they were both on board. Nurse Naomi and Dr. Leba had sat on either side of Mike. The nurse had agreed with everything her husband had said.

Mike had held both their hands in his and, in a quiet, soothing voice, told them that "I have made people disappear many times." The irony had not been lost on the young man. "This is what we're going to do." He'd narrated what he was going to do for them. He'd told them to follow the itinerary that his brother had paid for.

Mike had informed them he would meet them in Oahu.

There he would furnish them with completely new identities. He'd told the couple that they would no longer be able to see family and friends. Dr. Leba and Naomi had nodded their heads in agreement. They had no family or real close friends.

Dr. Leba had told Mike that they had considerable money still left in bank accounts in Fiji. Mike had let them know that a bank account would be set up in Maui, and their existing Fijian dollar amounts would be deposited. Mike had instructed them to immediately close the account once they retrieved their money. Naomi had given Mike a big hug, as she'd known that she and the doctor had considerable wealth, and she'd thought it would be lost.

Mike had then gone into the second half of the story. He'd asked the Lebas to write down on a piece of paper the new names they would like for the rest of their lives. Mike had told them that they shouldn't let him see their new names. The young Hudson had then asked them what other professions they might like. Being a doctor or a nurse would be out of the question.

The doctor and his nurse wife had done as Mike had instructed.

Dr. Leba had asked one too many questions. "How are we to die, and whose bodies will take the place of ours?"

Mike had smiled but stayed away from a cliché answer. Instead, he'd simply said, "The morgue has plenty of them."

Special Forces leader Mike Hudson had made one phone call, and mountains had been moved. He loved his brotherhood and his connections worldwide.

Morning arrived and Mike rose from his couch and headed toward the washroom.

48

GATHERING WAR-ROOM INFORMATION

BRENT WAS ALSO up early. His head was foggy from the amount of whiskey he'd drunk the previous night. He felt lucky that his head wasn't pounding like a hammer on an anvil. He knew what the agenda of his evening hours would look like, but for the daylight remaining, he would revisit the home of Lieutenant Josefa Gavidi. Brent had witnessed him returning home from Black Rock Camp several times, and before going into his house, he would go into a free-standing garage. Brent, up until now, hadn't been able to see how long he stayed in the garage because of other surveillance duties. Today he would investigate and see just what was so interesting in there to Lieutenant Josefa Gavidi.

Brent sat hidden in his car for three hours. He saw no

movement in the house or any activity in the immediate area. Brent suspected that if there were other occupants of this house, they were elsewhere. He felt relatively safe to investigate and explore the garage.

Safely inside, he immediately discovered what held the lieutenant's interest.

Brent decided it was time to exit the garage of Lieutenant Josefa Gavidi. He still had to purchase a jerrican of gasoline for the boat and go over his plan with Mike, once again about Captain Tui Nacola. Brent phoned Mike with the details of the entire plan. Brent returned home for a brief moment. With the gasoline safely stored in the trunk of his car, Brent left his house to go over to Black Rock Camp. He wanted to be in position for when Captain Tui Nacola departed.

Captain Tui Nacola's vehicle left right on time, and Brent followed it home at a safe distance. Nightfall set in, and Brent sat quietly in his car until Captain Tui Nacola decided to check his fishing nets. Right on time, Tui exited his home and settled into his car to drive to the beach. Brent followed him. Brent parked in the same spot—out of the way and out of sight. Captain Tui Nacola was a creature of habit and was soon shoving his boat off the shore and into the water.

In the dark, without the aid of a flashlight, Brent assembled the borrowed boat and motor. Brent could still see the lights on Tui's boat. He could not directly follow his target, as the engine noise of his own boat would give him away. Brent proceeded to do a zigzag pattern but far enough away so Captain Tui Nacola's boat would drown out the sound of his motor.

The Hudson clan always knew the whereabouts of both boats because of Daniel's tracking devices.

Brent's boat sat quietly in the ocean, and Tui had his motor on idle. Brent thought he was probably at his net and taking in the day's catch.

James broke the silence with a voice riddled with nervousness. He reported that a car was traveling the dirt road to the beach.

Mike, in a calm, reassuring tone, reported back. "I am in a position to intercept." Mike suggested to James that he abandon his post and help him deal with the vehicle.

The vehicle parked right next to Captain Tui Nacola's car. Two fishermen exited the car, took a few steps, and stopped to look for their boat, but their boat was missing.

James and Mike popped out of the darkness and held the two fishermen at gunpoint. James retrieved his car and brought it to the shore.

The two fishermen were handcuffed. Then one was led to the passenger seat of James's car and the other to the fishermen's own car. They were then handcuffed again to the passenger seat armrests. Mike drove James's rental car to the designated jailhouse, and James followed him in the fishermen's vehicle. Doctor Sumner and Mike had secretly discussed the whereabouts of the doctor's safehouse. This was in case the location had to be used in an emergency.

James was left pondering why he didn't even know that there was a jailhouse. That would be a question for another time. Right now, executing an improvised plan for success was the priority.

Mike let Daniel know that the sole responsibility for the well-being of the Golden Goose was in his hands.

Daniel slipped on a black wet suit and donned scuba gear.

He would be Brent's protector at the fishing net and would act as ocean rescue.

After what seemed like a lifetime, Brent heard Captain Tui Nacola's motor throttle up. Tui was headed back to shore. Brent used his GPS to mark the exact location of the fishing net. He used the same zigzag pattern on the return to land. Brent had to stay silent and short of landfall until Captain Tui Nacola cleared the beach and started for home.

Mike and James had just managed to return the fishermen's car to its original parking spot before Tui could recognize that anything was amiss. Brent was finally safe to land his boat. He didn't bother to return the beach to its original state as he knew, before the night was over, he would be returning. Instead, he jumped into his well-aged car and sped over to Captain Tui Nacola house.

Just as Brent expected, Captain Nacola's night was not over. Tui was at his outdoor, fish-cleaning station and filleting the catch of the day. He then packed them into buckets of ice and put them in the back of his car. Tui put his car in gear and drove away into the night.

Brent decided to follow him. Captain Tui Nacola drove straight to Black Rock Camp and through the guard gate. Brent laughed to himself. Tui was selling his fish to Black Rock Camp. As Brent drove away, he knew there would be a job vacancy after tomorrow night.

Brent drove back to the beach. He still had work to do. He got back in the boat and returned to the fishing net. Brent gathered up the entire net and put it in the boat to take back to his house. There, he would do some alterations so the net would catch the fish he had his sights on. Tonight, would be a late night for Brent.

Brent didn't sleep well. He tossed and turned throughout the remainder of the night. Morning found him sitting out on the back deck with a coffee. He was in a melancholy mood. He was wrestling with his morals and justifications. Brent had spent his entire life dedicated to saving lives and properties. Tonight, he would kill a man.

Brent weighed his own scale of justice. "These four fuckers killed my wife. The judicial system in Fiji is nonexistent. The military and the police covered up the murder. The medical professionals buried the pertinent paperwork." On the other side of the unbalanced scale was the murder of his most cherished and loved one. Without her, he was not. Brent would try to balance the scales.

In the end, Brent prayed to God, then humbly asked him to close his eyes.

49

NET FISHING

BRENT SPENT MOST of the day on the deck enjoying the swaying palm trees and the warm ocean breeze. Late afternoon found Brent completing the rest of the alterations needed on the fishing net. Afterward, it was time to think about dinner. He decided to eat in town. When Brent drove past the Hard Rock Cafe, his emotions were mixed. He had tears in his eyes and fury in his heart. He settled on a local family-run eatery. The place was quiet and would give him the time he needed to go over his plan once more.

Even if one hadn't known Brent, one would have sensed that he was deep in thought about something. He was counting with his fingers and rehashing the plan in chronological order. He was satisfied with everything except what to do with Captain Nacola's vehicle. In the end, he decided to just leave the car at the beach. Brent wanted the world to know that someone hated Captain Tui Nacola, and he wanted to avoid tracing the incident back to himself. Because of his years on the fire department, Brent knew that when the tones went off, it was game time. Brent looked at his watch. It was game time.

Brent arrived at the shoreline where the boats were docked. Brent hauled the fishing net from the trunk of his car. He meticulously laid out the folds on the bench seat nearest the bow on Tui's boat. The two pen markings were situated in the correct place. Brent went back to his vehicle and took out a small duffle bag that housed the rest of the materials he would need. He drove his car back to where it had been hidden the previous days. He had nothing to do now but wait.

Captain Tui Nacola drove down the familiar dirt road with nothing on his mind except how many fish might be in his net. He was delighted with the spot he'd found, as it was yielding him a bounty of fresh fish to sell to Black Rock Camp. He parked in his usual spot and proceeded to attach his motor. Something was wrong. Why was there a fishing net already placed neatly near the bow of his boat? Then he heard the words, "Don't move, motherfucker, or I'll blow your head off."

Brent then instructed Tui to move slowly and sit down on the middle seat.

Tui did as requested, as he feared for his life and couldn't figure out what Brent wanted from him. "Why all this to steal my fish?"

Brent handed Captain Tui Nacola two plastic zip ties. He told Tui to put them around his wrists and pull them snug. Brent then explained that the next two zip ties were to go under the ties on Tui's wrists and then be attached around the top of the net at the two previously defined marks. This meant that Captain Nacola's wrists were now handcuffed and attached securely to the fishing net.

Captain Tui Nacola then spoke, "What are you doing? I have no money. I don't understand."

The anger in Brent was rising to the surface. He decided to interact with Tui. Brent started with, "Do you remember, just a little less than a year ago, when you and three of your military buddies got all piss drunk and went to the Hard Rock Cafe?"

Captain Tui Nacola went white. He knew that his military brothers would not have spoken to anyone about that night. Brent pushed the boat off the shore and engaged the motor.

Captain Tui Nacola spoke out and said, "I didn't shoot anybody, and I didn't know that would happen."

Brent stopped Tui there. "Why didn't you inform the police?"

Captain Tui Nacola told Brent about his fear of Major Lala Tavai. He remembered Etak dancing with a white woman.

Brent interjected, "My wife."

Captain Tui Nacola's voice began to quiver as he went on with the story. Tui told Brent that "It was Major Lala Tavai who shot you in the back after you punched Etak. When Captain Etak Wainiqolo pulled himself off the floor, he took out his gun and put the second shot into your back." Tui went on to explain that "Your wife regained consciousness, then she crawled to protect you." Tui softened his voice when he said, "That was when Major Lala Tavai shot your wife in the head." To end his sad tale, Captain Tui Nacola repeated his innocence and added that he and Lieutenant Josefa Gavidi never even left the table.

Brent thought it was ironic that the first two of the four

fuckers to die had likely had the least to do with Laura's death. Brent increased the throttle, and the boat sped up to just over idling speed. He spoke loudly so Captain Tui Nacola could clearly hear him. Brent said, "If your crew is robbing a bank and your only role is driving the getaway car, you're still guilty of bank robbery."

Brent's GPS was alerting him that he was approaching the area where Captain Tui Nacola had his fishing net. Brent throttled down and put the motor in the idle position. He surprised Tui with a pistol whip to the top of his head.

Tui winced with pain.

This allowed Brent to affix heavy-duty masking tape to his mouth. Brent wasn't too concerned about Tui yelling out, but the tape would make sure Tui's words would never be heard.

Mike, equipped with night-vision goggles, could see plainly from the water the two occupants in the boat. If anything went amiss, he could be on the scene in seconds.

Daniel was in position on the Bayliner.

Brent had to persuade Captain Tui Nacola to push the net overboard. Tui was reluctant. Brent informed him that he would shoot him right now. Tui put one end of the fishing net into the water. Brent started the motor and proceeded to unravel the net. The entire length of the fishing net was approximately the length of a football field. Heavy weights were on each end to keep the entire fishing net from drifting away with the currents. At the halfway point, Tui unceremoniously exited the boat because of the drag on the net.

Brent laid the last half of the net before returning to Tui. Brent had customized the net by eliminating several of the floating buoys. The fishing net where Captain Tui Nacola was zip-tied was 2/3rds of a meter below the surface of the water.

Captain Tui Nacola was in a tough spot; his arms hung almost straight down. If he tried to rest his feet on the net, the fishing net would sink because of the weight of his own body, and his head would slip below the surface. Even if he were able to tread water, the weight of the fish that would get caught in his net would eventually drag him under. It could be a long and cruel death for Captain Tui Nacola, but death would come. Brent started the motor, took one last look at Tui, and then headed for shore. One-quarter of his work was done.

Mike communicated from the water with the rest of his team. After his detailed report, he knew his crew was waiting for further instructions. They came in short order. Mike instructed James to monitor the Golden Goose. Mike thought for a moment before he gave his final orders. He knew his father had done what he'd set out to do, but to leave Captain Tui Nacola's vehicle in the open would lessen the likelihood of his father remaining undetected. Mike came back with his orders. "I will take and dispose of the target's vehicle."

Daniel was to hold his position until Mike arrived at the boat.

Mike had to make another life-altering decision. What his father was doing to Captain Tui Nacola was equal to, if not worse than, anything he had done on this mission. His dad was being deliberately cruel. Even this battle-worn veteran had never delved into the world of darkness that was currently surrounding his father. Mike made an immediate decision to be more humane to Captain Tui. He swam up to Captain Tui Nacola and, with no words spoken, cut the target to hasten death before his exit.

50

POST INCIDENT AND REVIEW

MIKE HELD A post incident analysis and review, or PIAR, with his brother and brother-in-law.

Overall, Mike thought the Tui operation had gone very well. He did have some issues with two facets of the operation. The first was the malfunction of the one tracker. The solution was to test every tracker before they put them into operations.

The second issue was more of a discussion by the three of them on the pros and cons of how they'd disposed of Captain Nacola's vehicle. The vehicle had been driven to a deserted area. The vehicle identification number, or VIN, had been removed along with the license plates. The vehicle had then been torched with the gasoline that had remained in the plastic gas cans.

One can of gasoline had been found in the boat that the Golden Goose had used and the other found in Tui's trunk.

Once ignited, a plume of black smoke had filled the sky above the area. This had caused an emergency response from the Nadi fire department. This meant that some sort of incident report would be generated and possibly become a link between Tui and anyone looking for him.

In the end, after hashing out the situation before them, they unanimously agreed it had still been the best avenue to take. The link between the car being burned and anyone looking for Captain Tui Nacola was of little probability. Leaving the vehicle at the beach was a no-brainer. If the vehicle had been found at the shore, it would have pointed directly to Tui's fishing net. If the vehicle had been parked back in Captain Tui Nacola's driveway, in no time at all someone would know that something was amiss. The police and military would both have started investigating right away. The absence of a vehicle would cause bewilderment for a time and delay an investigation for as long as possible.

Mike's last order of business was to inform James and Daniel that Lieutenant Josefa Gavidi was the likely next target. Mike communicated to his team what was in Josefa's garage and the probable way he would exit this earth. The former JTF2 leader then looked toward Daniel for his expertise.

This took James by surprise, and he listened intently as Mike spun his sobering tale.

"Once Father kills Josefa, the shit is going to hit the fan. Captain Etak Wainiqolo and Major Lala Tavai aren't stupid people. They will put two and two together, and the entire dynamic of our mission will change. This will be the point where Daniel's skills are going to be tested with life-and-death consequences." Mike asked Daniel to tell them what he had done to hide their tracks and identities of the entire Hudson team while on this mission. He went further and informed Daniel that he and Dr. Alec Sumner should mostly be OK, as they were in SAS safe houses.

Daniel's short reply was, "Legally or illegally?"

Mike didn't care how he'd done it, only that it was done. Mike got the answers from Daniel he was looking for and pressed on for the rest of his wants. Mike wanted to know if Daniel had all the necessary information technology devices needed to help render safe the Golden Goose.

Daniel assured Mike that he was fully capable of mission success. Secretly, he was somewhat enthusiastic about playing James Bond. Daniel gathered everything he would need for the magic of keeping the mission incognito. The gravity of what he was doing set in. Daniel knew that the lives of everyone else involved would depend on how well he could pull off his wizardry. Daniel told Mike what the situation was to this point. Daniel reported that "There has been no traffic of concern inquiring about anyone within the Hudson realm. I was able to falsify everyone's identities, but a smart immigration administer could undo my work in no time if one is a curious sort." Daniel was banking on the complacency of the government employees not to dig into more areas than necessary. His duty was to tell Mike and James about all the possibilities. Daniel did this like a good soldier.

Mike then looked at his brother and got straight down to business. He reiterated some of the conversations they'd had before. Mike asked James, "Do you still have the resources to fund this mission?" Mike was genuinely concerned about how much money his brother was going through.

James, in his business voice, stated that "Money will never be an issue." They'd lost their mother and had only one parent left alive. James then lessened the stress by telling Mike that he had done very well in the Bitcoin market, so it was all just play money to him.

Mike indicated to all that that a rapid escalation of events was truly going to take place, and soon.

Mike told James that "Our father is very likely going to pay Lieutenant Josefa Gavidi a visit very shortly. We're going to need a rendezvous point once this mission is complete. The meeting point has to be fluid with many different locations considered, because it must work for every possible scenario and phase of our mission. The transitions could be as simple as walking to the plane or as complex as running for our lives with the police and military in pursuit."

This was the first time that James felt like he was part of the mission. He was not going to fuck it up. He told Mike, "Leave the meeting points and escape routes to me."

51

WHERE'S CAPTAIN TUI NACOLA?

THE FIRST DAY Captain Tui Nacola missed work his fellow officers thought it was, unusual for him not to call in the reason for his absence. When Major Lala Tavai was informed that Tui had missed work again, he became alarmed. Lala assigned Captain Etak Wainiqolo to look into the situation with Captain Tui Nacola.

Three days later Captain Etak Wainiqolo parked his car in the military fleet parking Lot. He went immediately to Major Lala Tavai's office. Once inside and comfortably seated in a chair, he started his report. He told the major of all the places he had been and of all the conversations he'd had with people who might know the whereabouts of Captain Tui. Etak told

Lala of his findings at the shore where Tui had landed and stored his boat.

Major Lala Tavai listened intently, all the while processing even the most minuscule detail of information. Lala looked at Etak and told him that "Tui's unknown whereabouts are troubling. But for now, we shall see what tomorrow brings." Lala asked Etak, "Would you mind, after your shift, going back down to the shoreline where Tui's boat and motor are located?"

Captain Etak Wainiqolo told Major Lala Tavai that "I will go back to the shoreline. I know when and approximately where Captain Tui Nacola went to check his fishing net." Etak qualified his answer. "I haven't accompanied Tui too many times, but I have on the rare occasion."

The major and the captain left it at that, but both hoped that all was well with their friend.

52

HEAVEN HOIST US

BRENT METHODICALLY ASSEMBLED the equipment he would need to carry out the murder of Lieutenant Josefa Gavidi. He tied a 30-meter utility rope to his belt. In his backpack was a series of odds and ends that might be needed for a yet unforeseen reason. He did pack an iron bar that had a definite purpose. Brent was going to use it as a club to render Josefa harmless. The last thing he made sure of was to pack his fully loaded pistol in case his best-laid plan to eliminate Lieutenant Josefa Gavidi went down the tubes.

The drive from Brent's dwelling to Josefa's house seemed eerily quiet. So quiet, in fact, that Brent turned on the local radio station. His mood was robotic. He was devoid of feelings; his entire focus was trained on what he had to do. He looked at his surroundings, and it was just about dusk. Lieutenant Josefa Gavidi would be home from his work at

Black Rock Camp in about a half hour. Brent used this time to park and hide his car, get in position within the garage to surprise Josefa, and make sure the hydraulic engine lift was operationally sound. Time seemed to stand still as Brent waited in ambush.

Josefa was through his shift for the day and couldn't wait to get home to finally drop the reconditioned engine into his 1955 Ford Fairlane. He was done all the bodywork, the brand-new paint job was to die for, and the interior was all spit and polished. With his new motor installed, he would be the envy of all his friends, and it didn't hurt that his antique car would probably turn the heads of a few girls. Yes, he thought to himself, he was a lucky man and blessed by the man upstairs.

Lieutenant Josefa Gavidi drove up his driveway and parked his car. He hustled inside to change out of his military uniform and into his overalls. After work he usually changed and went immediately into the garage, but tonight he was hungry. He reheated himself a few leftovers.

The wait was killing Brent. This was a break in the pattern. Brent figured out what the delay must be and bided his time with his metal club at the ready.

Josefa walked slowly out to his garage. It was now dark outside. He opened the door and went to turn the lights on. Just as the lights came on, the metal pipe landed on the crown of Lieutenant Josefa Gavidi's head. Josefa fell to the ground like a tonne of bricks. Brent had opened up a pretty good gash on Josefa's head.

Brent knew he had hurt him pretty badly. Brent took his utility rope off his belt. He put a loop around each of Josefa's thighs. He then put a loop around Josefa's chest, just under his armpits. In effect, Brent made a firefighter's self-rescue seat with just a few alterations. The last thing Brent did was put masking tape on Josefa's mouth, just in case he woke up before he was in position. Brent used the utility rope to drag his target under his Ford.

The adrenaline running through Brent had caused him to hit Josefa hard enough to kill him. Fortunately for Brent, Josefa survived the blow. Further investigation of Josefa's skull allowed Brent to see that he had crushed a portion of his skull. Brent thought for a moment and then repositioned the body so that the engine would crush Josefa's head. He quickly undid the ropes to make the killing scene look as natural as possible. Brent started up the hydraulic lift and slowly lowered the engine until it rested on Josefa's chest and head. Brent lowered the motor just a bit more until he heard ribs breaking. He again checked to see if the engine was in the proper place to kill his target. Brent felt that everything was in the perfect position. He took a second to reflect on his love for Laura. He bent down and took the masking tape from Josefa's mouth.

Josefa opened his eyes and stared into Brent's eyes. As blood streamed out of his mouth, he spoke and asked Brent, "Why?"

Brent replied, "Hard Rock Cafe."

Josefa's eyes let Brent know that he knew.

That was enough for Brent. He stood back up, put his hand on the controller of the hydraulic hoist, and pressed the down button. Brent heard bones cracking and Josefa's skull being crushed. The motor did its job. Lieutenant Josefa Gavidi was vital signs absent.

53

RECAP AND RESUPPLY

MIKE'S POSITION AT Lieutenant Josefa Gavidi's garage was right outside the door so he could vividly hear the awful sound of bones being crushed. It was time to scramble to the back, outside corner of the garage. Mike preferred not to allow his dad to know that he was there. Mike was cloaked in darkness before his father exited the garage. Once Brent retrieved his car and was safely out of sight, Mike entered the death scene. Mike could see that there was still work to do.

Mike asked Daniel and James to join him in Josefa's garage. He told them to be extremely careful not to attract attention to themselves. Mike took his time and methodically surveyed the mayhem that lay before him. The first task was to eliminate the blood spatter from when Brent had hit Josefa with the iron bar. There was blood on the side and top of the Fairlane. More was found on the wooden rafters above and still more on the joists in the garage wall. Mike thought about how hard his father must have hit Josefa to cause his blood to fly such great distances.

He was glad to see his brother and brother-in-law show up. He read the horror on Daniel's and James's faces. Nothing could prepare one for the blood clinging to everywhere. They settled into the cleanup task at hand, which took a couple of hours.

The last thing Mike had to accomplish was to make this look like a true accident scene. Mike reminded himself of the old adage: "People don't plan to fail; they fail to plan." Mike released his family members at this point. They had seen enough.

Unfortunately, if his father had been trying to make this seem like an accident, he'd failed miserably. For the vehicle engine to end up on Josefa's face and chest, it could only have been caused by a malfunction. The only way for that to happen was for hydraulic fluid to somehow leak out of the cylinders. The hoist was in perfect working order, which could only mean that someone had lowered the engine deliberately to kill Josefa.

Mike achieved the look of a malfunction by first removing some fluid and then replacing it with water. This would look like a failure to maintain proper pressure in the cylinder, which would worsen fluid leakage from the seals. Mike knew that to the untrained eye, this would look like an accident, but to a machine mechanic, it wouldn't pass muster. All in all, he was satisfied that the alterations he'd made to the pseudo accident scene would at least buy time. Before he left the garage, he took a long look at Josefa. Mike felt no remorse.

"You murdered a mother and a wife. You paid for this injustice with your life."

Mike drove back to his safe house. He closed and locked the front door. He had to make more phone calls. He poured himself a drink and decided the order in which to communicate with the others. His first call was to James and Daniel on a conference call. Mike brought them up to speed on how he staged the accidental death of Lieutenant Josefa Gavidi. What was more concerning to Mike was the probability of what would happen from this point on. He realized that, up until now, he and his team had been a security detail. Now, the possibility of skirmishes between the Fijian military and the Hudsons was becoming more of a reality. Mike went over the weaponry available and what they might need to complete the mission. The telephone line went momentarily silent as nothing else, so it seemed, needed to be said on that point.

The hesitancy in Daniel was quickly vanishing. Just as an added afterthought, he stated that "We might need a rocket-propelled grenade launcher (RPG). This might help us gain an equal footing against the firepower of the Fijian foot soldiers."

Mike agreed and would put the wheels in motion to secure one in Port Moresby back in Papua New Guinea. Mike made a cursory inquiry as to how the two fishermen were making out in captivity.

Daniel jumped to answer Mike's question. He said he had been in touch with Dr. Sumner and that they were doing just fine. They were getting three square meals a day, and $1,000 was placed into their hands at the end of every day. Daniel laughed and reported that "The fishermen want you to know that you're not to rush this mission. You're to take your time and do it right."

Mike thanked his family members for their participation in the mission so far but alerted them that "From here on is when we will all start to earn our money." Mike asked Daniel, "Could you perform your wizardry once again and get the jet through Fijian immigration?"

Daniel waited for Mike to finish and updated him on the fact that he could still hide all their identities but couldn't hide the ownership of the Hudson Reinsurance jet. Therefore, Daniel went on to say, James was taking it out of play. He said that "James will give you an update on that situation." To end his part of the conversation, Daniel told Mike that "Getting everything through immigration will not be a problem."

James overheard Daniel talking to Mike about the Hudson jet. James told Mike, "I'm sending the Hudson jet home, and it has already been replaced with another leased Learjet."

On that topic, Mike stopped his brother and asked him, "James, do you want an assignment?"

James was quick to agree. James was instructed to fly to Port Moresby to pick up and pay for an RPG and a plethora of ammunition. James was then to return to Fiji and after he landed at the airport, Mike himself would fetch the gun. James was just to go straight through customs.

Mike then inquired as to how James's escape plans were coming along.

James let his younger brother know that "I have secured a helicopter that will seat our entire group." He had rented a Learjet. This allowed Daniel to hide the identity of the person renting the jet. James was also moving the jet from airport to airport so that no one could track it. James also indicated that he had a speedboat available to him. It had enough seating to accommodate them all. James went on to say that everything else was in a fluid situation depending on the trouble that Brent got them all into.

Mike did ask James one question. "Where is the heliport located?"

James laughed and replied, "On the yacht I rented. When you told me to rent a yacht, I rented a yacht."

Daniel piped up to say he was living in the lap of luxury.

54

THE PLAN CONTINUES

BRENT SHUT OFF the ignition in his car and unlocked the house door. The first thing he did was pour himself a stiff shot of whiskey. He sat down on the couch and laid his head back. He closed his eyes and thought of the day's events.

Brent was generally happy with his day but didn't want to dwell on what had happened. He wanted to figure out the future and how he was going to get near either Captain Etak Wainiqolo or Major Lala Tavai. Brent leaned toward leaving the major to the end. He was the actual person who had put the bullet in Laura's head, but he would take more planning.

Brent rose from his couch, walked to his war room, and studied the investigation wall. When he looked under Captain Etak Wainiqolo's and Major Lala Tavai's names, very little information was available. He decided that more time surveilling both would have to be done. The last thing he did was fetch the Fiji Times from his mailbox. He didn't read the entire paper but read enough to assure himself that Captain Tui Nacola's body hadn't been found yet.

55

VENASIO PULLS SOME STRINGS

NOTHING CONCRETE HAD come in, but the rumor mill was alive and active. Venasio heard that the Fijian military was trying to find out the whereabouts of one Captain Tui Nacola. The young police officer called his contact at immigration. The message back to him was that everything was normal, and nothing was suspicious on their end. Venasio hung up the phone and immediately called his good friend at the Ministry of Housing.

His friend said he might have something for him.

Venasio stopped him right there and, with a raised voice, demanded to know why he hadn't already been informed of this new possible development.

His contact told him he'd just gotten back from his holiday, and if the police officer would give him an hour, he would furnish him with the information he had.

Venasio slammed his Fiji Times onto his desk and stood up, doing a little dance shuffle in his head. Almost right to the hour, his Ministry of Housing contact called him back and told him he had found two numbered companies that fit his criteria. Venasio was told that the two numbered companies, after a deeper dive, were owned by Hudson Reinsurance. They were renting properties on a monthly basis. The renters on record were James Hudson in a condo and Brent Hudson in a detached house.

Venasio thanked his friend and once again made him aware that this was a hush-hush operation. When he put the phone down he joyfully stated, "Gotcha now, you bastards." He could not wait to get to his home to sit down and plan his next moves.

The sun had long since settled, giving way to the night. Venasio was a smart, young man, and he was methodically planning out his next moves. He would focus on James Hudson. He was the CEO of Hudson Reinsurance. That was where the money was.

Venasio showered and changed into his police uniform. This should get him past reception in the downstairs lobby. It not only got him past the condo staff, but the receptionist also gave the police officer a key card to James Hudson's penthouse condo. Venasio drew his gun a few steps from the condo door. He quietly activated the card lock and entered James's rental. James was nowhere to be found, but the intruder did hear the shower going in the back bedroom. He decided to just take a seat on the couch and wait for his target to appear.

James entered the living room wearing only a pair of

boxers and a T-shirt. His heart rate immediately soared as he was faced with a police officer pointing a gun at him.

The perpetrator waved his gun around and told James to sit on another couch directly across from him.

Naturally, James did as he was told. James remembered a life lesson that he'd learned from his father years ago: "Panic breeds panic." He would suppress his and hopefully de-escalate the current situation.

Venasio introduced himself to James as the man who rodent poison couldn't kill.

James immediately knew that his brother Mike had inadvertently left a footprint alive. He was thinking that footprints can indeed trample on one's best-laid plans. James called him Venasio and congratulated him on his nine lives.

The young police officer was surprised that James put a name to him. Venasio went into his well-thought-out proposition. He told James that he and his family were going to have to pay him one million American dollars to buy his silence and his forgiveness.

This let James deduce that Venasio was operating as a lone wolf and that his superiors weren't aware of his dalliances. James took hold of the conversation. He looked the young man in the eyes and said that this was a money transaction, and his gun was out of place for this arrangement.

Venasio agreed and placed the gun on the coffee table in front of himself.

James had been able to reduce the intensity of the situation, but he realized that this would be a never-ending cash transaction and that there would be no end to the money they would have to pay this tin god. James decided that it had to be handled here and now. Venasio was a strong, young man, but James had at least the element of surprise. He hoped that would be enough.

He agreed to the extorter's conditions and offered him a drink. Venasio happily complied, and James poured them both a two-finger rum and coke. He walked slowly and relaxedly and went to hand Venasio his drink. Venasio had thought James would be an easy target, except James turned the tables and smashed the police officer's drink right in his face. In essence, it was an old-fashioned glassing.

Blood poured from the open wounds in Venasio's face. As they struggled, they overturned the coffee table, and the gun went flying. James knew he was fighting for his life against a much stronger foe. The condo was being trashed by the two combatants in this epic struggle. James was getting hit with punches all over his body and they hurt. He was losing any advantage he'd enjoyed off the start. James remembered some key spots to hit from sparring with Mike. He lashed out at Venasio's groin. Then he slammed the palm of his hand directly into his opponent's nose. That seemed to temporarily slow down Venasio. The oldest Hudson boy got a glimpse of the bloody pulp he'd created out of Venasio's face. He had no time to dwell on the officer's face as his own survival was still not assured. James felt that nothing was totally working to slow the onset of Venasio's punches. James was finally able to maneuver himself behind the young man and put him in a choke hold.

Venasio knew he was in trouble, and he pushed back against James as hard as he could. They both started stepping backward at a very fast rate. All of a sudden, James felt his head break a mirror. They both fell down in a heap. Shards of glass were everywhere. During the fall, Venasio had gained the upper hand. The older of the two combatants was tiring.

James was in trouble. Venasio was now repeatedly beating away at his face. A sixth sense helped James feel along the floor. He came up with what amounted to a glass shiv. He plunged it between Venasio's ribs. The oldest Hudson son heard the air leave the police officer's torso. James continually plunged the shiv anywhere into Venasio that would hurt. After three more stab wounds, the young man's eyes rolled backward, and he collapsed in a heap on top of James. Venasio was dead.

James got himself to the couch. He looked around the room and saw broken furniture and blood everywhere. He took a minute to assess his own wounds. He was beat up pretty badly, and blood was seeping from the back of his head where he'd hit the mirror. Worse, the shiv he'd used to kill Venasio had cut the shit out of his own hand, and the gashes looked like snarling wolf teeth.

There was something to be said for taking a man's life. It was a line crossed that one could never uncross. The older Hudson son began to shake uncontrollably. James started to cry. No amount of money or influence could help one in hand-to-hand combat. One couldn't outspend one's opponent. One could only outwill them or, as James realized, be luckier. He took a moment to compose himself.

James found the portable satellite radio and gave his family a conference call. He also included Dr. Sumner. His family immediately heeded the call. First to arrive was Daniel. He burst into tears as he looked at the battered and bloody body of his loved one. The rest of the Hudsons appeared a short time later.

Dr. Sumner spied James and immediately went to work

trying to piece him back together again. Brent and Mike were responsible for body removal and were able to get Venasio down the freight elevator and onto the speedboat. No one was the wiser about this operation. They took the young man's body out to sea and just threw him overboard. Trying to hide their tracks was impossible. The condo was ruined, and the reception staff had to know that Venasio had been there.

When the father and the younger son arrived back at the condo, Daniel and Dr. Sumner were doing what they could to erase the blood trail throughout the condo. Daniel planned to throw money at the condo owners to fix and repair their condo.

The Hudsons took a minute to have an impromptu meeting. It was agreed that James would have a short-term stay with the doctor and then rent himself a different penthouse condo, definitely in another part of Nadi. The rest of the family would return to their abodes.

Mike had the last say. "If Venasio knew where to find us, who else knows?"

56

Etak's Green Lights

THE NEXT DAY found Brent in his observation post, safely tucked away in his old car, just outside Black Rock Camp. He was witness to both Captain Etak Wainiqolo and Major Lala Tavai reporting for duty. Today he was going to take a closer look at their homes and see what obstacles he would have to overcome to take out each of the men.

He decided to drive to Captain Etak Wainiqolo's house first. Again, as he always did, he parked his car in a discreet location. When looking at Etak's house from the dirt road, the first thing that came to Brent's mind was that this was a lot of house compared to the money that Captain Etak Wainiqolo was making with the Fijian military. It was a two-story, white stucco home with a circular driveway at the front. The front and sides were lined with Fiji fan palms. Brent surmised that to Etak, these palms gave beauty as well as some privacy to his property. To Brent, the palms could be used to hide behind, especially around dusk. The backyard contained a gorgeous pool that was surrounded by designer rocks and manicured flower gardens. The back property line was defined by a hedge of Fiji fire plants that were standing just over a meter high and immaculately groomed. Jungle stood beyond that point.

Brent committed to memory that although Etak might think it was a secure location, it was a false sense of security. Etak had an outside camera, but the scope and range were limited to the front of the house. Brent heard a vehicle driving toward him in the distance. That was the thing about a dirt road—it was noisy. He took the time to get out of sight in hopes the vehicle would pass on by without seeing him.

Instead, the vehicle slowed down and turned into Etak's driveway. It happened to be the pool company that took care of Etak's swimming pool.

Brent watched the driver go around the side of the dwelling and put his hand into a Fiji fire plant located against the house wall. The pool man came out with a key. This got Brent's curiosity as he continued to watch.

The pool man proceeded to some sort of lockbox about two meters further down the stucco wall. He put the key into the slot, opened it, and flipped a switch. The guy carried on with his business to clean the pool. When he was finished, he reversed his procedures on the sidewall.

Brent waited for the pool man to safely leave. He then retraced the pool man's steps. The use of the key was for the purpose of activating and deactivating an infrared alarm system. Brent sarcastically thought this might be good to know as he returned to his car and drove away.

Brent immediately headed for Major Lala Tavai's place.

On arrival, he quickly discovered that it was somewhat of a fortress. Three-meter, stone walls with broken shards of glass on top surrounded the entire perimeter. To Brent, it looked like Lala had an entire day crew looking after both the inside and outside of this rather impressive homestead. The house looked like a white mansion one would see on an old Georgian plantation. It was funny to Brent that the location of Major Lala Tavai's place was rural, but the hive of activity on the Lala property seemed like a busy city. Brent knew it would take intricate planning to get the upper hand on Major Lala Tavai. Brent would focus on Captain Etak Wainiqolo.

57

THE MISSING

MAJOR LALA TAVAI was in his office at Black Rock Camp when he was informed that Lieutenant Josefa Gavidi had not reported to work. Lala asked the clerical worker, "Has Captain Tui Nacola reported for duty?"

Again, the answer was no.

Major Lala Tavai had gotten to his rank in the military because he was smart. He was very highly regarded in the strategic, tactical, and task facets of the military. He was a leader, and to be a leader, the major was respected, but he really wasn't well loved. If he invited his fellow soldiers out for beers, they went because they didn't want to feel the wrath of the major.

Major Lala Tavai called Captain Etak Wainiqolo into his office. When Etak arrived, Lala gave him the news that

Lieutenant Josefa Gavidi was also absent from duty. They both looked at each other with confused faces.

Etak was first to speak. He said, "Do you want me to go and check on Josefa?"

Lala shook his head to indicate no. Major Lala Tavai, in a solemn, quiet voice, inquired, "You don't think Josefa has anything to do with Tui, do you?"

There was silence in the room as they both tried to think of scenarios that would tie Josefa to Tui. Neither allowed the other to answer that question. Instead, Major Lala Tavai told Etak to assign a private to go to Josefa's house and check on his well-being.

Etak left Major Lala Tavai's office with dread swirling around in his head.

Major Lala Tavai was weighing the probabilities of each scenario he had visualized in his head. A cold chill ran through his body when he delved deeper into the proverbial worst-case scenario. He would hold his final opinion until he heard news about Lieutenant Josefa Gavidi.

58

THE FOUND

THE PRIVATE TOOK a military vehicle and headed toward his assigned task. Once he got to the correct address, he noticed that Josefa's truck was parked in the driveway. The private's mindset was that Lieutenant Josefa Gavidi was probably home sick and had forgotten to telephone that he would not be there for duty today. The private knocked on the door several times. There was no response. He decided to check the garage. He opened the side door and was about to step in when his nose made him aware of a pungent odor within. The private closed the door, stepped back, and had a few dry heaves. He had no desire to go back in the garage. The private returned to his car and exited the driveway.

"Fuck me," were the next words uttered by the private.

He stopped the car and returned to Josefa's driveway. He went to recheck the garage. He wanted to make sure that no dead animal had somehow gotten in there and died. He put his hand over his nose and entered. What the private saw, no one should ever see. He saw the bloating, crushed, and decaying body of Lieutenant Josefa Gavidi. He was pinned under the motor he had been trying to install in his old, vintage car. One didn't have to be a coroner to see that this was an obvious death.

He rushed out of the garage, seeking fresh air. He was physically sick to his stomach and enduring that disgusting, icky sweat that made one cringe. Not sure what to do, the private decided to drive directly back to Black Rock Camp and report his findings. He made his way to Major Lala Tavai's office and, with an ashen face, reported that Josefa was dead. The private told Lala that "Lieutenant Josefa Gavidi was crushed by his car engine because the hydraulic hoist malfunctioned and gave way."

Major Lala Tavai dismissed the young man and said, "I'll take it from here."

59

THE POSSIBILITIES

MAJOR LALA TAVAI rose from his desk and walked around his chair. This was a horrible turn of events. Lieutenant Josefa Gavidi had been a decent man. He had been somewhat aloof but had been depended upon to do his military duty and, at the same time, keep his mouth shut when need be.

In particular, Lala was referencing the protection and extortion business that he and Captain Etak Wainiqolo were involved in. The store owners in Port Denarau were paying Etak, Lala, and an unknown silent partner protection money to render their businesses safe from harm. Strategic members of the Nadi Police Department were paid by these two military men to turn a blind eye. All in all, it was a very profitable undertaking.

Lala thought it possible that one of the extorted store owners had had enough and was on a rampage to eliminate this shakedown. Major Lala Tavai wondered if Captain Tui Nacola and Lieutenant Josefa Gavidi's tiny role in his business had ended up causing their demise. According to Captain Etak Wainiqolo, they had only been used for noncontroversial envelope pickups.

As he continued to pace, another unthinkable canvas was being painted. Major Lala Tavai vividly remembered the altercation with the Canadian couple at the Hard Rock Cafe. Lala refreshed his memory about putting a bullet in the lady's head. He knew the adult male had survived but, according to information he had been given, the man was reportedly in bad physical shape. Lala didn't really have any way to confirm or dispute the condition of the Canadian male, as Dr. Zayn Leba and his wife Naomi had drowned in a scuba diving accident. Still, the likelihood of one person with two bullet holes in his back causing all this havoc seemed doubtful.

Major Lala Tavai sat back down in his chair and immediately telephoned the superintendent of police in Nadi. Superintendent Jeet Singh. Singh was Major Lala Tavai's silent business partner in the shakedown of the Port Denarau merchants. This was information that Captain Etak Wainiqolo was unaware of, which was exactly the way the two partners wanted it. When Jeet picked up his private telephone, Lala told him that there had been an accident at Josefa's place. Josefa had been killed. Jeet informed Lala that the police would respond. Lala went on to explain that Captain Tui Nacola had also been missing for the last few days. No one could find him, and it was time to start getting worried.

Superintendent Jeet Singh took all the information offered and said that the police would start an investigation into Tui as well.

Major Lala Tavai did communicate to Jeet that both Josefa and Tui had acted as bagmen in their other business activities. Superintendent Jeet Singh ended the conversation, telling Lala that "I will take care of the police investigations." Then he chastised Major Lala Tavai by saying that "You take care of the business, find out what's going bad, and get your house clean!" Jeet hung up the telephone, leaving no doubt as to what would happen next.

Hours later, Major Lala Tavai summoned Captain Etak Wainiqolo to his office. Etak was told to sit, and Lala informed him of the where and how of Lieutenant Josefa Gavidi's death. Lala ran his two possible scenarios by Etak.

Etak also agreed there might be a problem with disgruntled merchants.

Major Lala Tavai was starting to stress. He told Etak, "You are going to revisit everyone concerned with the business. I want you to seek out any malcontents and put them back in line. If you come in contact with the person or persons who might have killed Josefa and Tui, immediately eliminate the problem." The last order from Major Lala Tavai was for Etak to "Return to the shoreline where Tui puts in his boat. If the motor is still on the boat, take the boat out to Tui's fishing net to see if he has harvested his catch in the last while."

Captain Etak Wainiqolo stood up on his feet and exited the major's office. Captain Etak Wainiqolo knew what he had to do and knew he had the blessing of Major Lala Tavai to get it done. He informed the duty sergeant that "I was just assigned other duties by Major Lala Tavai that will take me away from Black Rock Camp for the immediate future."

The duty sergeant took his name off the roster.

Etak decided to drive home before anything else. It was

already a hot day, and he certainly wasn't going to investigate anything in his uniform. Once home and with a feeling of freedom, he decided to take a swim. His time was his own, and he was going to enjoy it. Once he was done in the pool, he watered the flowers before getting dressed to address his investigative responsibilities for the day.

Etak drove his car past Josefa's house. There were a multitude of police officers on the scene and one big, black hearse. Etak wondered what Josefa's body must have looked like after the motor he'd been working on had crushed his bones. It must have sounded like snapping toothpicks. One of the vehicles on the scene wasn't marked. That didn't matter to Etak because he knew who the vehicle belonged to; it was Superintendent Jeet Singh's. Etak thought that, for him to be at the scene, the police were taking this a lot more seriously than he was. Etak leaned toward Josefa's death being an accident. Still, he couldn't discount problems in the food chain with the protection business. Right now, his task was to investigate the shoreline where his friend Tui launched his boat.

60

EMPTY THE NET

ETAK ARRIVED AT the shore and took a 360-degree scan of the area. Nothing seemed out of place except Etak puzzled over why Tui had left his motor in plain sight and attached to the stern of his boat. The tide was out, so it was a long struggle to get Tui's boat in the water. Etak knew where the fishing net was likely to be, so he put the motor in gear and headed in that direction. Twenty minutes later, he put the motor on a slow idle as he was nearing the net. The day was hot, and the sun shining on the water caused Etak's eyes to squint. The reflective glare was causing a problem for Etak to see great distances.

Etak finally saw the end buoy keeping Tui's net afloat. As he scanned toward the middle of the net, he could just make out a black blob. He steered the boat in that direction. Etak noticed that the top of the net was well below the surface. He thought to himself that the net must be full of fish. Etak looked again and noticed that many buoys were missing, which would normally help keep the net at the surface of the water. Etak's eyes went wide open when he saw something other than fish caught in the net.

What he was seeing was a grotesque, bloated, and half-eaten human body. It was facedown and only attached to the net by one arm. The other arm was free of the net but barely hanging on at the shoulder. The entire body seemed to have either net gouges or fish bites throughout. On closer examination, Etak found that the arm still attached to the net was encased by a plastic zip tie. In this case, the plastic zip tie was being used in place of a handcuff. The other plastic zip tie was a hollow loop, but Etak surmised that Tui's decaying flesh had fallen away from the wrist and hand area, allowing the arm to float free. Captain Etak Wainiqolo couldn't physically see Captain Tui Nacola's face to make a positive identification, but neither was he going to try and position the boat to allow that to happen. It was just too ugly a scene, and Etak could only think of distancing himself from the horror show he was living in. Etak didn't need to see his friend's face to know it was him.

"Who else could it be?" He put the boat back in gear and headed for shore.

Etak was glad the tide was rising, as he could get closer to the original resting point of Tui's boat. Etak kept the boat at full throttle until the propeller almost grounded on the bottom. He then raised the motor and was able to sand surf many meters closer to where the boat could be secured to its original beach location. Etak took a minute and just sat in the boat. He had to think about what to do next. Captain Etak Wainiqolo decided to call Major Lala Tavai before the police.

Lala picked up his phone and listened as Captain Etak

Wainiqolo told him of the wretched scene that had confronted him.

Etak said, "I think we will have to call the police."

Lala said, "Etak, you continue with your investigation of the store merchants under our control, and I will definitely inform the police."

When Major Lala Tavai ended the call with Etak, it was quite apparent to Etak that Lala was putting more significance on the deaths than Etak was.

Major Lala Tavai felt an awful pit in his stomach. The feeling of suspecting but not knowing was eating at the very fibers of his body. Lala did what he had to do. He made another dreaded call to Superintendent Jeet Singh. He informed Jeet of the death of Captain Tui Nacola. Lala took Jeet through the report that Etak had recited to him.

The superintendent said he would get the police to investigate. He also told Lala that the preliminary report on Josefa was that it had been an accidental death. The hydraulic hoist had malfunctioned and dropped the engine on Josefa. The superintendent also indicated that a forensic engineer would be coming in from Suva to further investigate and confirm that the hydraulic hoist was the culprit. The forensic mechanic wouldn't be able to be at the scene until tomorrow. Before Jeet hung up the phone, he again chastised the major about getting his troops in line.

Lala hung up the phone and decided to bury his head in paperwork for the rest of the day. He just didn't want to think about a world that was currently turning to shit.

Captain Etak Wainiqolo hung up, put his head in his hands, and gave a loud shout of anguish. He now had time to mourn his friend. They'd had a long history going way back. They had not only been military men, but they'd also been brothers in many ways. It had been Etak who had persuaded Tui to pick up envelopes from store merchants in the Port Denarau vicinity. Etak's business was essentially run like a series of paper routes. Each route had about twenty-five customers each. He had six employees and out of them all, Tui had been the nicest and the most proficient collector he'd utilized. Etak wiped the few tears that were left on his cheeks and drove away from the shore.

Etak proceeded to drive to all his handlers' homes. He wanted to speak to them to see, what they had to say about the store merchants they handled. If anyone was going to lie to him, it would be face-to-face. After many hours of one-on-one conversations with the handlers, Etak came to the opinion that, first, none of them had gone rogue. Second, the store merchants seemed to be as happy as they could be considering they were being extorted. Etak concluded that someone had to be very clever to pull off this vigilante murdering spree. He assessed the mental capacities of everyone involved in his part of the operation and felt safe that none of them were involved. It was going on midnight when he finished his interviews, so he decided to end the night with a few drinks at the Hard Rock Cafe.

Major Lala Tavai spent the evening at home racking his brain to come up with something that made sense out of Tui's and Josefa's deaths. The evening couldn't come to a close fast enough for Lala; all he wanted to do was go to bed and make this nightmare disappear. The night didn't yield any nightmares because Lala spent the time awake, tossing and turning.

It was four o'clock in the morning, and he had had enough. He rose and got out of bed and telephoned Captain Etak Wainiqolo.

Captain Etak Wainiqolo, in a groggy voice, answered, "Hello?"

A conversation ensued between the two of them about the protection gambit that Etak was running for Major Lala Tavai. Once Etak had exonerated his entire crew from any wrongdoing with Tui and Josefa, Lala's heart began to sink. He challenged Etak to admit that "It must be the Canadian man who is responsible for all the carnage."

Etak pushed back against Major Lala Tavai's assumption. Etak said, "I find it hard to believe that the shot-up man from a year ago could heal or have the wherewithal to come back to Fiji and kill our friends." He offered that "There must be another option. Perhaps Captain Tui Nacola got mixed up in the turf war between the charter boat captains and the local net fishermen. The captains of the charter boats depend on tourists renting their boats and fishing with rod and reel. Whereas the local fishermen fish for a living with long nets strewn across the ocean. The captains are upset because their livelihood is being usurped by locals overfishing the Fijian area of the ocean. In the past, locals have been killed and their nets slashed."

Major Lala Tavai hung up his phone, far from being convinced by Captain Etak Wainiqolo's tale.

Lala went to work at Black Rock Camp early. Today was the most unsettled he had ever felt in his entire life. Lala was the one who everyone looked to for answers. In this case, he had none. He busied himself with his paperwork, and half the morning had elapsed before his phone rang. The person on the line was Superintendent Jeet Singh.

The conversation was extremely short with the last line being, "Get your ass over here now!"

61

THE PUZZLE PIECES FIT

MAJOR LALA TAVAI called for his driver and went to the police headquarters in Nadi. Lala went straight to Superintendent Jeet Singh's office. Once inside, he closed the door and took a seat.

Jeet was on the telephone. When he hung up the phone, he took a deep breath and stared directly at Lala. Dispensing with the pleasantries of the day, Jeet started directly into what he had to say. "Major, it took forensics less than ten minutes to establish that the hydraulic hoist had been sabotaged. What we have here is a homicide," barked Jeet. The superintendent then dropped another bomb on the major. "I got in contact with Immigration to see how many North American tourists we currently have in Nadi. I was told that a police officer by the name of Venasio Tubuna had already inquired about this information. They'd told him they couldn't help him, but Immigration had actually felt that he'd lacked the correct approvals to inquire so they'd pushed him away."

Immigration had furnished Superintendent Singh with the names and addresses of all numbered companies renting accommodations in Nadi and the surrounding area. This had helped point Singh to the Ministry of Housing. The superintendent told Major Lala Tavai that he'd run into another contact that Venasio had used. This ministry employee had been very helpful. He'd furnished Singh with the same names and addresses that he'd given to Venasio. Superintendent Singh looked straight into Major Lala Tavai's eyes. "Venasio Tubuna is missing, and my guess is that he is dead. We know Captain Tui Nacola, Lieutenant Josefa Gavidi, Mark Volau, and Dr. Zayn Leba and his wife Naomi are dead. They are all dead. What does that say to you?"

Major Lala Tavai knew immediately what that meant. The Hudsons had arrived back in Fiji, and they were looking for justice for the death of Laura Hudson. He took a moment to gather his thoughts and then he suggested that the police and military do simultaneous late-night raids on the two residences.

Singh interrupted the major by saying, "There are a couple things wrong with your plan." He went on to say that his police force was washing its hands of the whole operation. Singh reminded Lala that he'd already covered up for the military when the first tragic incident had happened at the Hard Rock Cafe. He was not going to continue to jeopardize himself or his police force's good name. The police superintendent also informed the major that he was aware that the Australian SAS safe house was currently occupied and that he bet it was another Hudson staying there.

The telephone rang, and Singh picked it up and listened. He said absolutely nothing and then quietly hung up. He looked sarcastically at Lala and stated, "Police Officer Venasio's nine lives have run out. His body just washed ashore with several puncture wounds to the torso."

62

THE RAID

MAJOR LALA TAVAI couldn't get back to his office fast enough. He immediately called Captain Etak Wainiqolo to come to the strategic war room just beyond his office. When Captain Etak Wainiqolo arrived, Major Lala Tavai briefed him and apprised him of the situation. He also informed the captain that he was to coordinate and command the raids on the three addresses. Lala then rose from his chair and left Etak to handle the strategy of the raids. Once Etak had it worked out, he was to report back to Lala and run it by him for his approval.

Two hours later, Captain Etak Wainiqolo summoned the major back to the strategic war room. There, he laid out his plan, which met with the approval of Major Lala Tavai. It would be go time at 0100 hours that night. There would be no moon, and the night would be dark. All three residences would be attacked at the same time.

Etak would send twenty-five soldiers to the condo in Nadi occupied by James Hudson. The SAS safe house and Brent Hudson's dwelling were relatively close together, so precision timing would be necessary. Etak would dedicate seventy-five soldiers to these two houses. They would park their transport vehicles a distance away to use the night and their quietness to surprise both the occupants. Twenty-five of his men would head directly to the jungle a kilometer away. They would stay there until the raids started. Then they would march through the jungle and brush to force anyone in the jungle to a designated spot. Twenty-five more of his men would sneak up and quietly capture Brent Hudson. The last twenty-five soldiers would follow at a safe distance and capture whomever was in the SAS safe house. It didn't matter to Captain Etak Wainiqolo if the Hudsons were captured dead or alive.

63

RESULTS

0100 HOURS ARRIVED, and the operation started.

Brent Hudson was the first to become aware that something was amiss. His sentry was barking and carrying on. Brent knew that hesitation would be his downfall, so he immediately jumped out of bed, grabbed his portable radio, slipped on some good footwear and dashed out the back door. In stealth mode, he made his way to the jungle. Brent was able to hide and witness the raid on his house. They went in with guns blazing. They exited the back with guns still blazing and headed his way into the jungle.

Brent drew on lessons he'd learned from his Ojibwa friends. While being hunted an alerted hunted animal would test just how much a predator wanted it. The quarry would run deep into the thickest, dirtiest, and hardest-to-maneuver part of the jungle. If the predator wasn't all that hungry, or in a human's case plain lazy, they would not traverse insanely thick bramble. For the most part, Brent's chess game with the military was working for him.

The Fijian military still didn't know for sure who was in the safe house. They did, however, suspect it could be Mike Hudson. Their research let them know he had been a member of Canada's elite JTF2. The foot soldiers were on high alert, as they knew how dangerous this man could be.

High alert or not, one of them activated a trip wire that Mike had put in place after Venasio had been killed by James. Mike knew then that the gig was up. The primitive tin-can alarm worked. He scrambled out of bed and grabbed his survival backpack and headed for the jungle. He, too, could watch as the Fijian military shot up his safe house. He made a mental note to himself that his Aussie friends would have to change safe houses.

Mike retreated to the jungle. He had the foresight to warn the rest of his family members. He did an all-call on the portable radio.

Brent was able to say he was safe and deep in the jungle.

Daniel came on the air and stated that there was no activity in his surrounding area.

Dr. Alec Sumner also responded that he was safe, with no activity in his neighborhood. He went on to say that he didn't think the Fijian government knew about his safe house.

Mike was waiting for a response from his brother, James. He suspected the worst. James finally answered, although he seemed excited in his speech. The older Hudson brother ran from his bed and immediately went to the balcony of his luxury penthouse condo. James immediately knew what the situation was. He told Mike that the military had likely raided his last condo location. They must not have known that he'd moved.

Mike informed James that they didn't have time for a conversation and that he was to wait for Daniel to arrive with the speedboat and go with him to the yacht.

James hung up and proceeded to the docking area in Port Denarau.

Mike took a moment to assess what the Fijian military was trying to accomplish. He very quickly figured out their plan. They were executing a pincer movement. They'd prepared for him and his dad making it to the jungle out back. They were now doing a squeeze and funneling their prey into one small area. Once the military maneuvered him and his dad into position, they would be surrounded and likely disposed of right there.

He couldn't let that happen. He slung his backpack high in a tree. He knew his father, because of all the training he'd had, would know to not just look ahead or around but up as well. After disposing of his backpack, he headed toward the military soldiers with his hands above his head. He knew that he had to surrender himself to give his father any chance of escape.

The spotlights from the soldiers blinded Mike, and he heard the words, "Get on your knees."

Brent could see from his location exactly what Mike had done. He sat down on a dried-up, dead log. The father had himself a good cry. It broke his heart to see his youngest son sacrifice himself for his dad. Brent stayed hidden until the daylight hours. He was able to retrieve the survival backpack and have some dried food to eat. The Hudsons had to regroup, and he knew it. He put out over the all-call that everyone was to meet up at Dr. Sumner's safe house.

The last one to show up at the doctor's place was Brent himself. He had to be very careful. It was daylight and he could see, but what he saw alarmed him. The military still had a thick presence, although they were haphazardly placed. Brent sensed that they weren't really looking for him. Rather, they were just trying not to be eaten alive by mosquitos and no-see-ums.

Brent wasn't immune to the bites of these insects either. He found some wet earth and wallowed around until he had a good coat of mud on his naked body. Thick mud wasn't a cure-all for mosquitos but, with the added clothes from Mike's survival pack, it would create an additional layer for the little vampires to get through. With considerable ease, he was able to outflank the military and break free into more jungle. He had at least three or more kilometers of jungle to traverse before he arrived at the meeting place.

Brent was relieved that finally after the rigors of traversing the jungle he arrived at the safe house. He opened the door and, by doing so, startled the rest of the Hudson team. He was quite a sight with swollen, red eyes and a body covered in thick mud. Still, everyone greeted him with open arms. They were glad he had been able to escape. Brent told them all about the heroic sacrifice that Mike had made to save his father. He excused himself and went for a shower. His shower was not refreshing. It was stressful and tiresome as he racked his mind for some kind of plan to rescue his youngest boy.

Brent sat down with the others on the team in the living room of the safe house. Their conversation went round and round as they tried to determine where Mike could have been taken. The general consensus was that he was a prisoner at Black Rock Camp. An aura of gloom and doom filled the room. They all knew the difficulties they would have to overcome to penetrate this fortress.

Out of the back room came a voice that stated, "I think we can help with your problem."

Brent had told Dr. Sumner to bring the two fishermen to the living room. Once everybody was in the same room, Brent asked them for their story. They introduced themselves as Joni and Kona Patel. They were brothers and also had no love for the Fijian military. They reminded the Hudsons that the coup had taken away all the Fijian peoples' civil rights. It was military rule. The freedom of the press was greatly curtailed, to the point where newspapers were being shut down and reporters exiled to foreign lands. Some even vanished with no reason supplied as to why.

Joni impressed the Hudsons when he told them that he and his brother knew who they were. Not necessarily by name, but by an incident they recalled. Joni suggested that they were either family or friends of the Canadian couple who had been shot at the Hard Rock Cafe a year ago in Nadi. All the Fijian people knew of the cover-up by the police and the military but were rendered harmless to do anything about it. Brent and James nodded their heads in agreement with the Fijian fisherman.

Kona took it from this point. "Your captured friend will never end up at Black Rock Camp. If he were brought to camp, it would expose the crimes committed by the military men a year ago. The people responsible can't allow that to happen. The military, according to local knowledge, has a concrete structure in the jungle on armed forces land. No entry is allowed by the local people. Legend goes that the purpose of this secret jail is to quietly get rid of prisoners that they want to be sure will never be found again. Interrogations and torture are also involved. The tower is high, and the lowest of three jail cells is located 30 meters in the air. Security around this tower is minimal. The tower has an unguarded door at the base of the structure."

The Hudsons, to a man, furrowed their foreheads wondering why that was.

Kona was quick with the answer. "The jail cells are locked with a combination number pad. The only way to enter is to know the intricate numbering sequence. The pad is wired into a sophisticated explosive charge designed to violently detonate with one wrong move. If the bomb were triggered, the rescuer is killed. Further, the prisoner, due to the shock wave created by the explosion, is blown out the open fourth wall to his death."

Daniel spoke, "They built a tower with only three sides?"

Kona answered, "Yes."

Joni summed up the entire story line by saying, "It's called Rapunzel's Tower after the girl with impossibly long hair who lived alone in a tower."

64

RAPUNZEL'S TOWER

BRENT HAD HEARD enough. He knew that time was of the essence. Like sand sifting through an hourglass, he knew that Mike's life was draining away with every grain of sand that succumbed to gravity. He asked the Patel brothers which one of them knew the whereabouts of Rapunzel's Tower. They both knew, but Brent selected Kona simply because he looked more weatherworn and seasoned to the rigors of a hard life.

Brent was happy to see that Kona was as delicate in the bush as he was. Brent was just about to take a mud bath to ward off some mosquitos, but Kona stopped him.

He said, "No need to get all dirty with a cure that only half works when eucalyptus trees grow in the jungle and work beautifully to give us an aura of smell that mossies hate."

Brent ceded to the local knowledge.

They silently crept up to where they had a good vantage

point of the entire concrete structure. It really did look very primitive, but it served the military's purposes. Brent was observing through his binoculars when he heard the unmistakable cries of his youngest son screaming out in pain. It was hard for a father to bear.

Kona put his hand on Brent's back as they both lay on their stomachs. It was a gesture of compassion for the father who had to listen to the torture of a family member. This evil process lasted for over an hour. Then, as quick as it started, it stopped.

Brent didn't know if his son was alive or dead. He buried his head in the dirt, praying whichever way it was that God showed his son mercy.

When they retreated, Kona stopped Brent and told him that his son was most likely still alive and had passed out over the amount of pain he had been enduring. If Mike had died, they would have simply kicked his body out the open fourth wall and let the lifeless corpse plummet to the earth below. Both strangers hugged and proceeded back to Dr. Sumner's house.

Before Kona and Brent went in the doctor's front door, they agreed that the others didn't have to know about the screams of pain they'd heard coming from Mike.

Once inside, Brent took the lead in trying to formulate a plan to rescue Mike. His prime idea was already fixed within his mind. Brent needed to know if they had access to utility rope.

Joni immediately stepped up to say that they had a plentiful amount of this rope because it was needed for their fishing nets.

The retired firefighter took a moment and then told the

rest of the group what the plan was going to be. He started out by saying that Mike was no Rapunzel; in fact, his hair was rather short. The utility rope was going to double as Rapunzel's hair. Brent had spied a water tower on the roof. The piping looked strong enough to hold a man's weight. In this case, it would have to hold the weight of two men. He was going to enter the cement structure and head right to the roof. There, he was going to make himself a firefighter's self-rescue seat. He was going to also tie the other rope to this pipe. This would eventually become Mike's rescue seat. Brent was then going to rappel down to Mike's jail cell. There, they were both going to rappel the rest of the way down until they set foot on land. The last thing he said was that Daniel, James, and Dr. Sumner would protect the perimeter. Brent gave special instructions to the doctor to bring medical supplies that might be needed for Mike's wounds.

The two brothers were back in an hour with the utility rope. Brent tested it and it would suffice. The actual rescue would take place under the cover of darkness. The reasons were obvious. Time was important, and Brent was quietly dying inside and worried that he wouldn't be in time to save his son. He prayed to Laura to protect their baby for just a little while longer. Brent thanked the two brothers, Joni and Kona, for their help and told them that they could go home.

James peeled off another $1,000, which added to the substantial amount of money they already had and thanked them for a job well-done.

The brothers gracefully accepted the money and left.

65

THE RESCUE

BRENT'S ENTIRE TEAM was bathed in eucalyptus oil. The ground crew took up their positions and left Rapunzel's Tower to Brent. The retired firefighter trudged his way up the length of two football fields of stairs. He easily broke the lock of the roof hatch and got access to the pipes of the water tower. Everything looked good. He tied the knots that were second nature to him from many years on the fire department. He looked down and let the slack in the rope fall first. Then he grabbed the taut rope coming from the pipes and lowered himself to Mike's cell.

He popped into the open fourth wall and scared the shit out of his son. Mike was lying down, resting. The father and son embraced for what seemed to be forever. Brent broke the hug when he said it was time to go. He asked his son if he had ever rappelled before, and his reply back was in the affirmative. Brent smiled and said that he hadn't rappelled like they were about to do, ever! The father called it strong-arm rappelling. If your arms were strong, you might survive; if not, you perish.

Brent made his son the rescue seat. Mike said that it might not work because they'd used a battery-powered cow prod on him, and his entire genital area was swollen.

Brent lightened the mood when he said, "Niki would surely like that, but for right now, we go, pain and all." The wily, old vet told his son which rope he had to grab. He hammered it home by saying that the wrong one would turn the rappelling into a bungee jump, and he couldn't vouch for the elasticity of the ground. Out of Rapunzel's Tower they went and smoothly traversed all obstacles until they were on level ground.

Once on the ground, Dr. Sumner went to attend to Mike. He had cuts and abrasions on his face. The doctor went to check Mike's groin. He got a quick rebuke when Mike let him know that he would be killed if he went anywhere near his nuts.

They looked around and saw James and Daniel. They had been quietly busy handling their own responsibilities. Following them were two tied soldiers, muzzled and with bags over their heads. Granted, their prisoners were inebriated but they had still been rendered harmless to the Hudson operation.

They tied the soldiers to a tree, and the successful operation came to a completion. The Hudsons would return to the doctor's safe house and give Mike all of one night to recuperate.

James, asked him, "What did you do when they were torturing you?"

Mike replied, "I screamed, the Beastie Boys song "No Sleep Till Brooklyn" at the top of my lungs

They both laughed.

The Hudsons' presence was not a secret anymore, and things had to happen quickly. The Fijian military was proving to be a more than adequate enemy.

Brent put Captain Etak Wainiqolo back on the menu.

66

SIDEBAR

MAJOR LALA TAVAI met with Superintendent Jeet Singh at police headquarters in Nadi. Tavai informed Singh about the simultaneous raids and the success of capturing Mike Hudson. The major bragged that they had him in Rapunzel's Tower. He bragged to Singh that the tower was impregnable and that he had put the fear of God into the rest of the foreign adversaries.

Superintendent Jeet Singh looked at Major Lala Tavai like he was an idiot. He informed Lala that, the Hudson's are not on the run, the Hudsons would never leave anyone behind. The police superintendent reminded Lala that, so far, more of his men had died at the hands of the Hudsons than the Hudsons at the hands of Major Lala Tavai.

Lala reluctantly agreed. He told Singh that it would not be necessary to put guards at the tower. He would just put more around the surrounding perimeter. Lala got up and left.

Singh just shook his head in disbelief. Something had to be done to protect Etak from the Hudson's. Singh quietly assigned a protection detail consisting of four men to safeguard Captain Etak Wainiqolo.

67

Hardware Store

BRENT CLOSED HIS eyes and visualized walking through Etak's yard and the security systems employed by his target. He remembered the pool in the backyard and the utility shed where the pool equipment was stored. Brent was saying the same four words over and over, "House, yard, pool, shed."

After multiple times saying this chant out loud, his eyes opened wide. Brent's back bolted away from the back of the sofa. His eyes stared straight ahead as his mind began formulating his plan. One by one, Brent checked off and built upon each section of the plan. At the end of it all, the conception of his plan was confirmed by logic. His plan should have a great chance to succeed. He talked to Mike.

His youngest son let him know that he was fit and able for their next mission. He also told his dad it had better be soon.

Brent told him and the others to hold tight at the safe

house and that he would be back shortly. Brent picked up Dr. Sumner's vehicle keys, got into the car, and headed for Port Denarau. It was there that he would get the ingredients to complete his recipe to kill Captain Etak Wainiqolo.

Brent's first stop was no surprise; it was the Denarau hardware store. On the way, he noticed an increased police presence. Less than a kilometer to the hardware store, he witnessed several cars pulled over at the side of the road. The drivers were being asked for their paperwork by the Nadi police. What stuck out like a sore thumb was that every driver was white and male. They were all driving in their shiny rental cars. Brent took the safety off his pistol and laid it on his lap. He was not going to go down without a fight, especially knowing what the military had tried to do to Mike. By the grace of God, all the police officers were busy, and he was able to drive right past the spot check.

Brent parked outside the hardware store. Inside, he found the automotive section and picked up one of the ingredients that he needed. Then he went off to the sports and recreation section and another ingredient was added to his shopping cart. The last thing he needed was a twenty-liter, plastic gas container. After he exited the hardware store, he made a quick stop to get fuel for his vehicle and still more to fill his gas container. Brent then headed back out of Port Denarau and toward Captain Etak Wainiqolo's home.

68

ETAK'S HOUSE

MIKE SHADOWED HIS father until it became absolutely clear what his destination was. Mike allowed himself a moment of triumph for predicting his father's moves.

He phoned the safe house and got the Hudson crew to meet him at a designated location. They were to be armed with pistols and knives. When the team was assembled, Mike confirmed that Captain Etak Wainiqolo was the target.

Brent was very careful to discreetly park his vehicle out of sight. His next obstacle was to avoid the cameras at the front of the house. He elected to enter Etak's property on the same side as the infrared alarm system.

He left the ingredients to complete his mission temporarily hidden in the palm trees. Brent rendered harmless the infrared alarm system, but that was as far as he went. He didn't know if the inside of the house was also alarmed. Brent would wait for Etak to return home and allow him to disengage any alarms himself. He looked at his watch and estimated that Etak wouldn't be home for half an hour. Brent elected to wait in the scrub forest behind the house. The members of the Hudson crew were also in place. Daniel and James could see Brent's hiding location from their positions in the back jungle.

Sunset had long passed; it was time for the entire team to switch to night-vision goggles. The team's senses were on high alert. The team knew that if security assigned to Etak did exist, deadly hostilities would likely occur.

Etak turned the corner and headed down the dirt road that led to his house. Etak had not thought too much more about the words of Major Lala Tavai in previous conversations. He was sure the Hudsons would be long gone. Who would stand up to the Fijian military? Pulling into his driveway, all Etak could think about was the oppressive heat and getting out of his uniform. He sauntered up to his front door, opened it, and disarmed the alarm system. Etak went upstairs, undressed, and took a cool shower.

Brent saw lights coming down the dirt road. He listened and, sure enough, the car pulled into Etak's driveway. Under the cloak of darkness was Brent's opportunity to advance his position from the scrub jungle to the thick Fijian fire hedge at the back of the house, where he had a clear view through the patio doors. He watched as Etak entered the front door. The first thing Etak did was turn the alarm off. He then switched on the lights. He bent down to take off his shoes, then proceeded upstairs.

Brent rushed to the back patio door. From his days in the fire department, he'd learned a trick for how to remove a glass patio entry door from its tracks. He put both his hands on the outside aluminum trim, just below the locking mechanism. He then moved the entire door up and down within the aluminum casing at a rapid rate. The locking mechanism flipped to the off position, and now egress into the house was available.

Brent quietly entered the back of the house. He pulled the curtains slowly closed to protect himself from being seen from the outside. He pulled his gun and put himself in position to surprise Etak. The last thing Brent did was remove several plastic zip ties from his pockets.

69

THE DANCE OF DEATH

OUTSIDE, ANOTHER DEADLY game was about to start. Special Forces Dr. Alec Sumner was the first to see a vehicle coming toward them on the dirt road. The car turned into Etak's driveway, and Dr. Sumner identified the driver as Captain Etak Wainiqolo. Once Etak was in the house, Dr. Sumner watched the main floor light come on and, shortly after that, lights on the second floor illuminated the windows. Daniel reported that the Golden Goose had changed position to a closer vantage point.

Once the light on the top floor was turned on, the Golden Goose broke through the back patio door and was in the house. Daniel reported that his sight line was gone because the patio door curtains were pulled close. Dr. Sumner reported that an additional vehicle was coming their way on the dirt road. He also informed his team that a second car, which had been directly behind the first car, appeared to have continued straight ahead on the paved road. "Heads up," reported Dr. Sumner. He went on to say that the car on the dirt road contained two occupants.

The car parked, and the engine and lights on their vehicle were turned off. It appeared that the new arrivals were on guard duty.

Mike had been correct again in his assumption that Captain Etak Wainiqolo would also have a four-sided security detail. Mike quietly radioed his team and let them know that this likely meant there were another two protectors not yet accounted for.

It didn't take long after the lead car parked on the dirt road for James to break the silence. He reported the addition of a second vehicle stopped on the paved road.

Mike issued rapid-fire commands. "Doc, you are to eliminate the two targets in the car on the dirt road. James and Daniel, can you carry out a silent kill on the occupants of the second vehicle?" Mike got a query back that he dreaded answering; both of them inquired about what a silent kill was.

Mike replied in a loud whisper, "Use your knives." Mike stayed focused on the Golden Goose.

Doc opted to use the darkness to cloak his advance on the vehicle. His footwear allowed him to be very stealthy while using the ditch as the route best suited to achieve his goals. His first objective was to get to the back trunk area of the vehicle. Once this was accomplished, he then proceeded to the driver's-side window to take out the driver first. If he eliminated the passenger before the driver, the possibility of the horn being activated greatly increased. Silently, Doc cocked his gun, checked to make sure his silencer was tight, stood up, and put one bullet in the driver's head. He used hollow-point bullets so that he would not have to shoot more than once. In a nanosecond, he changed his target to the passenger and shot at his torso three times. Hitting body mass was the best way to incapacitate the farthest target. The special forces soldier paused for three seconds to confirm his targets were dead. Then he put one more bullet into the driver's and the passenger's heads. In effect, it was to kill them twice.

James and Daniel waited, camouflaged within the trees, surrounded by darkness and a moonless night. Etak's last two guards were taking up their positions in the rear of the house. It had been them who had drawn the first watch in an outside position with the mosquitos for company. They took solace in the knowledge that after four hours, they would change positions with the two lucky guys out front sitting in a nice, comfortable car.

James took a step that snapped a dry twig. He might as well have banged cymbals, as the sound traveled like a crescendo at the end of an epic symphony. Now all four combatants were aware that something other than themselves was in the bush.

Perhaps it was an animal? Perhaps it was not?

Etak's guards had guns in hand as they half stepped their way quietly to their posts.

James was ready to pounce and could see Daniel with his night-vision goggles. He gave the silent order with his hand, and they both attacked the two guards. James sunk his serrated knife blade into the abdomen of his target. He then swiftly employed an upward motion of the knife, and it was life over for his adversary.

Simultaneously, Daniel ambushed his target. He plunged his knife into the midsection of his target but, before he could give a deadly swift yank upward, the target got off a shot that penetrated his torso. Daniel had been shot.

James rushed to assist his husband by stabbing the target in the back. This severed his spinal cord, and down to the ground the quarry fell. James finished the task at hand by slitting his throat from ear to ear.

Both of Etak's guards at the rear of the house were eliminated, and James was attending to Daniel's gunshot wound.

Daniel was bleeding, but it looked like he would survive the injury.

James couldn't be sure but he thought that the bullet must not have come from a very powerful gun. He reported this to his brother, Mike, and his orders were to take Daniel to the doctor's safe house and stay with him. Mike informed James that he, Doc, and their father would join them when this mission was complete.

70

BRENT AND ETAK'S REUNION

BRENT WAITED FOR Etak to come back downstairs after
his shower. Brent heard a gunshot that seemed to come from
somewhere out back of the house. He wondered if someone
was poaching game at night.

Etak also heard the gunshot. He was alarmed but not panicked. He knew his security system would warn him about tres-
passers. He felt safe, so he would just go downstairs and rearm
his interior security system. Etak was on the last stair when a
voice broke the stillness.

"Touch that alarm and I'll kill you, motherfucker." Brent
had his gun sharply focused on Etak's torso. Brent ordered Etak
into the living room and told him to bring a kitchen chair with
him. Brent got him to sit on the chair.

Etak looked at Brent with eyes that knew everything Major
Lala Tavai had suspected about the deaths of Tui and Josefa was

true. Etak still couldn't believe this one family from a country half the world away could get the drop on three of Fiji's finest military men.

Brent threw Etak four plastic zip ties. Brent instructed him to handcuff his own ankles to the legs of the chair.

Etak knew to put one zip tie around each ankle and the third was to link the first two.

Brent instructed him to make sure he put the third zip tie around the horizontal spindle.

Etak started pleading for his life, saying things like "Sorry. Forgive me." He insisted that he had not been in his right mind the night of the unfortunate event.

Brent pretended that he cared and let on that he knew it was Major Lala Tavai who had put the bullet in his wife's head. Brent asked Captain Etak Wainiqolo, "How much money do you have available right now?"

Etak was optimistic it might be possible to pay his way out of this predicament. Etak told Brent, "Name your price."

Brent instructed his prisoner to take a plastic zip tie, put it around his wrist and secure his wrist to the arm of the chair. Brent made sure to spell out it was Etak's right hand he wanted to be tied.

Etak accomplished this and watched Brent step forward to fasten his left hand securely at his wrist and around the chair armrest.

Brent stood back, picked his gun up off the coffee table, and put it back in his belt. He was confident that Etak was secure.

Etak continued to try and talk himself out of harm's way.

Brent unsettled Etak when he excused himself and left through the back patio door. Etak was given a ray of hope, or so he thought. He believed his infrared alarm system would be activated by Brent and send alarm bells through the night air and activate a silent alarm at Nadi Police Department. Etak was surprised when Brent re-entered the house.

Brent tossed the key to activate or deactivate the infrared alarm system on Etak's lap. Brent said, "Are you looking for this?"

Etak sensed he was not dealing with an uneducated bumpkin. Rather, he was face-to-face with a very shrewd man. Etak started to worry more about his well-being. He again reverted to sweet talk and promises of riches.

Brent, for his part, played right along with Etak's pleading. Brent walked over to Etak and nonchalantly doused him with twenty liters of gas.

Etak sputtered and stammered and kept his eyes closed to try and keep them from burning.

Brent played a very compassionate jailer. He got a dish towel from the kitchen and wiped Etak's face and eyes.

Etak thanked him and tried a different tact on the same approach. He tried to play to Brent's better angels but that wasn't close to being successful. He decided to revert to offering money for his life.

Brent thought for a moment. He looked Captain Etak Wainiqolo in the eyes, smiled, and said, "I have a deal for you. I will not light the gasoline. If you sit in this chair the entire night, I will inform you as to the amount of ransom I want."

Etak was thankful that his life was going to be spared.

Brent smiled and thought to himself, "There's the lob ball." Brent retrieved the bag of items he'd left in the kitchen. He came back in and checked the plastic zip ties on Etak's wrists. He added to them and told Etak it was because the gasoline might eat away at the plastic during the night. He then squatted down and refastened Etak's ankles. At the same time, he took a container of calcium hypochlorite, which was commonly used in chlorine. The same ingredient was used in backyard pools. Brent then took the cap off the container of brake fluid. He waited to pour it onto the chlorine crystals. Brent, still crouching, asked Etak, "How sorry are you that you caused my wife's death and shot me in the back?"

Etak went to great lengths, including crying like a baby, to tell Brent just how horrible he felt about what he had done.

Brent listened and finally said, "I'm a Christian man. I'll see you in the morning."

Etak thanked him truly from the bottom of his heart.

Brent poured the brake fluid onto the chlorine and left through the back patio door without saying another word. He looked at his watch as he returned to his hidden vehicle. One minute went past and then a huge whoosh sounded, followed by the agonizingly piercing screams of Captain Etak Wainiqolo.

Brent had known that a flash fire would ensue if he mixed calcium hypochlorite and brake fluid. Brent had estimated that once he mixed the two, he'd have about a minute to clear the house. Sure enough, one minute, six seconds in total was all it had taken to ignite his mixture, which burned extremely hot. The added attraction was that this flame would ignite the vapors of the gasoline, and another flash fire would occur. The two fires combined would make sure that Captain Etak Wainiqolo endured a horrendously painful death.

Brent started the old Ford and said to himself, "And that's hardball."

Driving away from Etak's house, Brent could see the glow of the fire in the rearview mirror. He wondered just how much of the house would burn before the Nadi Fire Department would be able to extinguish the flames. One thing he did know was that Captain Etak Wainiqolo, the son of a bitch who was responsible for starting the misery that Brent was enduring, was now dead.

Brent was about halfway to the safe house when he heard sirens. The sound was coming toward him. Brent wondered if he was going to come across fire trucks and police cars before he reached the safe house. He was finally relieved when his car was parked in the driveway, and he was safely tucked away inside the house.

Brent sat down at the kitchen table and poured himself a drink. He was processing and manipulating data that was roaming in his head. It occurred to him that no one else seemed to be at the safe house. He got up to investigate. Brent went into a bedroom and found Daniel wounded and lying on the bed. James was in a chair beside him, worrying for his loved one and waiting for the impending return of the rest of the Hudson gang.

A vehicle was coming up the driveway. Brent scurried and found a semiautomatic rifle. The front door opened, and in stepped Mike and Dr. Sumner rushed immediately to tend to Daniel's wound.

Mike and his father sat down and discussed the two-phase operation that had taken place at Etak's house. Mike suggested that his father put to an end, once and for all, his rogue one-trick-pony show.

Dr. Sumner and James came back out after attending to Daniel. Dr. Sumner reported that the bullet might as well have come from a pellet gun for all the damage the bullet had done. Daniel was going to be fine, and no organs were affected. A nice bandage around his waist and, in a few days, he would be fine.

71

MAJOR LALA TAVAI
ON THE MENU

MIKE THOUGHT HE would give the group some of his own thoughts. He stated that the weaponry they were using would change from guns and knives to military-grade automatic machine guns. These would only be used by himself and Doc Sumner. Mike told Brent that he and James would be using AK-47 semi-automatics. Mike knew that there was a world of hurt between automatic and semiautomatic. Mike was comfortable with this because he knew his dad was an experienced hunter. James was a wild card, but Mike had to put his trust in him being at least adequate with a rifle.

His dad was used to one pull of the trigger giving him one bullet out of the business end of the semi-automatic. An automatic was compared to a Machine Gun: One pull of the trigger held long enough would empty the chamber and the rest of the reserve bullets in the metal clip.

It was time to discuss the discrepancy between them and the military in terms of both manpower and military assets. Mike suggested that their element of surprise was over. They were onto Brent and his family being in Fiji after Captain Etak Wainiqolo's death.

Part two of Mike's discussion involved the protection that would surround Major Lala Tavai. Mike suggested that the major's movements would be limited to home, work, and then back home until the threat against him was terminated. Mike made sure that everyone knew that the meaning of terminated was the elimination of all those who sat in this crowded kitchen. He then opened the discussion to suggestions on how to attack their very sizable problem.

All suggestions were in, with some good and some bad.

It was now Brent's turn to give his two cents' worth. Brent started with a story. He stated, "To me, this is like a hunt. It is no different than trying to stalk an animal in a forest." Brent used the example of a deer. "It lives a basic life, somewhat like the limited day-to-day movements that Major Lala Tavai now does. The deer goes from its bed and travels to its feeding area and then vice versa. If the deer is not bothered during its travel stage, it will keep relatively to the same route. The deer is most alert when it's on the move, and all its defensive shields are operational. Trying to take out Lala when he's on the move is not the best of choices."

Brent went into comparing deer with Major Lala Tavai in respect to feeding and bedding areas. "In the feeding area, the deer lowers its guard in very short spurts. When its head is removing the food from the source, the senses are lowered, but when it's chewing, the radar is back up. Blue jays are the tattletales of the forest and warn the deer of intruders." Brent's thinking, as it applied to Major Lala Tavai, was that "The feeding area in this case is the major's actual home. He also has blue jays in the form of armed guards to protect him."

Brent suggested, "Major Lala Tavai's true bedding area is Black Rock Camp. A deer will sneak into its bedding place and lie down with relative comfort. Yes, the deer will always be somewhat alert to its surroundings. However, it's definitely less alarmed knowing it's not moving around attracting predators; plus it has the cover of the forest to protect itself. If the cover breaks down, then the deer has already situated itself with a predetermined escape route away from the impending invader.

"There is only one scenario where the deer is extremely vulnerable. Just before the deer can lie down, it has to prepare the bed. The deer becomes occupied with this chore; thus, its guard is down as much as it will ever be." Brent looked at the others and confidently stated that "It's much the same with Major Lala Tavai. Once inside Black Rock Camp, he is nested and as safe as he will ever be. Just like the deer making its bed, Lala must enter through the guard station. His vehicle has to stop to let the guards manually raise the security arm. The two military guards are complacent in this task that they have been performing forever. Major Lala Tavai's security detail are on motorbikes. When everything ahead or behind them is stopped, they have to put a foot down to balance their bikes. They, too, are most vulnerable at this point. This is when we hit."

Mike thoroughly endorsed this idea but suggested small alterations and made it a plan. Most importantly, Brent agreed with Mike's finalization of his thoughts but still agonized over putting his two boys in harm's way. Mike ended the meeting at around 4 am.

Zero hour would be at 6 am. the following day. This would give Mike and Brent time to do a critical assessment of all facets of the mission. At the same time, it would selfishly give the Hudsons what may be their last day with family.

72

FIJIAN ROMAN CANDLE

THE QUIETNESS OF the night was broken by the sound of sirens. The Nadi Fire Department was responding to a house fire. The owner of this dwelling was Etak Wainiqolo. The first fire truck on the scene immediately called dispatch to activate a second alarm to this response. This would give the first arriving crew additional assistance with the fire. The back half of the house was already fully engulfed in fire.

Superintendent Jeet Singh's telephone rang.

It was the night sergeant at the police station. He was calling to inform Jeet that two people had been found at the front of the house that was on fire. They were deceased and sitting in a vehicle. The sergeant indicated that they had been shot. The victims had initially been found by firefighters.

Superintendent Jeet Singh cringed as he asked the sergeant for the address of the fire. In his heart, he already knew that it was Etak's house.

The sergeant only confirmed Jeet's thinking. The sergeant let his boss know that two police cars were en route to the address.

Jeet informed the night sergeant that he would also be attending this response. Superintendent Jeet Singh feared his worst possible nightmare was coming true. All the Hudsons were still alive and proceeding with their plan to erase everyone involved in the death of Laura Hudson. Nobody had to inform Jeet that Etak's body was likely right in the middle of this house fire.

When Superintendent Jeet Singh arrived at Etak's house, he immediately walked over to examine the murder scene. Jeet, with his own eyes, confirmed the two deceased victims were two of his police officers.

He was met by the coroner, who reported that these two officers had already been dead when the felon or felons had chosen to, in effect, execute them again.

Jeet knew exactly what the coroner meant. This homicide had either been committed by someone in a rage of hate or it had been surgically done by a well-trained assassin. Jeet amassed all of his subordinate officers at this response and told them to spread out and search the area. He assigned two officers to the rear of the dwelling as well. They were to begin their search in the scrub grass and small woods behind the premises. Superintendent Jeet Singh didn't have to wait long before an excited officer called him on his portable radio.

The officer excitedly said, "We found them. We found them. They're both dead. Looks like they were stabbed." He went on to indicate their location.

Superintendent Jeet Singh hustled to their locale, as he wanted to see with his own eyes the method employed to kill his men. Jeet went hands-on with the physical investigation of the two dead bodies. He was particularly interested in the wounds themselves. Superintendent Jeet Singh was able to confirm what he had always suspected. The knives had been serrated. They had been thrust straight into the bodies. Once buried, a sharp upward motion had then been employed, at least to one of his men. The wounds had been delivered by a trained killer or killers.

He was informed that one of his dead officers had managed to get a shot off.

Jeet wondered if maybe one of the perpetrators had received a gunshot wound. Superintendent Jeet Singh surmised that he was dealing with well-trained operatives. He estimated that there were between three and at most five enemy combatants. He addressed the officers on the scene once again. Jeet then separated the officer in charge of this response from the others. Jeet left explicit orders for that officer to send the incident response report directly to him and no one else.

Superintendent Jeet Singh returned to his unmarked vehicle and departed the scene. He pounded his steering wheel in anger. His entire undercover protection detail for Etak was eliminated.

72

JEET AND LALA
MEET LATE AT NIGHT

SUPERINTENDENT JEET SINGH looked at his watch and, even though it was after midnight, he decided to drive straight over to Major Lala Tavai's compound. Jeet had concerns, not just about Brent Hudson and his crew, but also about how he and Lala were going to handle all the logistics. More had happened about a year ago than just the murder of Laura Hudson and the shooting of her husband, Brent. The cover-up of this event was going to rear its ugly head again. They had been able to censor the media last time, but all bets would be off on the negative press reporting this time.

Jeet entered the compound through the guarded gate and was met at the front door by Lala. The two of them settled into the sitting room.

Before they could begin their conversation, a message was heard over Superintendent Jeet Singh's portable radio. The message was that an unidentified adult male had been found deceased in the dwelling.

Jeet knew it must be Etak. Superintendent Jeet Singh opened the conversation by retelling the series of events that had happened in and around Etak's house.

As Major Lala Tavai listened, the blood in his face was physically draining. He looked ashen. His eyes resembled those of a lifeless person. His pupils looked dilated and fixed. He was a dead man walking. By the time Superintendent Jeet Singh finished recounting the events of the night, Lala was in a cold sweat.

Major Lala Tavai entered the conversation with what he thought was a bona fide plan. He suggested that they shut down all of Nadi, including Port Denarau. They would employ numerous spot checks, effectively monitoring all travel in the area. They would secure all other modes of transportation including land, water, and air. They would check all hospitals for anyone who had been admitted with a gunshot wound. Major Lala Tavai told Superintendent Jeet Singh that, between the police and the military, these foreigners absolutely would be caught or killed. Lala told Jeet that the military would double the resources of the police to create a circular spiderweb. "There will be no escape for the Hudsons!" Lala roared.

Superintendent Jeet Singh gave Major Lala Tavai a sarcastic look and rose from his chair. He went and looked out the window. Jeet was trying to lower his blood pressure and formulate a response to Lala. Jeet took a moment and just stared out into the darkness. He wondered how in the hell he'd even gotten involved in this charade. Superintendent Jeet Singh turned and faced Lala and began his cautionary tale.

He told Lala, "Take your mind back to the night you called me asking for help." Jeet wanted Lala to revisit the drunken phone call that they'd had. Jeet asked Lala to "Think back to the skirmish that happened at the Hard Rock Cafe, and the two tourists you stated were likely dead because of it." Jeet looked Lala right in the eyes. "Your story never seemed to add up." Jeet couldn't equate a minor occurrence being met with such a level of deadly force. Jeet told Lala, "I told you this at the time."

Nonetheless, the two men had history.

Both Jeet and Lala had been recruited by the military and had worked side by side with each other. They'd eventually gone their separate ways but remained friends. Jeet had chosen a police career and had had great success. Equally, Lala had flourished in the military. Both men had risen to the top of their fields.

Jeet asked Lala to remember the steps they had taken to keep their crimes from being detected. Way back then, the police incident report had been produced and handed directly to Superintendent Jeet Singh. Jeet had put this report under lock and key. The media, including TV and print, had been nosing around. They had been given information from someone who had been working at the Hard Rock Cafe that night. Superintendent Jeet Singh had been able to deflect and cast aspersions on that Hard Rock Cafe employee. Jeet said he'd ruined the young man, all in the attempt to keep what Major Lala Tavai had done out of the focus of the general public. Jeet told his friend Lala that they had not been able to control the Internet then, and they wouldn't be able to control the

Internet this time either. In fact, conspiracy theorists were already saying Brent Hudson and his boys were back in Fiji. They were touting them as a crack commando crew serving justice to those who'd killed their family member.

Major Lala Tavai listened for as long as he was going to. He told Superintendent Jeet Singh, "You are in this as deep as I am, so never mind lecturing me. What the fuck are we going to do about this crew we're facing?"

Jeet fired back, "we are going to do nothing! My police force is out of this. If anyone, including the press, makes inquiries about this investigation, all I'm going to tell them is that everything is on the table. This investigation will lead us to wherever the facts dictate."

The two old friends laid both their cards and friendship on the table.

Major Lala Tavai didn't like the hand he had just been dealt. He looked at his old friend and replied, "Jeet, can you at least suppress the police report on your men's homicide investigations?"

Superintendent Jeet Singh nodded his head in agreement.

It was no secret to either of them that the possibility of this powder keg blowing up in their faces was very real. They knew they had to come up with both an attack on Hudson and his crew and a defense against the same obviously capable crew. Superintendent Jeet Singh would carry on with his murder investigations in the hopes of perhaps snaring some or all of the Hudsons within that net. He would elevate his police presence in the Nadi area, but not to a level that would cause undue attention to his management of these investigations.

Major Lala Tavai would have to take care of himself. The major was reminded by Jeet that he oversaw the entire military at Black Rock Camp. Lala elected to flood the zone with his military forces in Nadi and the surrounding area. He would take over the vehicle spot checks. Lala would have roving military vehicles to enhance his chances of discovering backstreet movements by his enemies. Lala would increase the security at his compound and limit his own movements between his home and Black Rock Camp. Last, Major Lala Tavai would add two more security personnel to his motorcade. That would mean he would have three motorcycles in front of his car and three in the rear.

Daylight was just right around the corner, so Superintendent Jeet Singh and Major Lala Tavai decided to end their meeting. Sleep would be limited, as they both agreed that keeping the same routines was essential. That meant they would go to work for the start of their shifts.

73

HUDSONS' DAY OFF

THE HUDSONS SPENT the day in introspection. They all
knew that tomorrow might be their last day on this earth. They
all handled it in different ways. Those who had loved ones and
family stole away and made one last phone call.

James and Daniel tried to get in touch with their son,
Brady. They finally tracked him down at his aunt Niki's house.
It seemed he had been there for a few days. Secretly, they were
glad that Niki had taken it upon herself to scoop up Brady and
put him under her wing. They were not so happy about the
earful they received from Niki about their cloak and dagger
operation. James and Daniel did have a short, happy-go-lucky
call with their son, Brady. They told him that they would be
home in a couple of days. When they hung up the phone,
they embraced each other. It had been a tough call for them,

and all Brady had wanted to do was get off the telephone to go and play with his cousins.

Mike made his phone call to Niki. Niki entertained the small talk from her husband and then put both of their children on to say hello to their dad. After the children were finished, they left to continue playing games in the basement. Niki got back on the phone and was not going to be entertained any longer. She knew the why and where of Mike's mission.

Niki didn't chastise Mike for lying to her. She knew that wasn't the first lie that Mike had told her. Niki realized that sometimes Mike had to downplay events so she wouldn't become an emotional cripple. Niki let Mike know that she loved him very much and told him to make sure he returned home to her. She subtly let Mike know that she knew all and then she requested to speak to his father.

Mike knew the gig was up.

Brent said "Hello," and Niki let him know about his grandchildren and how much they missed him. Brent said that he missed them as well.

Niki ended the conversation by urging Brent to take care of his sons and bring everyone back home safely.

Brent hung up and immediately sat down on a chair. He looked up at Mike with watery eyes and inquired, "How do they know?"

74

THINGS GET SERIOUS

THE SUN WAS starting to set on another blistering day in Fiji. Under different circumstances, Mike thought he could enjoy a week or two on one of Fiji's many islands.

Special Forces Dr. Alex Sumner called Mike on his portable radio. He informed Mike that Major Lala Tavai was safely back in his compound. Doc reported that the major had picked up another two security personnel to add to his entourage. There were now three motorcycles in front of Major Lala Tavai's vehicle and three behind.

Mike asked his dad if the major had still left home to report to work at 5:00 a.m. and, more importantly, had he entered through the guard gate at 5:45 a.m.

Brent's answer was in the affirmative.

Mike then instructed Doc to return to the safe house. Once Doc was back at the safe house, Mike left to see with his own eyes the situation at Black Rock Camp and Major Lala Tavai's compound. While driving, he did observe the elevated presence of military vehicles, but he was surprised to see that there were no police spot checks. The guard post into Black Rock Camp was the picture of normality with two men on duty. Major Lala Tavai's compound however was now a fortress, with armed guards surrounding his house, and outside the three-meter walls. Everything was how his father had said it would be. His Ojibwa friends had taught him well. Mike returned to the safe house and slapped the Fiji Times into his father's hands. The headline on the first page read, "House Fire Claims Life."

Brent read the entire article and then told whoever would listen that "The body has yet to be identified, and there is no mention of the four guards being killed." This puzzled Brent.

Mike told his dad to reflect on how his attack and Laura's murder had been covered up. Then he said, "The same is happening this time."

Daniel, the quiet one, opened his laptop and began talking to the group. He cited that the Internet was well aware of what was happening. Daniel told Brent that people knew of his counterattack against the military and that the topic was trending. He smiled at his father-in-law when he said, "You are the Canadian James Bond."

The kitchen clock read midnight. The entire crew was going to have their last orders given to them by command.

Mike pulled a whiteboard from behind the dresser in his bedroom. On it was a schematic drawing of the guard post at Black Rock Camp. Everyone in the room had a predetermined location drawn on the big board. Mike's mind flipped between being a brother, brother-in-law, son, and commander. He started with Daniel. Mike asked him how his wound was.

Daniel said, "Good."

Daniel was to go to the crossroads and keep his presence unknown. He was to radio that Major Lala Tavai and his escorts turned left at the crossroads. When Daniel radioed that would give the rest of the unit forty minutes before Lala and his escorts turned into the guard post at Black Rock Camp. Mike instructed his brother-in-law to wait for three minutes and then follow them toward their awaiting trap. Daniel, at the sound of the first shot, was to bring his Humvee up to the entrance of Black Rock Camp. The rest of the Hudson crew would board the vehicle Humvee at this time and head off to Port Denarau.

Mike and Doc would have that amount of time to ambush and silently kill the two sentries assigned to the guard post. Upon the arrival of Major Lala Tavai, Mike would wait until the three lead motorcycles came to a complete stop while waiting for the security arm to go up. Mike would eliminate them and, from that point on, protect the road leading to and from Black Rock Camp. Doc would vacate the guard house position and lie in wait. James would take up his position at the rear. Simultaneously at the sound of the first shot from Mike eliminating the three front motorcycle drivers, James would eliminate the rear three motorcycle drivers.

Once that was accomplished, James would safeguard Daniel the getaway driver. Doc would cripple the engine of the major's car and see to Major Lala Tavai. Brent at the same time would shoot out the visible front and rear tires. This will make sure the car is disabled. He would then eliminate the driver. Doc would use the RPG to first take out the engine compartment and then reload and shoot at the back seat passenger compartment of the vehicle.

Mike said that if all went well, they could execute the

escape plan. "The escape plan will consist of the following. I will enter the front passenger seat of the vehicle that Daniel is driving. Brent will make his way over to the same vehicle and enter the rear passenger side. Doc and James will go to the rear driver's side. Daniel will drive our vehicle to Port Denarau where we will board the speedboat. We will travel by sea to Lautoka. We will pick up our rental car and drive to the Bath Airport. It's about thirty kilometers away either by road or by sea from Nadi." Mike was now prepared to accept questions from his team.

Doc asked, "Is Bath Airport big enough to handle a Learjet? I'm speaking specifically about the length of the runway."

Daniel supplied this answer. He replied, "It is 45 meters long enough, so long enough."

Doc just shook his head and smiled.

It was at this point when Brent asked his son Mike if he could speak to him outside. Once outside in a blanket of darkness, Brent approached Mike to lobby for himself. Brent told Mike that it was he who had come all the way to Fiji to get restitution for his wife and the boys' mother. Brent solemnly said, "It should be me who stops the heartbeat of Major Lala Tavai."

Mike felt for his father, but the commander in him knew what he had to say. Mike looked at his father and said, "Dad, you weren't the only one who came on this mission, and you were never solo in any of your killings. Everyone in that house has contributed to mission success so far. It's my job, Dad, to keep everybody as safe as possible. I'm truly sorry that you won't be the one to kill Major Lala Tavai, but the most important focus of this mission will be accomplished. Major Lala Tavai will be dead, and that's what you really came here to achieve."

Brent was resigned and reluctantly agreed with his son. Brent and Mike returned to the others in the kitchen.

Mike had one more issue he had to discuss in private, and he asked Daniel if he would step outside with him.

Outside, Daniel was all ears.

Mike asked him if his connections in Fiji could attain four wooden caskets and load them on the Learjet in Bath. Mike spoke further with eternal hope that "We probably won't need them, but they're for a just-in-case scenario."

Daniel implied it would be done within the hour.

Mike shook his head with a sense of wonder. He had a new-found respect for the resourcefulness of his brother-in-law.

Daniel had no desire to carry on this conversation any further.

When Daniel and Mike went back inside, Mike again took command. He stated, for his last order of the night, that everyone would need to remember to stay quiet while he and Doc executed their mission to take out the guard post. Mike looked around the room with pride. Then he headed for his bedroom. Before he closed the door, he looked back at the kitchen and said, "Lights on at 3:00 a.m."

No one slept that night. It was a time to think of family and their own personal well-being. Deep in each of their sub-conscious minds was the fear of the mission possibly going bad.

Each prayed to the big guy upstairs that if things did go bad, "Please don't let it be me who fucks up."

75

MAY GOD HELP US ALL

GUNS WERE CLEANED and ready to hand out. James thought to himself that the combined amount of ammo that each shooter had available could start a war.

That was when Mike tossed Daniel an unregistered Glock handgun.

Daniel sarcastically inquired, "What am I supposed to do with this?"

Mike shot back, "Bake a cake."

Everyone piled into the Humvee and headed toward Black Rock Camp. The ride was uneventful, but Daniel was acutely aware of how loudly his spit echoed when he swallowed. Once in the area of the guardhouse, everyone exited their military-style vehicle and quietly snuck into their positions.

Daniel then drove to his lookout position.

Mike and Doc passed the guardhouse but didn't see any

sentries. They both reasoned that the soldiers were asleep in the guardhouse. They got in position and waited.

Everybody waited.

The world was waking up to greet the dawn. The sound of roosters boasting about their whereabouts could be heard throughout the Nadi area. It was going to be another hot and humid day.

Mike again thought that Fiji was really a beautiful country. It was just so unfortunate that they were experiencing such an ugly situation. He prayed that no one on his team would be injured or killed. Mike's thoughts were interrupted by the activation of his portable radio.

Daniel was on the other end saying that Major Lala Tavai had just turned left onto the road that led to Black Rock Camp. He further reported that the motorcade was as expected. The formation was three armed motorcycles in the front, then Major Lala Tavai's vehicle, which contained a driver and Lala in the back seat. The rear of this procession had three armed motorcycles.

Mike acknowledged his brother-in-law and said, "Don't forget to wait three minutes."

Mike made an all-call to everyone on his team, ordering them to radio silence until he and Doc finished taking over the guard post.

Major Lala Tavai was in the back seat of his chauffeured vehicle working on his phone. His superiors in Suva were on the cell phone inquiring about the conspiracy theories trending on the Internet. They also wanted to know why he'd approved a training exercise in Nadi in respect to searching out and capturing an active terrorist cell. Major Lala Tavai said he would discuss it further once he was in his office. Lala hung up the phone.

Doc and Mike moved stealthily toward the guard post. They opted for revolvers with silencers attached as their weapons of choice over their serrated knives. Security lights shone at the front of the guard station, so their direction of attack would come from the rear. The two could hear the guards in some sort of conversation that indicated they were not alarmed to their presence.

Mike did a finger count to three.

The two of them turned the corner, entered the guardhouse, and simultaneously killed both guards. They hauled the bodies outside and to the rear of the guardhouse. They obscured the corpses in the lush underbrush.

Mike did an all-call stating that they were now in control of the guardhouse.

Daniel was a bundle of nerves. He had been a pencil pusher all his life and now the getaway driver on a covert mission. He could feel the sweat on his hands and body. Daniel drove with his windows fully open. There was no way he was going to miss the sound of the first shot. He also paid particular attention to the speedometer. The last thing he wanted to do was catch up to Major Lala Tavai's motorcade.

"Fuck," Daniel said to himself as headlights shone in his rearview mirror. A military troop transport vehicle was gaining on him. He had decisions to make. It was all about timing. His was shitty. He looked around the Humvee and spied a cardboard box with a dozen grenades contained inside. The only thing he knew about them was from Hollywood movies.

He had to do something to protect the rest of the crew. It was a fine line between handling the problem he had and alerting the convoy of impending danger. Daniel assessed and rapidly decided that doing nothing was not an option. The immigration lawyer took a grenade out of the box. He pulled the pin and immediately threw it backward at the transport vehicle. It took about five seconds to explode. The blast killed a couple of trees but was nowhere near his intended target.

He did get the attention of the military transport. Rapid gunfire erupted with all muzzles aimed at Daniel's Humvee. Bullets were impacting everywhere on his vehicle. Daniel was crouched over, trying to be as small as possible. He knew this couldn't last long. He would be dead in no time. He grabbed another grenade and pulled the pin, but this time he counted to three before he threw it out the window. It was a Hail Mary, and he knew it. Two more seconds later, and after what seemed to be about fifty more bullet holes in the Humvee, the grenade exploded. It was a direct hit. The military transport vehicle turned sideways on the road and began to roll over. It rolled several times and burst into flames. Daniel was surprisingly cool, partly because he was still alive and also because his mission wasn't complete. The others were depending on him.

Mike had lain in wait for unsuspecting targets a thousand times. This was a little different for him. His family was part of the operation, and their lives were in his hands. If they lost their lives under his command, he would never forgive himself. Like any good commander, Mike rolled over and over in his mind the plan he had put forth. He couldn't find any holes or weaknesses. He took solace in the fact that expediency and surprise were his allies.

Brent and Doc had found the best position to carry out their part of the mission. The only negative issue was that it was very uncomfortable. The spot Doc had selected had them laying in a prone position right on top of an ant colony.

Brent thought that at least in the forest when he hunted, he still allowed himself some comfort. He could feel ants crawling over his body. Anywhere he didn't have clothing, he could feel the itch of their little feet. Some stopped to take a bite, but the pain was bearable. Brent had a newfound respect for special forces soldiers and what they went through to execute missions.

Major Lala Tavai's motorcade was in sight. Everybody heard the first explosion and gunfire that took place in the distance. Several more seconds after that, another explosion and fire lit the sky. The motorcade sped up. They had just pulled into Black Rock Camp and were nearing the temporary halt in front of the guardhouse. The rumble of motorcycle engines indicated that they were close to their location but not yet stopped.

Mike and Doc were seasoned combat veterans and knew the deadly ramifications of being early.

Mike left the sentry gate closed. He needed them to stop. There would be no running starts.

James heard the throttles power down to idle on the motorcycles. Then he heard the tap of the horn on one of the bikes.

Mike did a quick finger count and exited the guardhouse. A hail of bullets rained down on the three lead motorcycles.

James opened up on the three rear motorcycles.

Doc Sumner stood up and aimed his RPG at the motor of Major Lala Tavai's vehicle.

Brent shot out the tires and then opened up on the driver.

The RPG hit its target, and the vehicle was disabled.

Brent kept firing at the driver, but the latter was quick and able to exit the car and use it for protection.

Mike witnessed what was happening with the driver and right away knew that the man had special forces training. Most drivers would pause and panic if a deluge of bullets rained down all around them. This driver had catlike reflexes and knew immediately to exit this metal coffin.

None of Mike's team could expose themselves and eliminate the threat until Doc put the second RPG into the rear passenger compartment of the vehicle. Doc reloaded, stood up, and aimed his weapon.

One shot rang out, and Brent could feel blood spatter hitting the side of his face. Dr. Sumner had been shot.

Mike radioed his team and told them to pin down the driver with gunfire. He firmly said to his dad, "Pick up the RPG, and aim it at the middle of the car."

Brent had never even seen an RPG until this very day. He knew that he was too far away from the target to have any chance of hitting his mark. Brent loaded the RPG onto his shoulder and ran toward the vehicle. After about twenty steps, he stopped and knelt on one knee. He double-checked the sights and aimed. Brent pulled the trigger. He could physically see his shot nearing its target. Then the explosion happened.

Mike immediately dashed to the front of the vehicle to get an open shot at the driver.

Concurrently, James did the same thing from the rear. James made the kill shot on the driver.

Mike proceeded to look in Major Lala Tavai's vehicle. There were spot fires in the engine compartment, and the passenger section was devastated.

Brent's concern turned to Dr. Sumner. Brent wanted to

run and get in the escape car, but he knew he had to drag Doc with him. He ran back to his original location and found Sumner dead on the ground with a bullet hole in his forehead. Brent used the firefighters drag to move Dr. Sumner. After his first few steps Mike and James were at his location.

They took the doctor's body from Brent and immediately carried him away.

Brent ran toward Major Lala Tavai's car. He had to see if the man who had taken away the love of his life was no more. When he arrived at the car and looked in the back seat compartment, he was not disappointed.

The major sat with a vacant stare, and multiple pieces of his flesh adorned the interior roof and seat beside him. The proof that Major Lala Tavai was dead was right before Brent's eyes. The back half of Lala's skull lay on the trunk area of the car.

Three minutes was all it had taken for eleven lives to be extinguished. There were ten dead from the Fijian military and Dr. Sumner. Daniel's body count would never be known.

Daniel heard the gunfire. He increased the Humvee's speed to arrive expediently. Daniel was impressed that the vehicle was still drivable with all the bullet holes in it. When he was still about a minute and a half away, the orgy of bullets went silent. He truly hoped that their side had been successful; otherwise, he was driving into an ambush. When he did arrive, what he saw was like something out of a horror movie. It was all so surreal. Carnage was everywhere. There were more dead bodies on the ground than he had ever seen in his lifetime. There was no time to sit and stare at the horror. Daniel had functions he still had to perform.

Daniel witnessed the lifeless body of Dr. Sumner being

tossed into the back seat of the car. The Hudsons were crammed in, but they fit into the one vehicle. Daniel was parked in a position where he could just see the military parade of vehicles heading toward the guard post to confront the situation at the gate.

76

ESCAPE IFFY

WHILE DRIVING AWAY from the scene and heading toward Port Denarau, all eyes were peeled looking for possible trouble. Nothing happened until they hit the four corners. Two military jeeps were stopping traffic, and each vehicle contained two officers.

Nobody had to tell Daniel what he had to do. He faked slowing down but when he neared the military roadblock, he put the gas pedal to the floor and powered right through the minimal space left open by the two military vehicles.

Mike, James, and Brent aimed their weapons at the four military men and made short work of their feeble opposition.

Brent closed his eyes and leaned back on the headrest. He couldn't help but think about his first time operating an RPG and the bull's-eye he'd gotten on his very first shot. He believed that he wouldn't be able to hit that spot again even if he were given ten tries at it. Nothing like that had ever happened since the time he'd had to parallel park to pass his driving license test. He'd aced it that time, but he had never again been able to duplicate that feat.

Daniel was a better driver than Brent knew. He navigated the streets of Port Denarau with the professionalism of an off-road racer. He parked the vehicle, and Mike instructed every one of them to only take a pistol each out of the rented vehicle. They made it to the dock without incident but, as they looked down the wharf, they saw two military soldiers blocking their way.

Mike ordered everybody not to go any further. Mike continued to meander along the wharf leading to the dock where their speedboat was moored. He stopped to talk to the two guards. Within seconds, both of the guards lay dead on the wharf. Mike had used lethal punches in targeted spots to kill his enemies.

Brent, James, and Daniel stood in awe. They were impressed with the speed at which Mike had accomplished his kills. At the same time, they were terrified of the awesome power exerted by their family member.

Mike broke them out of their trance when he yelled to them, "Get your asses moving!"

Daniel again took the helm of their speedboat. He headed out of port and set a heading toward Lautoka. Once they got out to open sea, Daniel went full throttle and put the speedboat through its paces.

James was the first to notice a Fijian navy gunboat off their port side.

They all knew that the military boat couldn't catch their boat. It didn't have to. All the officers had to do was keep them in sight and when they turned to put their boat ashore, have people there to apprehend them.

Mike knew that the Fijian military would be monitoring their radio communications. He watched James pull out a different radio. It was foreign to Mike's knowledge. The radio wasn't tied into their communications network.

James spoke three words into his portable. He said, "Start her up."

Daniel could see that the navy vessel still had them well within their sights. He only hoped that they stayed out of range of their turret guns. Daniel put his eyes ahead and finally could make out the shape and location of their rented yacht. He altered his heading marginally but kept the throttle full out.

Brent twigged the heading change and spotted their destination.

Mike realized why James had his own portable radio. In the distance, he could see that the yacht had a helicopter idling on the helipad aboard the yacht.

The Fijian navy stepped up their game. They had another faster speed that the Hudsons were not counting on. Not only was the navy boat faster than anticipated, but the Hudsons' yacht was also well within the gunboat's strike area. A navy high speed gunboat shell whirled over their heads and landed just past the bow of the yacht. That was enough danger for the hired helicopter pilot, and he put his bird in flight. The Hudsons had lost their planned escape route. Now everything was liquid. The next navy round was a direct hit on the yacht. The Hudsons were now fucked.

Daniel immediately turned all the lights off on the speed-boat. He changed course and idled his way to a rowboat moored to a buoy in the middle of the darkness. He told everybody to jump in the water and board the rowboat. Daniel could see all the lights on shore, which surely had to be the Fijian military. They were in position to intercept the Hudsons when they came to shore. If that was what they wanted, that was what Daniel was going to give them. He did a wide circle around the rowboat, turned all the lights on the speedboat back on, and pushed the throttle to full speed. Daniel aimed this sea missile directly at the middle of the military shore blockade. As the speedboat roared past the rowboat, Daniel did a flying exit and landed hard in the ocean. He checked all his extremities and decided that he was OK. He swam toward the rowboat and got on.

The navy ship turned and headed back out to sea. The Hudson rowboat was alone. The speedboat had done its job and crashed on shore. Nighttime was running out, and the Hudsons felt that soon they would be sitting ducks.

Brent spied a blinking light on shore just about forty-five meters to the right flank of the military line. They had a quick discussion among themselves. Was it a trap? Was it salvation or possibly the light at the end of the tunnel? They decided they had no decision to make. They rowed toward the light.

When they got close to shore, all weapons were locked and loaded. Behind the light was a Fijian local waving them in. Apparently, no one was enamored with the military coup going on in Fiji. Once on shore, the Fijian farmer told them to follow him. He took them to his barn and hooked up his hay wagon to his horse team. Now there had to be an element of trust. The Fijian farmer had no idea where he was taking the Hudsons, and the Hudsons had no idea if they could trust this local.

Mike asked the farmer if he knew the way to Bath Airport. The farmer smiled and said to get on. All the Hudsons climbed aboard the hay wagon, along with the body of Dr. Sumner. They were going to ensure that he also got home.

The farmer was able to follow both bush-and field-roads on his farm. He never once had to veer anywhere near the paved roads of Queen's Highway. The trail was bumpy, but no one complained. The roosters were now announcing daylight, and they were safe. The farmer and his hay wagon pulled up within 6 meters of the Learjet. Everyone hustled off the farm appliance and onto the jet. The Fijian farmer immediately and quickly vanished back into his farm fields.

Mike could hear the sound and feel the roar of the jet engines throttling up. Mike looked out the window of the Learjet and saw the direction it was pointed. It was heading down the runway, but Mike thought this grassy field looked a little short. He grabbed his brother and inquired as to where the rest of the runway was hiding.

James realized that for the first time since they'd landed in Fiji, he was calmer than his special forces brother. James replied, "If everybody's had a shit today, we should have just enough runway to lift this baby off the ground."

Once on the airplane, everybody buckled up and the Learjet began its takeoff. The roughness of the grass runway was paramount in everyone's mind. No one wanted to believe that after all they had been through, their demise would be on an airfield in the middle of nowhere. The jet powered full throttle down the runway, but it seemed to take forever before they finally sensed the nose go up. Next, they felt the wheels leave the ground. At last, they were airborne.

They all cheered just like tourists did on commercial airliners. They flew into international airspace and that meant they were safe.

Mike gathered everyone around and said a prayer for their fallen teammate, Dr. Alec Sumner. They were going to fly to Papua New Guinea and land in Port Moresby. The Hudson's are sending the body of Doctor Sumner on a private flight from there to his family in Australia. The body of the doctor would be flown under the radar to his loved ones.

The champagne was broken out, and almost everyone was partaking in the festivities. Even though they had lost one of their teammates, the campaign had been successful, and the mission had had a favorable outcome. Not to be understated was that they were alive.

James and Mike spotted their father sitting alone on a sofa, away from the celebrations. They knew what they had to do. They weren't, for now, a CEO of a successful reinsurance company or a recently retired member of JTF2, Canada's most elite Special Forces Unit. They were sons, and their father needed them right now. They walked down to the sofa where their father was and sat on either side of him.

Brent looked at his two boys and sadly stated, "I have no home to go to."

James took his father's hand. He said, "Mike bought the house."

Mike added that "Dad, you will come and live with me, Niki, and our kids."

James looked at his father with tears in his eyes and choked out, "Dad, let's go home. It's time to put Mom to rest."

Made in United States
North Haven, CT
26 December 2023

46668946R00195